DOOM AND BLOOM

THE ENGLISH COTTAGE GARDEN MYSTERIES
BOOK THREE

H.Y. HANNA

CONTENTS

H.Y. HANNA

CHAPTER ONE

Poppy Lancaster stared at her opponents. There were six of them lined up in front of her: small, brown, and hairy, each with dark eyes set close to a pinched hole of a mouth... She clenched her fingers around the wooden ball, feeling its smooth surface against the sweaty skin of her palm, and shifted her hold, trying to get a better grip. Then she swung her arm back and heaved the ball forwards as hard as she could.

She held her breath. For a moment, it looked as if the ball might strike her target—then it sailed harmlessly between two members of the line and landed with a *thud* on the grassy ground behind them.

"Aww... bad luck. You almost got one," said the owner of the side stall with a grin. It was a coconut shy, a time-honoured funfair attraction where you could test your skill at aiming (or lack of skill, in Poppy's case). "Not as easy as it looks, eh? Got all those fancy computer games and whatnot these days, but I still say these traditional games beat 'em hands down. You were very close that time though…" He held out three more wooden balls and smiled persuasively, "Would you like another go? It's just a quid…"

Poppy hesitated. She knew she was probably throwing money away. On the other hand, it was only one pound and the money *was* going to a good cause. Besides—she glanced once more at the six coconuts propped up on sticks and her expression hardened—she was determined to knock one off if it was the last thing she did!

Several minutes later, Poppy was breathing hard, many pounds poorer, and in a very bad mood. She had thrown ball after ball, and still hadn't managed to knock a single coconut off its perch.

"Nothing like a traditional English country game to get the blood pressure up," came an amused voice behind her.

Poppy stiffened. She recognised that deep baritone and as she swung around to see the tall, dark-haired man standing behind her, she wondered why Nick Forrest always managed to come upon her when she was at a disadvantage. It was almost as if he planned it, just so he could always laugh at her!

"What are *you* doing here?" she asked.

He raised his eyebrows. "Everyone in the village has been invited to the fête."

"Yes, but I thought... well, I thought all you writers were anti-social introverts."

He grinned. "Oh, we can be persuaded out of our caves now and then. Especially when it's in aid of a good cause. This is the biggest fundraiser of the year for SOAR—South Oxfordshire Animal Rescue."

He nodded towards the small podium a few hundred yards away from them, where a table held hampers filled with various donated items: from jars of home-made jam to hand-knitted toys, gourmet cheeses to carved wooden ornaments. And one of them was filled with books. Poppy couldn't see their covers clearly from this distance but she could guess that they were all novels written by the bestselling crime author standing next to her.

"I usually just make a personal donation but this year, when they told me that they were planning this fair, I thought a hamper of my books might make a good prize too. Encourage more raffle tickets."

"I didn't realise you were such a big supporter of SOAR," Poppy said, looking at him curiously.

Nick made a wry face. "Yes, well, considering that I adopted that bloody cat from them, I suppose I feel a certain sense of loyalty—although God knows why. I constantly rue the day I brought that scrap of fur home eight years ago."

Poppy smiled to herself. She wasn't fooled by Nick's belligerent words. The "bloody cat" he was referring to was his talkative ginger tom, Oren, and while they seemed to spend most of their time bickering like two grumpy old men, she had seen enough to know that there was a deep affection between them. Nick might never admit it, but she was sure that he loved his irascible feline companion.

"So... you need help?" Nick grinned and nodded towards the row of coconuts on the other side of the booth counter.

"Uh... no, no! I'm managing fine," said Poppy quickly. She raised her chin. "I... er... I was just warming up."

Nick glanced at the grassy area around the coconut stands, which was littered with missed balls, and his lips twitched but he refrained from saying anything. Instead, he folded his arms and stood back to watch, his dark eyes alight with amusement.

Poppy turned her back and tried to pretend he wasn't there as she lifted a wooden ball again and took aim. It was the last ball she had. She took a deep breath and lobbed it forwards. It sailed tantalisingly close to a coconut but didn't make contact. From the corner of her eye, she saw Nick's lips twitch again.

"Give me another set!" she said to the stall owner, shoving a pound coin at him.

He took the money and handed her three balls. They were dispatched with equal force—and an equal lack of results.

"One more!"

Another three balls. Another three misses.

"Another!"

The man hesitated. "Miss... er... not that I don't like taking the money, but there's no shame in giving up, you know—"

"No, I'm not giving up!" Poppy cried. She plunged her hand into her pocket and pulled out a five-pound note. "Here! Give me the whole lot."

The man gulped, then took the money and deposited fifteen wooden balls in front of her. Nick started to say something, but Poppy ignored him and turned back to the coconuts. She hurled a ball at them, gasping:

"Take that!"

Thud.

"And that!"

Thud.

"And that! AND THAT!"

Harder and faster, Poppy flung the balls. She could see Nick from the corner of her eye, his hand over his mouth and his shoulders shaking, and the sight goaded her even more. Was he laughing at her? She'd show him! She began to throw even faster, her movements turning into a frenzy, her aim completely random. Balls flew wildly in all directions, bouncing and striking things.

"Whoa! Whoa!" cried the stall owner, ducking as a wooden ball narrowly missed his head. "Miss... you have to slow down—"

Gasping and panting, Poppy hurled her last ball. It struck the side of a coconut. She drew a sharp breath. The hairy brown fruit wobbled for a moment on its stick, then settled down again, but the stall owner lunged forwards and knocked it off its perch.

"Hurrah! You got one!" he said brightly, turning back to Poppy and presenting her with her prize.

"No, I didn't—that wouldn't have fallen off the stick. You swiped it off," Poppy said indignantly. "I wanted to win it on my own!"

"And you did, you did!" the stall owner babbled. "Best player I've had all day today. Here you are... here's your prize. Well done. Now, would you like to go and try another game?" He mopped his brow with a handkerchief.

Poppy took the coconut, slightly mollified, and scowled at Nick, who still looked like he was struggling not to laugh. "What's so funny?"

He chuckled. "Nothing. I just never realised how stubbornly proud and independent you are."

"What? I'm not—"

Poppy broke off as the air was rent by a terrified scream. She spun around, trying to trace the sound.

"It came from over there," said Nick, pointing to the marquee beyond the coconut shy. His eyes were suddenly alert and watchful, and Poppy caught a glimpse of the CID detective he had once been.

She dropped her coconut and rushed after him as he hurried over to the small crowd that was already beginning to form in front of the marquee. One woman's voice rose shrilly above the babble.

"Oh my God, he's dead! He's dead!"

The crowd parted and Poppy stopped short at the sight of the man slumped on the ground. He was lying face-down, with his eyes closed and his face deathly pale, and there was blood smeared along his temple. Poppy heard a loud gasp next to her and turned to see the woman who had been shrieking also staring down at the body. She clamped a hand to her mouth and looked up at Poppy, her eyes wide with horror.

"I knew this was going to happen! I saw a black butterfly this morning as I was leaving the house—it's a terrible omen! It means death is near..." The woman's voice rose hysterically again. "This is another murder!"

CHAPTER TWO

No, this can't be happening, thought Poppy, her mind reeling. It had barely been a couple of weeks since the last shocking arrest—surely there couldn't be another murder in the village of Bunnington so quickly? Even as she had the thought, the man on the ground began to stir and there were audible sighs of relief from the crowd.

"He's alive!"

"Quick! Help him up!"

Nick crouched down next to the man and put a gentle hand under his elbow, helping him rise to a sitting position.

"Are you all right?"

"Yes, I believe so... other than the most frightful headache," the man said, massaging his bloody brow.

He looked to be somewhere in his sixties; he had a lugubrious face, balding head, and a thin, almost puny figure, which was not enhanced by the dated brown suit he wore.

"What happened?" asked Nick.

"I... I don't know..." murmured the man, still sounding dazed. "I was just walking along... and then something hard hit the side of my head..."

"Something hard...?" Nick glanced at the ground around the man and his gaze sharpened. He reached forwards and picked something up. "Like this?"

Poppy look at the item he was holding and let out a strangled sound. It was one of the wooden balls from the coconut shy that she had been hurling recklessly around! It must have hit this poor stranger as he walked past.

Nick's eyes met hers and he looked like he was struggling not to burst out laughing. Poppy squirmed with horror and embarrassment. She was just about to step forwards to confess and apologise when there was a commotion at the back of the crowd. She turned and saw a middle-aged woman with a round, kindly face trying to push through.

"They said there's been an accident? Has someone been killed?" the woman gasped. She was panting, as if she had been running, and her eyes were wide and anxious.

"No, no—not killed, just injured," someone in the crowd assured her.

"Yes, it looks like something smacked him on the head and knocked him out for a moment," someone else said helpfully.

"Injured?" said the woman, still looking worried. "Oh dear! SOAR hasn't taken out proper insurance for the fête; what if—oh!"

She stopped short as she stepped through the crowd, arriving in the centre at last, and her eyes fell on the man who had been injured.

"*Norman!* What happened? Your head! All that blood!" She rushed to his side. "Are you all right? If you stay still, I'll call the ambulance."

"Goodness gracious me—there's no need for an ambulance! I'm fine," said Norman, attempting to stand up with Nick's help. He swayed slightly on his feet, but Poppy could see that his colour was already returning to normal. "I was just stunned for a moment, that's all."

"You've had a knock to the head and that needs to be checked out at the hospital. You could have concussion," said Nick.

"Nonsense, nonsense... I feel fine, I tell you! Perhaps just a nice cup of tea...?" Norman looked hopefully around.

The kindly faced woman stepped forwards. "Oh yes, there's some in the marquee. I'll take you there—"

"I'll help!" Poppy cried, keen to do something to make amends.

Leaving Nick with the crowd—many of whom had

recognised him and were starting to badger him for autographs—Poppy took one of Norman's arms whilst the woman took the other, and together they supported him as he walked shakily to the marquee. Inside the giant tent, a long trestle table had been erected along one wall and several ladies from the village were manning it, serving cups of tea and coffee, and little plates of cakes and buns.

Poppy was relieved to see a familiar old lady with a mop of grey curls and round apple cheeks standing beside the teapot. It was her friend Nell Hopkins, who used to be her landlady back in London and who had recently moved to Oxfordshire to live with her.

"Oh my lordy Lord, Poppy—what happened?" cried Nell as she caught sight of Norman and his bloody temple.

She hurried forwards, followed by several of the other ladies, and they surrounded Norman, fussing over him. Poppy was amused to see Nell bossily directing the other ladies to bring her the first aid kit and make a hot drink for the injured man. Her old friend might have only arrived in the village a few weeks ago but it looked like she was already establishing her position as Top Hen in the local pecking order!

Poppy stood back to let the other ladies tend to Norman and she heard someone talking next to her. It was the kindly faced woman, who had helped to bring Norman to the marquee; she was speaking into a walkie-talkie, and a minute later she shut off the receiver and gave Poppy a harassed look.

"I know Norman doesn't want any fuss, but I've called the paramedics anyway. He really ought to get his head checked out." She sighed and looked anxiously at the injured man, who was now parrying several offers of tea and cakes from the well-meaning ladies around him. "I hope he's all right. I don't understand what happened—"

"It's my fault actually," said Poppy, shamefaced. "I think one of the wooden balls I was using at the coconut shy struck Norman on the side of the head. I... er... I got a bit too enthusiastic and my aim must have gone wild."

"Oh! I see..." said the woman, looking slightly relieved. "Well, I suppose accidents happen. At least that's a simple explanation and it isn't anything more sinister. When I heard that someone had been killed—"

"I think the lady with the orange hair got a bit hysterical and jumped to conclusions," said Poppy with a wry smile.

The woman sighed. "Ah, yes... Sonia... she does tend to overreact. She's very superstitious, you see, and often gets upset about things. Still, sometimes you never know with these public events. One does try to plan for all eventualities, of course, but it is so difficult, especially with an event that takes place outdoors."

"Are you involved in organising the fair?" asked

Poppy.

The woman nodded, holding a hand out and smiling. "Yes, my name is Ursula Philips. I'm on the board for SOAR and also part of the committee that organises the annual fundraiser. This year's fête is probably the most ambitious thing we've ever attempted—although, I have to say, so far it seems to be the most successful as well." She turned and looked out of the entrance of the marquee to the elegant landscaped gardens around them. "We've been very lucky to have access to such a beautiful location, of course. This estate belongs to my aunt, Muriel Farnsworth, and she offered SOAR the use of the grounds at no charge. Duxton House isn't normally open to the public, you see, so that has been a draw in itself."

Poppy followed her gaze to the grounds outside and saw that the stalls and booths around the open lawn were surrounded by crowds of people milling about, all having a great time. There was the wonderful jovial atmosphere of an English village fête, with the colourful bunting that decorated the stalls fluttering in the breeze, and the sound of talk and laughter mingling with music and cheering. Several people were eagerly trying their hand at the traditional games on offer, from the hoopla and Hook A Duck to the infamous coconut shy—and others were admiring the entries for the Largest Fruit and Vegetable competitions, as well as the home baking, jams, and pickles on sale at the stalls.

"The villagers have been so kind," Ursula said with a grateful smile as her eyes roved over the various stalls. "Some have brought home-made cakes and jams and things, and others have volunteered to run the games, and they've all offered to donate the proceeds from their sales to SOAR. We're hoping to buy a new van to transport the animals to their foster homes, you see."

"I think I just funded half your van with the amount I spent at the coconut shy," said Poppy with a laugh. "But it was worth every penny. I only moved to Bunnington a few weeks ago and this is the first village fête I've been to—and I'm having a fantastic time!"

Ursula smiled. "Thank you. It's my first time organising an event of this scale and I'm delighted with how it's turned out. Charitable organisations rely on fundraising events so this kind of organisational experience is crucial for someone who wants a position on the committee." She gave Poppy a curious look. "You said you only moved to Bunnington recently...?"

"Yes, I inherited Hollyhock Cottage and the attached garden nursery—"

"Oh! You're Mary Lancaster's long-lost granddaughter!" cried Ursula.

Poppy flushed slightly. "Yes, I suppose—"

"What a coincidence! You're the very person I've been wanting to see. I heard that you were coming to the fête so I've been hoping to bump into you—I'm so glad to have found you at last."

"You were looking for *me*?" said Poppy in surprise.

"Yes, I—" Ursula broke off as a pair of paramedics hurried into the marquee, carrying a stretcher and other medical supplies.

Norman looked mortified and protested loudly as they attempted to carry him out on the stretcher. He flatly refused to go to the hospital, no matter how much Ursula pleaded with him.

"This is ridiculous! I've had a small knock to the head, that is all—there is no need to go to hospital for that," he insisted. "All I need is to rest for a bit, just until my headache lifts."

At last, they reached a compromise where the paramedics examined Norman as best as they could and then left him with some strong painkillers, instructions to take things easy, and a stern warning to go to the hospital immediately if he experienced any serious concussion symptoms. As soon as they'd left, Norman stood up and made to leave the marquee.

"Norman! Where are you going?" cried Ursula, putting a hand on his arm.

"I must go to my car to retrieve the items for the raffle," said Norman. "I've brought several pieces from my antique shop to donate—"

"Oh no, you're not going anywhere, other than into the manor house to lie down," said Ursula firmly. "You heard what the paramedics said. You need to rest and take things easy, not go around lugging heavy boxes."

"But—"

"I can go and collect the things, if you like," Poppy offered. "If you just tell me where your car is parked and give me the keys...?"

Norman dug into his suit jacket pocket and handed her a set of car keys. "It's parked right at the end of the field, underneath the elm tree. There are some ceramic items so—"

"Don't worry, I'll take the greatest care," Poppy promised, taking the keys and heading out of the marquee.

CHAPTER THREE

Several minutes later, Poppy walked slowly back from the carpark, carrying a cardboard box. She headed for the table beside the podium where the other donations for the raffle were being displayed. Included amongst the prizes was a large bouquet of fresh flowers that she had cut from her own cottage garden that morning. As she approached the table, Poppy was surprised to see that the group of women standing around the table were actually admiring her bouquet.

"It's just gorgeous, isn't it? So nice to see a simple bunch of country flowers in an arrangement," said one lady.

"Yes, one gets so tired of all those strange exotic things that you get at the florists nowadays," agreed her friend, making a face. "Monstera and eucalyptus and whatnot..."

"I always prefer to buy British and this is exactly the kind of thing I'm always looking for: a nice, simple bouquet of cottage garden favourites," said a third lady. She turned the arrangement to look at it from all angles. "This one really is fabulous. Look at the way they've combined the colours and even tucked in some ivy on the sides—"

"Oh yes, that's very clever!"

"I love the looser style of the arrangement too," said the first lady. "Not like those perfect, stiff bouquets that you get from florists. This one looks as if you've just picked these flowers yourself from the garden and tied them together."

"Mmm... yes, lovely!"

Poppy flushed with pleasure as she listened to their compliments. She hesitated, wondering if she should go over and tell them *she* had created the arrangement. Before she could make up her mind, however, the women turned and wandered off. As they moved away, Poppy noticed a stout lady in her sixties who had been standing a bit farther beyond them, grouping and arranging items to display them to the best effect in the hampers. Poppy realised that it was Mrs Peabody—one of the worst busybodies and biggest gossips in the village—and began to beat a hasty retreat, but it was too late. The woman had seen her.

"Ah—Poppy... I haven't seen you out and about in the village in days! Been busy with the cottage garden, have you?"

"Er... yes, well... you know my grandmother's property was very neglected and the garden was terribly overgrown. It's taken me a while to get on top of it. Actually, I'm still not completely done," Poppy said with a rueful smile. "There are still some things—like that monster rambling rose at the back of the garden and some overgrown ivy on the walls—that I haven't had the heart to tackle yet. But it's a *lot* better than it was."

"And I understand that your friend Mrs Hopkins has come to live with you at Hollyhock Cottage," said Mrs Peabody with a sniff. "*She* certainly hasn't wasted time in making herself known in the village."

Poppy hid a smile. Oh dear. Maybe Nell's bid for the Top Hen position *was* ruffling a few feathers after all.

"Is it true that Mrs Hopkins used to be your landlady back in London?" Mrs Peabody asked.

"Yes, that's right."

Mrs Peabody raised her eyebrows. "Your landlady? And now she's living with you?"

"Well, Nell has been wonderful—she helped to nurse my mother during her illness, and she's been so good to me since Mum passed away last year. She's really become more like family now."

"But of course, you still have your *real* family to find, don't you?" said Mrs Peabody quickly, with a gleam in her eye. "Surely you haven't given up your search for your father?"

Poppy sighed inwardly. She should have known that Mrs Peabody would start asking about her father again. The woman never missed an opportunity to pry into her background.

"Well, it was never much of a search to begin with, since I know so little about him," she said. "I mean, it's really like looking for a needle in a haystack. I wouldn't even know where to begin."

She didn't add, though, that she still couldn't quite break the habit of buying celebrity magazines whenever she could and flipping eagerly through the pages, searching the faces of male musicians for signs of similarity to her own features. To her relief, however, Mrs Peabody seemed happy to abandon the subject of her father, returning instead to the topic of the cottage garden nursery.

"I'm looking forward to seeing it when you officially reopen the nursery—and to being able to purchase plants in Bunnington again," said Mrs Peabody, rubbing her hands. "So... when will you be opening?"

"Oh... um... I don't know yet," Poppy mumbled. "I'm... ah... still working on some things. You know... er... laying the groundwork..."

She felt embarrassed to admit that she was struggling with the practical aspects of setting up and running a garden business. She had borrowed a pile of books from the local library and dutifully read them from cover to cover, as well as spent hours online researching plant growing, propagation, and "running a nursery business". She had tried to absorb all the information on business plans and plant licences, horticultural qualifications and gardening equipment, seed stratification and bottom heat, potting mixes and soil amendment... but all the research seemed to have done was make her feel even more intimidated. Now she felt too paralysed by the fear of "getting it wrong" to even take the first step.

Besides, even if she had felt confident about the business aspects of running a nursery, she was still stuck on a basic practical level. Her grandmother had specialised in cottage garden plants—flowers, herbs, and other traditional favourites—and that was what people would expect to find when they came to the re-opened nursery. After a rocky start, Poppy had slowly got the hang of sowing and planting seeds. She had a new batch of seedlings that seemed to be growing well, but most of them were perennials that wouldn't be mature enough to sell until spring next year, at the earliest. In fact, with autumn just around the corner and winter creeping up soon after that—a time when people retreated indoors and did very little in the garden—she had no idea how she was going to bring in an income.

When she had received that letter about her unexpected inheritance, Poppy hadn't expected to come to Oxfordshire and fall in love with the little stone cottage and the wild, romantic garden surrounding it. She had impulsively decided to stay and resurrect the nursery business that had been in her family for generations—even though the sensible thing would have been to sell up and take the money. However, since then, not a day had gone by when Poppy hadn't wondered if she had made the right decision. With no gardening skills or naturally green fingers, no experience of running a business, and barely any savings to her name... had she been naïve and reckless to think that she could take over her grandmother's cottage garden nursery? It was a worry that had kept her awake at night more and more in the past few weeks and now she squirmed under Mrs Peabody's shrewd gaze.

"There's no shame in admitting that you're feeling overwhelmed, especially if you've never had any experience of gardening or running a business before. Don't be like your grandmother, dear," said Mrs Peabody tartly. "She was a great plantswoman and gardener, but her pride was her downfall. She was always too proud to accept help or advice, too stubborn to admit that she might have made a mistake or done things wrong—and it cost her both her family and her health in the end."

Poppy swallowed, thinking of the gardening job she had just completed for John and Amber Smitheringale, a wealthy young couple who had bought a country home in the village recently. That had nearly turned into an absolute disaster because—it was true—she had been too embarrassed to admit her inexperience and too proud to ask for help when she had run into trouble. Thankfully, it had all ended up okay in the end, but she had learned a valuable lesson.

She took a deep breath and turned to Mrs Peabody with a shamefaced smile. "You're right... I *am* struggling a bit. Well, more than a bit, actually. I don't know what to do—I want to re-open the nursery but I don't have anything to sell! It's too late in the season to start growing flowering plants, and by the time they're ready, it will be autumn and nobody will be planting anything in the garden—"

"They will if it's winter bedding plants."

"Winter bedding plants?"

"Yes, things like pansies and violas and primroses that will flower in colder weather and early spring. And you could grow cyclamens—those are always popular in winter. People love having colour that they can bring indoors, to liven up the dark winter days."

"Oh. I didn't know... I was just thinking of the traditional cottage garden flowers, like hollyhocks and foxgloves and sweet peas and things. You know, the things that I've seen in the garden..."

"Ah... but you do know that gardens change?" said Mrs Peabody with a smile. "What you see now isn't going to be the same in a month's time. There will be different plants coming into their own and blooming. Dahlias, for instance, will be just starting to flower now, and rudbeckias too. Gardens aren't a static thing, dear. They change with the seasons. So there will be different plants that you can provide at different times."

"Yes, I see that now." Poppy felt her spirits lift, her optimism returning. "Okay, I'll sow some seeds for winter bedding plants as soon as I get back. Thanks for telling me!" she said enthusiastically.

Mrs Peabody put out a restraining hand. "But you know, dear... personally, I think you're trying to do too much. Rome wasn't built in a day. Maybe it's too ambitious to want to immediately re-open the nursery the way your grandmother had it. She had years of experience and knowledge. *You* need to learn how to grow plants well first and that takes time, and lots of trial and error. But you can make things easier for yourself, you know. For example, there's no need for you to grow everything from seed."

"But... but isn't that what nurseries do?" asked Poppy, bewildered.

"Well, technically, yes—nurseries propagate plants from seeds and cuttings. But many nurseries also buy in plug plants which they grow into bigger plants to sell. Then you don't need to worry about germinating and pricking out seedlings and all that nonsense." Mrs Peabody made a face. "It's a terribly fussy business and half the seeds never seem to germinate, and then the remaining seedlings die for no apparent reason or simply don't grow very well."

"Yes, that's exactly what happened to me!" Poppy

exclaimed. "I've finally managed to get one batch of seeds sprouted and growing well, but they're still really tiny and I keep wondering if they'll make it."

Mrs Peabody nodded emphatically. "That's why I say you need to get plug plants, dear."

"Plug plants?"

"Baby plants. You can get them very cheaply; I've picked up a tray or two from the garden centre myself a couple of times. It's a very economical way to plant up a flowerbed, you know. And I imagine you could get them cheaper from the wholesale plant suppliers," she added. "I'm sure your grandmother must have a list of suppliers that she's dealt with. Even *she* didn't grow every one of her plants herself from seed or cutting, you know."

"But... if people are coming to a nursery, won't they mind that the plants haven't been produced there from scratch?" asked Poppy, still unsure.

Mrs Peabody waved a hand. "Who's to know? People don't care about the details, dear. They just want something easy and pretty to plant in their gardens. Of course, they could get the plug plants themselves—like I have—but most people don't want the hassle of waiting for the plants to grow on. Everyone is dreadfully impatient, you know— especially young people nowadays. They always want everything available immediately and can't seem to bear waiting for anything! I'm sure they'd be more than happy to pay someone else to grow them a bigger plant that they can put straight into their gardens."

Poppy digested all this, feeling like she was suddenly getting a new perspective. *Starting with plug plants is like learning to ride a bicycle with training wheels,* she told herself with a smile. *Once I get the hang of growing bigger plants, I can try doing things myself from scratch!*

She looked at Mrs Peabody and felt a sudden surge of gratitude, and also of shame for her earlier uncharitable thoughts about the woman. Mrs Peabody might have been a nosy old biddy and a dreadful gossip, but she was also kind and unexpectedly wise. Poppy started to thank her but the older woman turned towards the box from Norman's car and said briskly:

"Hmm... right, now, let's see—what have you got there? Ah... those are from Norman Smalle's antique shop, aren't they?" She took each item as Poppy began unloading them from the box. "Hmm... hmm... yes, lovely old clock, this... and these glass paperweights are always popular... oh, and he's included a pair of bookends—very nice—and these little china figurines are very pretty too..."

Poppy retrieved the last item at the bottom of the box and looked at it curiously. It was some kind of knife, with a chunky wooden handle and a curved blade with a hooked tip. It looked almost like a miniature sickle, and as she turned it in her hand, she realised that the blade could be folded into the wooden handle.

"Is this some kind of pocket knife?" she asked.

"Oh no, dear, that's a pruning knife," said Mrs Peabody. "You don't see so many around anymore—I suppose people mostly use secateurs or pruning shears now—but back when I was a little girl, most gardeners and farmers had one of these. You can do so much with them, you see—prune roses and trim branches from trees and shrubs, harvest things from the vegetable patch, deadhead flowers, cut up twine…"

"Wow, this thing can do all that?" said Poppy, looking down at the knife.

"Oh yes, it's very sharp. Cuts through most things in the garden. Look…" Mrs Peabody took the knife and pressed it gently against one of the wooden spools that held a roll of ribbon. Poppy was impressed to see it slice right through the rim, as if the wood was soft butter.

"You have to be so careful with those, you know! My father once nearly cut off his finger with his pruning knife."

Poppy turned to see who had joined them and recognised the hysterical woman who had thought that Norman was a murder victim. Sonia—yes, that was her name, Poppy recalled. She was very thin, almost bony, with frizzy orange hair and a pale face that seemed perpetually puckered in a worried frown. She wrung her hands as she eyed the pruning knife and said in a breathless voice:

"You know, it's very bad luck to give a knife as a

27

gift—having this as part of the raffle prizes is a terrible omen! It could bring pain and misfortune on all those who buy a raffle ticket!"

CHAPTER FOUR

"Hush! What nonsense!" said Mrs Peabody loudly, giving a forced laugh and looking quickly around to see if any members of the public had heard. She lowered her voice and hissed: "Really, Sonia, you must stop believing in these silly superstitions, and you certainly shouldn't be repeating them!" She frowned at the thin woman. "You would think, as a member of the committee, you'd understand how important it is to encourage the public to donate. This raffle has been fantastic for raising funds and the last thing we need is for the public to hear any bad associations with—"

"What bad associations?"

Poppy turned to see Ursula approaching the table.

"It's nothing—just Sonia overreacting again,"

said Mrs Peabody with an irritable sigh.

Ursula, however, gave Sonia a patient smile. "What are you talking about?"

Mrs Peabody cut in before Sonia could answer: "It's just a pruning knife that was amongst the items donated by Norman, from his antique shop. But really, Sonia is just being very silly and—"

"I'm not being silly!" cried Sonia indignantly.

Ursula cleared her throat and held her hand out. "May I see this knife?"

Mrs Peabody handed it to her but somehow Ursula's fingers slipped and the knife fell to the ground. The blade flipped out as it fell and stabbed into the hard earth as it landed, making the knife stick up straight with its handle to the sky.

Sonia gave a shriek. "NO! No, that's a terrible omen! Dropping a knife is bad luck and it's even worse when it lands sticking into the ground!" She looked around, her eyes wild. "It's a death omen—it means that someone you know will die soon!" she wailed.

"HUSH!" snapped Mrs Peabody, scowling at the hysterical woman. She looked worriedly around at the crowds, where several people were starting to look at them curiously. "That's enough, Sonia! You're going to cause a mass panic if you keep going on like this!"

Ursula reached out, patted Sonia's arm, and said in a soothing tone, like someone speaking to a frightened child, "It's all right, Sonia. Calm down—

nothing bad is going to happen."

"But it fell to the ground—"

"I'm sure that doesn't mean anything," Ursula said reassuringly. "You know, superstitions only have power if you believe in them. Now, I'll tell you what: there are so many other wonderful items in Norman's collection already. I'm sure nobody will mind if the knife isn't in there." She took the pruning knife. "I'll return it to Norman when I see him."

Sonia gave a dramatic sigh of relief, which had Mrs Peabody compressing her lips in annoyance.

"Why don't you go and arrange the rest of Norman's things in a hamper?" suggested Ursula with a smile.

Sonia's face brightened and she went off happily to the other end of the trestle table with the cardboard box and an empty hamper. As soon as she'd moved away, Mrs Peabody leaned forwards and hissed in an undertone:

"You shouldn't pander to her, Ursula—you'll just make her worse and worse! Sonia needs someone to give her a good shake and tell her to stop being such a ninny, not soothe her like a baby."

Ursula sighed. "I just feel sorry for her—"

"That's your trouble," said Mrs Peabody, shaking her head. "You always feel sorry for everybody. My mother used to say: 'One good turn never goes unpunished.' It's all very well being charitable, dear, but one of these days, you'll regret being so nice to everyone."

"Yes, but—" Ursula broke off as they were suddenly joined by an elderly lady carrying a toy poodle under one arm. "Ah! Aunt Muriel..." Ursula turned to Poppy and smiled, gesturing to the elderly lady beside her: "Poppy, I'd like you to meet my aunt, Muriel Farnsworth."

There was no family resemblance between the two women but, even if there had been, they couldn't have been more unalike. Ursula was quiet and unassuming in her pastel floral-print dress, with her brown hair pulled back in a loose bun and her round face enhanced only by minimal make-up. Her aunt, by contrast, was lavishly dressed in an expensive silk blouse with pearls at her neck, and despite her age—which was probably somewhere in the seventies—was wearing several layers of heavy make-up, including bright pink lipstick which looked very odd on her thin, puckered lips. As she moved her hands, Poppy caught sight of jewelled rings sparkling on her gnarled fingers—and they were matched by similar gems sparkling on the collar of the toy poodle she was carrying.

"You'll remember I said I was looking for you," Ursula continued. "Well, it was really for Aunt Muriel. My aunt is looking for someone to help her with a gardening project."

Poppy's ears perked up. Another gardening job would certainly help to assuage her worries about income, giving her a bit of breathing space until she got the plant stock ready for the cottage garden nursery.

She smiled brightly and held her hand out. "It's lovely to meet you, Muriel—"

"Say hello to Flopsy," Muriel commanded.

"Oh! Er..." Poppy paused, then turned to the white poodle who was eyeing her with suspicion. "Um... hello, Flopsy..." She put out a cautious hand.

The little dog snarled suddenly, her fangs bared, then she lunged forwards to sink her teeth into Poppy's fingers.

"*Yikes!*" Poppy cried, jerking her hand back just in time.

"What did you do to her?" Muriel snapped.

"N-nothing," said Poppy. "*She* tried to bite me."

"Rubbish! Flopsy would never bite anybody... would you, Flopsy-pooh?" Muriel turned to the poodle and said in a baby-voice: "Did that silly girl upset you?"

The poodle squirmed in her arms and Muriel set her down on the ground. Flopsy shook herself, then looked around, her pink tongue poking out as she panted lightly.

Muriel gasped. "Oh! The poor darling is hot! She needs water." She looked around. "Kirby? KIRBY? Where *is* that man?"

A man in his mid-thirties came rushing up to them and whipped out a bottle of mineral water, which he proceeded to pour into a dainty ceramic bowl and place in front of the dog. Flopsy approached the bowl and sniffed it disinterestedly, then wandered away.

"That's Evian!" said Muriel, glaring at the man. "You know Flopsy only drinks Perrier."

"Well, I thought she wouldn't notice the difference—"

"Of course she would know the difference!" snapped Muriel. "She has an incredibly refined palate and will not settle for anything less. I expect any pet nanny of mine to know that."

"Yes, of course, so sorry, ma'am," said Kirby, hunching over in an obsequious way. "I'll go back to the house and get some Perrier right away."

Poppy tried not to stare. She knew some people really loved their dogs, but this seemed ridiculous! Then she froze as Flopsy trotted over to her. The toy poodle looked so harmless—in fact, she looked almost like a cuddly toy with her woolly fur clipped into pom-poms at her tail and paws, and the pretty pink ribbon atop her head—that Poppy almost wondered if she had imagined the earlier attack. Still, she wasn't taking any chances and she held her breath as the little dog sniffed her legs suspiciously.

"I'm glad you're wearing cool tones," said Muriel, looking Poppy up and down approvingly. "Flopsy doesn't like warm colours. They hurt her eyes. And she doesn't like synthetic fabrics either. Her canine therapist says it's because she has such a sensitive soul and she can sense the chemical pollutants in the fibres. Isn't that amazing?"

"Er... yes, amazing..." said Poppy. *Canine therapist?* She stole a glance at the old lady, wondering if the whole thing was an elaborate joke. But Muriel seemed completely serious.

"Of course, what her therapist says she really needs is to reconnect with Mother Nature—to absorb the healing energies of the Earth and rediscover her inner pup," the other woman continued. "That's why I want to build her a Doggie Scent Garden."

Poppy looked blankly at her.

Muriel frowned. "You *have* heard of scent gardens?"

"Um... well, I..."

Ursula came to her rescue and said, "Research shows that scents from plants and herbs and flowers can fight depression and anxiety or even have physical effects, like cure headaches or lower your blood pressure, and sensory gardens have been used to help people with mental health issues or children with autism—"

"Yes, yes, but I'm talking about a sensory garden for dogs," Muriel cut in impatiently. "I want to create a personal scent garden for Flopsy, so that she can have a wonderful buffet of smells to enjoy. I want plants that will soothe her nerves and stimulate her creative energies..." She fixed Poppy with an assessing look. "I spoke to Amber

Smitheringale the other day and she says you did very good work for her—helped her create a cottage garden in her new place. Well, I want a personalised service like that. I want someone to join Flopsy's canine staff as her personal gardener and nurture her outdoor needs... can you do that?"

Poppy glanced down at the poodle, who was now standing by her sandals and examining her exposed toes with great relish. She had a bad feeling that she would be nurturing Flopsy's appetite for body parts more than anything else, but she reminded herself that she needed the money. She pinned a bright smile on her face as she shuffled backwards out of Flopsy's reach, and said:

"Um... yes, of course. I'd be delighted to be Flopsy's... er... personal canine gardener."

"Good. You can start tomorrow morning. Come at ten." Muriel turned and pointed towards the manor house. "I want it in that area around the side of the house. There's currently an old rock garden there, but you can—" She was interrupted by the sound of a voice on a megaphone:

"And now, ladies and gentlemen... boys and girls... it's time for one of the highlights of the day. It's FAST! It's FURIOUS! It's the Totally Thrilling Terrier Racing! So come down to the main lawn with your hairy hounds, your manic mutts, and your pocket pooches—and let's see who's got what it takes to win the race!"

CHAPTER FIVE

Shouts and cheers filled the air, and crowds of people began streaming towards the large open lawn alongside the stalls. Poppy realised for the first time that there had been faint sounds of excited barking and yipping in the background—which were now growing louder and louder.

"Ah—the Terrier Racing!" Mrs Peabody said, taking charge once more. "Muriel, remember, you are presenting the trophy to the winner. You had better go over to the finish line. There is a trophy table there where you can sit."

"Come with Mummy, Flopsy," said Muriel, scooping the toy poodle up and bustling off.

Ursula started to follow, then paused as her mobile rang. She answered it, struggling to hear above the din of the dogs' barking.

"Hello? Hello...? I'm sorry... I can barely hear you..." She placed a hand over her other ear, trying to shut out the noises around them. "HELLO? Yes, that's right—I'm Ursula Phillips... I'm sorry? Pardon?" She frowned, then said, "Can you hold on a second? I just need to find somewhere quieter..." She glanced up and gave them an apologetic look, saying: "I need to take this call first. You go on without me."—before turning and hurrying towards the marquee.

"Ah well, I'm sure she'll catch us up," said Mrs Peabody, hustling Sonia and Poppy with her as she started towards the race course.

Poppy felt the atmosphere of tension and excitement as she neared the crowds that lined the edge of the long, wide lawn. At the far end was the trophy table, where she could see Muriel sitting, with Flopsy next to her. Beside them, a wall of straw bales had been set up to cushion the dogs' arrival at the end of the course. Just behind the bales was a strange contraption—something that looked like an upturned bicycle—and someone was sitting on it, pedalling it experimentally, winding and unwinding a long cord around the wheel. The cord seemed to be part of a pulley system and it extended, through the straw bales, all the way down to her end of the lawn.

At this end of the lawn, a small group of people were congregating next to her, each with a dog straining on a leash, tongue hanging out and eyes bulging, barking at the top of its voice. There were bouncing Jack Russell Terriers and feisty Westies, self-important Schnauzers and yapping Yorkies— and a variety of other mixed-breed terriers. They all seemed to be fixated on something small and furry that was moving in the grass in front of them and Poppy realised that it was the lure attached to the end of the cord. As the cord was pulled back and forth by the bicycle contraption, the lure jerked forwards and backwards, and the dogs worked themselves into a frenzy as they eyed the tantalising scrap of fur a few feet in front of them.

Their pure, unadulterated doggie excitement brought a smile to Poppy's face. Then her smile spread even wider as she saw a familiar-looking, scruffy black terrier in the melee. It was Einstein, the feisty little dog that belonged to her eccentric neighbour Dr Bertram Noble—known to his friends as Bertie. In fact, she could see Bertie now, hanging on to the leash with difficulty as Einstein barked and flung himself at the lure.

"Bertie!" cried Poppy, rushing over. "I didn't realise that you were coming to the fête?"

A brilliant scientist and madcap inventor, Bertie was nevertheless also very reclusive, and Poppy had rarely seen him out and about in the village. *Which is probably just as well*, she reflected, eyeing him askance. The villagers already treated him with incredulity and suspicion, and looking at Bertie now, you could hardly blame them. He was dressed in his usual haphazard fashion, in a bizarre pair of baggy trousers that looked like fisherman's waders, held up by elasticated braces, and a red flannel shirt. On his head, he wore a helmet with a large weathervane attached to the top, and in one hand he carried a polka dot umbrella. And to top it all off, he had a pair of spectacles perched on his nose that looked more like swimming goggles than glasses, and which magnified his eyes to an enormous size.

"Ah, Poppy, my dear... how nice to see you." Bertie beamed. "I hadn't planned to come, but then I heard about the Terrier Racing—and I just had to bring Einstein! He does so love running around and chasing things, you see, and I fear that I have been badly neglecting him these past few weeks, as I have been so immersed in my experiments... so I decided it was time I took him for a nice day out."

"Has Einstein done Terrier Racing before?" asked Poppy.

"Oh no—but he is such a clever dog, I am sure he will pick it up very quickly," said Bertie. He leaned over and pointed to his head, adding: "Besides, my Weathercock Helmet should help to establish wind speed and direction, so I can send Einstein off at the best angle."

The voice came over the megaphone again, urging all competitors to take their places on the starting line. Bidding a hasty farewell, Bertie dragged Einstein over to take his place next to the other terriers. Poppy retreated to the edge of the crowd, trying to find a space to watch the race.

"Poppy—over here..." someone called.

She turned to see Nick Forrest nearby, his tall frame standing out amongst the other spectators She went over to join him, squeezing into a gap beside him.

"Hit anyone else with a ball lately?" he asked with a grin.

Poppy gave him a withering look. "That was an accident. It could have happened to anyone."

He laughed and began to say something else, then his eyes slid beyond her towards the starting line and the smile faded from his face.

"What the hell is *he* doing here?" he growled under his breath.

Poppy followed his gaze to where Bertie was crouched with Einstein next to the other owners. She stole a glance at the man next to her. Nick was taller and more muscular, and his eyes were dark compared to Bertie's soft brown, but now that she was looking for it, she could see the family resemblance: the same strong eyebrows and determined jaw, the thick unruly hair (grey in Bertie's case), the same sensitive, mobile mouth that could quirk into a smile of childlike delight (Bertie) or settle into a scowl of moody impatience (Nick).

When she had received the bombshell a couple of weeks ago that Bertie and Nick were father and son, Poppy had been completely gobsmacked. They lived so close—their houses on either side of Hollyhock Cottage—and yet never had anything to do with each other. They didn't even talk to one another! Poppy was desperate to find out why they were so estranged, but as a new neighbour who had barely been there a month, she didn't feel that she could pry into something so personal.

Now, she wondered if this was the perfect opportunity to bring up the subject. But before she could reply to Nick, she felt someone grab her elbow. She turned around to see Mrs Peabody next to her.

"Have you seen Ursula?"

Poppy shook her head.

Mrs Peabody made a tutting noise. "She should have come by now. I've sent Sonia back to the marquee to find her—I don't want her to miss the race. It was Ursula's idea, you know, to include Terrier Racing in the programme for the day and she'll be delighted to see the attendance. My goodness, we hadn't expected to attract so many people!" She smiled with satisfaction as she took in the cheering crowds around them.

Poppy turned to look back towards the starting line again. The barking was deafening, and the excitement was reaching fever pitch, with every terrier lunging, choking on their collars, their eyes fixated on the lure that was being jerked teasingly in front of them. She felt her heartbeat quicken as the voice came over the megaphone again:

"*Well... it looks like our canine competitors are raring to go! Look at them... look at that excitement! Do you think we should start the race?*"

The crowd roared and yelled and hooted.

"*Righto then... Are we ready?*"

Every dog strained forwards. Poppy held her breath, her eyes on the scruffy black terrier in the centre of the line. *Come on, Einstein!* she cheered silently

"*Get ready to release your dogs... On your marks... Get set... GO!*"

CHAPTER SIX

The dogs exploded from the starting line, legs pumping, ears flying, as they tore after the lure which was being reeled in as fast as the person on the bicycle could pedal. Poppy squealed with delight as she saw that Einstein was amongst the dogs in the lead—in fact, the scruffy black terrier was second in line and he was rapidly gaining on the Jack Russell in front of him. For a moment, the two dogs were neck and neck, tongues hanging out and legs churning. Then Poppy's heart skipped a beat as she saw Einstein begin to pull ahead.

"*Woohoo!* Come on, Einstein!" she yelled, jumping up and down, and waving her fists.

The scruffy black terrier put on another burst of speed, surging ahead of the other dogs as he chased the lure with single-minded determination. He was reaching the end of the course now. The lure disappeared through the gap between the straw bales and the winning dog was supposed to dive through the opening after it, but Einstein ignored the hole, launching himself into the air and leaping over the bales instead.

The crowd cheered, delighted with his acrobatics, and waited expectantly to see him grab the lure on the other side. But to everyone's surprise, instead of pouncing on his prey, Einstein kept running... straight up to the trophy table where Muriel and Flopsy were sitting. He sprang onto the table and rushed up to Flopsy, who jumped back, startled.

The two dogs faced each other, then Einstein gave an inviting bark and dropped into a "play bow", his tail wagging. Flopsy stared at him and, for a moment, Poppy thought she was going to take a chunk out of the terrier's nose. The poodle lifted a paw, looking uncertain, an expression of snooty disdain mingled with reluctant interest on her furry face. Pampered and protected as she was, Flopsy had probably never mixed with "common mutts" and certainly never had another canine come up to her and introduce himself in this way. She looked like she didn't know how to respond to the cheeky terrier.

Her owner didn't seem to share her feelings, however. Muriel sprang up with a cry of outrage as Einstein continued bouncing up and down in front of Flopsy, trying to invite the poodle to play.

"Ugh! Get away from her!" cried Muriel, waving her hand. "Get away—you disgusting mongrel!"

Einstein paid her no heed. Instead, he darted forwards and stuck his nose boldly into Flopsy's bottom, going straight in for a canine hello.

"Aaaahh!" Muriel shrieked, her eyes bulging. "How dare you smell her bum, you filthy animal!"

She tried to pick Flopsy up but the poodle had jerked away, a scandalised expression on her furry little face as she whirled to face the terrier who was sniffing her backside. Flopsy lifted her lip, showing her teeth, but Einstein was undaunted. He gave another cheeky bark, then turned and presented his own bum to her, his tail wagging invitingly. The poodle hesitated, then—trying to look nonchalant— stretched forwards to take a delicate sniff. Soon, the two dogs were circling each other, noses to bums, and Muriel was shrieking with horror.

"What are you doing to Flopsy? Get away! Get away!" she cried, flapping her hands and trying to shoo Einstein away. "Kirby! KIRBY! *Where are you?*"

The pet nanny came running out of the crowd and attempted to catch Einstein, but the scruffy terrier was too fast for him. He darted aside at the last minute, causing Kirby to trip and fall over himself. The crowd roared with laughter. They were enjoying the drama immensely—it was even more entertaining than the race! Several people began cheering Einstein on, but Poppy also saw some of the fête organisers rushing to catch the terrier. She was relieved when Bertie himself hurried up to the trophy table and grabbed Einstein's collar.

Muriel snatched the poodle into her arms and glared at Bertie. "How dare you let your dog harass Flopsy like that?"

"I'm terribly sorry," said Bertie. "Einstein is very friendly. I'm sure he just wanted to say hello—"

"He was tryin' to find himself a girlfriend," someone from the crowd called out, laughing. "It's a real case of 'puppy love'!"

Muriel did not look amused. She gave a contemptuous sniff and said: "Flopsy would never associate with a scruffy mutt of no breeding! She is descended from some of the top show poodles in the UK and I'm very careful about who I let her mingle with. If she ever were to have a 'romance', it would only be with select stud dogs from approved breeders and certainly not with some common mongrel!"

"Oh, Einstein isn't a mongrel," said Bertie earnestly. "They didn't know his exact parentage at the rescue, but they were sure that he has a lot of Cairn Terrier in him, although—" Bertie tilted his head and looked at his dog assessingly, "—he *could* also have Skye Terrier in his breeding or Norwich Terrier or even a touch of Westie... I've often thought of extracting some DNA and sequencing his genome to determine for certain—"

"I don't care what he is!" Muriel roared. "He's certainly not good enough for my Flopsy!"

Cuddling the poodle close to her chest, she turned her back pointedly and retreated to the other side of the trophy table. It was incredibly rude and it left Bertie standing alone, looking rather lost and bewildered. Poppy felt a pang of pity for him and broke out of the crowd, hurrying up to him.

"Never mind, Bertie," she said gently, taking his arm. "Come on, let's go."

The old inventor clipped Einstein back onto his leash and tried to lead him away but the lovelorn terrier resisted. He strained on his collar, his eyes still on Flopsy as he was pulled away from her. His sad whining was heartbreaking, and the crowd booed and hissed angrily. Several people began shouting at Muriel.

"Poor thing! You're breakin' his heart!"

"Aww, come on—they were only having a bit o' fun!"

"Yeah! They were cute!"

"What about the race?" someone suddenly demanded. "Who's the winner?"

"The black terrier—he was the fastest."

"Yeah, but he left the track—doesn't that mean he's disqualified?"

"That Jack Russell should be the winner!"

"Yeah—look! He's still got the lure!"

Everyone turned to see the Jack Russell with his teeth clamped on the lure, shaking it furiously and growling like a demon. Two men were trying to prise his jaws open to make him release the furry bait, and they were practically lifting him into mid-air, but still the little terrier wouldn't let go. Some people began to laugh, whilst others argued passionately about who should be the winner and still others booed Muriel and cheered for Einstein. It was total mayhem and Poppy heard the voice from the megaphone shouting desperately to make itself heard, trying to calm things down and restore order.

Then a sound pierced through the hullabaloo—a terrified scream that sent a chill down Poppy's spine. She turned and saw a woman running from the marquee. It was Sonia. She was gasping and panting, and her eyes were wide with horror.

"There's been a murder!" she cried. "Murder!"

Someone in the crowd guffawed loudly. "Yeah, right—you're not going to fool us again!"

"Murder, my foot!" someone else scoffed.

"Nice try, lady!"

Sonia stared at the crowd in disbelief. "I'm serious! There's been a horrible murder!"

She was greeted with more laughter and Sonia looked as if she would burst into tears. Mrs Peabody marched up to her and said impatiently:

"Sonia! You've *got* to stop these hysterical outbursts! I'm sure it's just your wild imagination again—"

"No, no... it's not!" Sonia shook her head vehemently. "You've got to believe me!"

But the crowd just jeered and laughed even

more. Then, to Poppy's surprise, she saw Nick Forrest push his way out of the mob and go up to Sonia. His voice was gentle as he took her arm and asked:

"What happened?"

Sonia turned and pointed a shaking hand towards the marquee. "It's... it's..." She broke off and started sobbing.

Nick let go of her arm and started towards the marquee. The jeering and laughter faded away, to be replaced by an uneasy silence. Several people began whispering and talking in urgent undertones. Poppy hesitated, then ran after Nick, catching up with him just as he was about to enter the marquee.

They stepped in together. The large tent was empty, all the ladies who had been serving tea and cakes having left to watch the Terrier Racing, and the only movement was the steam rising lazily from the spout of the kettle on one end of the trestle table.

Then Poppy caught her breath. There was a body slumped on the ground next to the trestle table. But this time, the victim did not stir and sit up, complaining of a headache... Poppy swallowed convulsively. No, this victim was not going to be sitting up ever again.

Ursula lay face down, her arms thrown out and her legs splayed in a funny position, the skirts of her long floral dress tossed around her ankles. Her face was turned away but there was no doubt that she was dead. A dark red pool was spreading ominously from beneath her body and Poppy could see a vicious tear in the fabric of her dress, just between her shoulder blades, where something sharp had stabbed into her body, then pulled out again, leaving a deep wound.

Sonia was right: it was murder.

CHAPTER SEVEN

Poppy sighed wearily as she pushed open the rickety wooden gate, ducked under the hanging vines of fragrant honeysuckle, and stepped into the garden. The stone walls encircling the property seemed to shut out the world outside, and she felt instantly transported into a place of fairy-tale enchantment as she gazed around.

Hollyhock Cottage had the quintessential English cottage garden: wide, rambling beds brimming with flowers and lush foliage, with bees buzzing merrily amongst the abundant blooms and climbing roses festooned with romantic rosettes of pink and cream. Everything was crammed together in a harmony of colours and a profusion of shapes and sizes. Plants spilled onto the narrow gravel path which wound from the gate to the front door of the cottage, as well as branching off into tracks that led to the rear of the property. After the grandeur and formality of Duxton House, with its carefully clipped hedges, well-chosen plantings, and landscaped grounds, it felt wonderfully refreshing to step into a wild, unstructured place which looked as if had sprung up exactly as Nature intended.

Poppy sighed again but this time with pleasure. The mayhem of the day at the fête, with the jostling crowds, the constant hubbub of talking, the hysterical screams, and the horror of the discovered murder, slowly began to fade away as the peace and beauty of the garden surrounded her.

It was early August and the days were beginning to draw in, the sun starting its slide down the horizon a little bit earlier each day. It was low in the sky now, casting a warm orange glow on the landscape, with a few rays glinting off the bronze pointer on the stone sundial in one of the flowerbeds. Poppy smiled as she saw an enormous ginger tomcat, with big yellow eyes and a glossy orange-striped pelt, perched on the edge of the sundial. He glanced reproachfully at the time on the sundial, then looked at Poppy and meowed, sounding as he always did to her ears as if he was saying:

"N-ow?"

"Sorry, Oren..." said Poppy with a rueful laugh as she stepped off the gravel path and waded between the plants, making her way towards the sundial. "I *had* planned to get back earlier, but who would have known that a day at a nice village fête would end in murder?"

The ginger tom jumped down and trotted over to her, pausing beside her legs to rub his chin against her knee.

"N-ow!" he said, looking up at her.

Poppy dropped down next to him and reached out to pat him. Touching his soft fur was strangely soothing and there was silence for several minutes as she crouched beside him and moved her hands rhythmically down his body. As she stroked him, her gaze wandered around the garden again, lingering thoughtfully on a section of the stone wall farther down which was covered by ivy and looked very overgrown. The ivy had been left unchecked for several months and was now a matted mass of stems and leaves clinging to the stone wall; as she had mentioned to Mrs Peabody, untangling it was one of the jobs she hadn't had the time or heart to tackle yet.

"N-ow!" said Oren, butting her hand with his head and reminding her that she was supposed to be stroking him, not staring into space, thinking.

Poppy chuckled, wondering what had possessed her to fall in love with such a noisy, demanding feline. Then she heard the garden gate creaking open and steps hurrying up the gravel path. She turned her head and caught a glimpse of Nell walking towards the cottage, her arms laden with carrier bags.

"Hi, Nell—do you need a hand?" asked Poppy, rising up from where she had been crouching.

"Poppy! Oh my lordy Lord—you gave me such a fright!" cried Nell, clutching her chest. "What on earth are you doing, hiding in the bushes there and jumping out to scare people?"

"I wasn't doing it on purpose," said Poppy. "I just crouched down to stroke Oren."

The ginger tom followed Poppy as she joined Nell on the path and he marched over to inspect the carrier bags, sniffing them inquisitively.

"*N-owww?*" he said, looking up at the older woman.

"Don't you '*N-ow*' me, you rascal," said Nell with mock severity. "There's nothing in here for you! Really, I have never known a cat to be so greedy and always asking for food." She gave Poppy a stern look and wagged a finger. "It's all your fault, you know. It's because you keep feeding him—that's why he comes over every night expecting it now. I'm sure he gets more than enough food at home."

Poppy sighed. "Yes, I know Nick feeds him, but Oren always looks so hungry—"

"Rubbish!" said Nell, putting her hands on her hips and frowning down at the ginger tom, who gave her an innocent look in reply. "He just knows how to wrap you around his paw."

"Well, you feed him too—I know you do," said Poppy defensively. "I've seen you giving him a dab of cream or some bits of chicken or bacon when you're cooking."

Nell's cheeks reddened. "That's... that's different," she insisted. "I'm just giving him scraps that would have been thrown out otherwise. Anyway," she added, briskly changing the subject, "why are we standing out here? It's going to be dark soon. Come on—time to draw the curtains and turn on the lights."

She bustled towards the cottage, with Oren a few steps ahead of her, his tail up in the air. He stopped by the front door and looked expectantly at them, for all the world as if waiting for his staff to open it for him. Nell muttered something under her breath, but Poppy noticed that her old friend paused to let Oren enter the house first and she smiled to herself. Once in the kitchen, Oren trotted up to the pantry door and gave them another expectant look. Ignoring Nell's disapproving expression, Poppy retrieved a tin of cat food from one of the pantry shelves and filled a bowl, which she set down in front of the ginger tom. Soon, the kitchen was filled with the sound of his loud purring as Oren polished off his second dinner of the day.

"I thought you had left the fête already— otherwise I would have waited for you," Poppy said to Nell.

"I was helping some of the other ladies clear up in the marquee," said Nell. She shook her head, tutting. "What a dreadful way to end the fête... Poor

Ursula... The other ladies were so upset, you know. Everyone loved her. Nobody can understand how anyone would want to kill her."

"Don't the police think it was just a tragic case of Ursula being in the wrong place at the wrong time?" asked Poppy.

"Pah! What a load of nonsense!" Nell made a face. "That's what happens when they send an inept sergeant instead of a proper detective inspector. Why wasn't she there—that pretty lady inspector?"

"Suzanne? I don't know—maybe she was busy on another case," said Poppy with a shrug. "The CID handle other serious crime, you know, like kidnapping and sexual abuse, so Suzanne doesn't just deal with murder investigations."

"Hmm... well, he should have called her," said Nell.

"Who?"

Nell jerked her head towards the kitchen window that looked out on the large house next door to Hollyhock Cottage. "The crime author chap. She's *very* chummy with him, isn't she?"

"Nell..." Poppy resisted the urge to roll her eyes. Her old friend was so nosy when it came to other people's love lives—or past love lives, in this case. "Suzanne is Nick's ex-girlfriend, and yes, they're still on good terms—but that doesn't mean that she can drop everything she's working on just to come when he calls."

"In fact, I wouldn't be surprised if Nick *did* try to

call her," added Poppy, thinking of how impatient the crime author usually was. "That's what happened when I first arrived here and discovered the body in the garden. Nick just bypassed the usual call to emergency services and rang Suzanne directly. But obviously this time she couldn't come and sent her sergeant instead. Anyway, I'm sure Sergeant Lee knows what he's doing," she added with more conviction than she felt.

"Oh, that twit doesn't know anything," said Nell with a contemptuous sniff. "Just look at his ridiculous theory about Ursula being the victim of a vicious mugging."

"But I thought the police arrested someone in the crowd who was a convicted robber—"

"That man has done his time and he was out on parole for good behaviour!"

"How d'you know that?" asked Poppy in surprise.

"Because Mrs Rogers heard it from Mrs Wilmott, who was chatting to the vicar before he left the fête, and he happened to be nearby when the officers arrested that man and he heard them questioning him."

Poppy shook her head and laughed. She still couldn't get over the power of the village grapevine.

"But people do relapse," she pointed out to Nell. "Maybe this man assaulted his victims in the past."

"So the police think that an ex-robber who happened to be out enjoying a nice day at the village fête would suddenly decide to throw his chance of freedom away by attacking a woman he doesn't know?" Nell asked with uncharacteristic sarcasm. "And what on earth was he trying to steal anyway?"

"I don't know... I think I heard that Ursula's mobile phone was missing?" said Poppy. "I was with Mrs Peabody, helping to calm Muriel Farnsworth, when the police came to ask her about it. They couldn't find it anywhere."

"Mobile phone thieves don't go around stabbing people," said Nell scornfully. "The police are barking up the wrong tree. I'm telling you, this wasn't an unfortunate accident from a robbery-gone-wrong; this was a deliberate murder."

"But you said yourself—everyone loved Ursula, so who would want to kill her?"

"Ah..." Nell's eyes gleamed. "Well, you know they say there's a thin line between love and hate."

Poppy groaned. "Don't tell me—you think this was a crime of passion."

"Why not?" said Nell. "Maybe it was a jealous ex-lover or... a frustrated wannabe-lover."

Poppy did roll her eyes this time. Her old friend was an avid reader of romance novels and seemed to spend half her time imagining melodramatic interpretations of real-life situations.

"Don't you roll your eyes, dear!" said Nell tartly. "There's a lot of gossip in the village about Ursula and Norman, you know."

"Norman? Norman the antique dealer? The man I

hit—er, I mean, the man who was knocked out by accident?"

Nell nodded. "He's been mooning after Ursula for years. He's always finding excuses to visit Duxton House and taking little antique curios to her as gifts... Everyone thinks it's rather pathetic."

"But if he's in love with her, why would he want to kill her?"

"Well, maybe he saw her with another man and flew into a jealous rage... or maybe he confessed his feelings and she laughed at him... or...or—" Nell's eyes gleamed as she warmed to her subject, "—maybe he was so overcome by passion that he tried to grab her and kiss her, and when she rejected him, he became furious and decided that if he couldn't have her, then nobody would!"

Poppy burst out laughing. She thought of the weedy, balding man she had met earlier that day. She had trouble imagining him overcome with passion, never mind forcing himself on a woman or killing someone in a jealous rage. Norman Smalle hadn't seemed strong enough to stab a piece of cake with a fork!

"What's so funny?" asked Nell, looking slightly annoyed.

"Oh Nell, this is real life—not one of your romance novels! Besides, how can you assume that his feelings were unrequited? Maybe Ursula liked him too." Poppy raised her eyebrows. "In fact, I'm surprised that the village gossips don't already know that."

"Well, apparently Ursula was always a very private person. She's nice to everyone, you know, so it's hard to tell if she favours anyone in particular. She was always very kind to Norman, even when he's being a bit of a nuisance... She just had such a compassionate heart."

"Yeah, I only met her briefly and I noticed that," said Poppy, thinking of the patient way Ursula had treated the hysterical Sonia. She said with sudden fervour, "I really hope they find her killer. She was a lovely lady and she deserved so much better."

"They certainly won't if they keep on following that silly theory of theirs," said Nell. "You mark my words: Ursula wasn't killed by a random criminal, she was murdered by someone who knew her."

CHAPTER EIGHT

The next morning felt strangely anticlimactic after the drama and excitement of the previous day and Poppy lingered over breakfast, wondering what to do with herself. She had originally planned to go over to Duxton House and start work on the canine scent garden, but she had received a message first thing that morning saying that the meeting had been cancelled. It was understandable, of course, given Ursula's death, and now she didn't know if Muriel Farnsworth still wanted to go ahead with the project.

Poppy's heart sank slightly at the thought of losing the lucrative contract. She had been delighted to have a new gardening job lined up—and it had sounded fun too! In fact, she had been so excited at the thought of designing and creating a canine scent garden that she had spent several hours last night poring over her garden books again, as well as doing some research online. And she'd been pleased to find several of the recommended scented plants right here at Hollyhock Cottage, such as meadowsweet for arthritis and thyme to help skin irritations—

An indignant cry broke into her thoughts. Poppy looked up, startled. It had sounded like Nell... She sprang up from her chair and hurried through to the greenhouse extension at the rear of the cottage. The door that led into the back garden was open, and through it she could see Nell staring aghast at something. She rushed out to join her friend.

"What is it, Nell?" she asked.

"Ooh... those blasted boys!" fumed Nell. "If I ever get my hands on them—!"

Poppy followed the direction of her gaze and saw that someone had spray-painted ugly graffiti onto the outside wall of the cottage. The stone surface was now covered in lurid pink paint which depicted male genitals in gross detail.

"Ugh!" cried Poppy. "That's awful!"

"It's that dreadful gang of teenage boys," said Nell. "I heard the other ladies complaining about them in the village. They've been sneaking about, causing all sorts of damage to the houses and shops. It's driving the residents crazy. They never had this kind of trouble in the village before, you know. Bunnington is still the kind of place where most of the residents leave their back doors unlocked."

"It's probably the summer holidays," said Poppy. "Kids are bored and looking for stuff to amuse themselves."

"I don't care what they are!" said Nell. "That's no excuse for vandalism! Their parents ought to have taught them better." She sighed and looked at the graffiti again. "Well, I suppose it could have been worse. At least it's at the back and not the front, so visitors won't see it as soon as they arrive."

"Yes, this would really ruin the 'pretty cottage garden' ambience," said Poppy with a grimace.

Nell began rolling up her sleeves as she headed back into the cottage. "I'd better get some soap and water, and see if I can scrub it off..."

Poppy followed her. "I'll help you, if you like. It's not as if I have much else to do this morning..." she added in a dejected tone.

Nell glanced at her. "Are you worrying about the garden business again, dear?"

Poppy sighed. "Yes, sort of. I mean, I have a better idea what to do with the nursery now after talking to Mrs Peabody yesterday—in fact, I rang one of my grandmother's suppliers this morning and put in an order of winter bedding plants! But I've still got to figure out a way to bring in some money while I'm waiting for them to grow big enough to sell." She sighed again. "I was so happy when I got the new gardening job from Muriel

Farnsworth yesterday, but now that's all up in the air because of the murder..."

"You know, dear, you could use the flowers in the garden."

Poppy looked up in surprise. "What do you mean?"

"There were so many people admiring your arrangement at the fête yesterday and I'm sure a lot of them would gladly pay for something similar. You could make up flower arrangements from the cottage garden and sell them to local homes and businesses." Nell smiled proudly. "And you do have a wonderful touch with the flowers. Your arrangement looked so beautiful and professional— but also had a lovely, fresh, home-made look which feels so much more special than a fancy bouquet from a commercial florist."

Poppy smiled, flattered and pleased. "But... but I don't have any florist training—"

"That doesn't matter! No one is going to demand to see your qualifications before they buy a bunch of flowers from you, are they, dear? As long as they think it looks pretty—that's all that matters."

"Hmm..." Poppy considered the idea. Selling cut flowers had never been in her plans—she had always thought she would just re-open the nursery and sell plants, like her grandmother had done. But in fact, she remembered now that her grandmother did have a cutting patch and the original sign outside the gate had read: "*HOLLYHOCK COTTAGE*

& GARDENS: Garden Nursery and Fresh Cut Flowers". And besides, even if her grandmother hadn't done this, it didn't mean that she couldn't branch out, do things differently. She could strike her own path. Especially if it would help to bring in some ready income...

She smiled at Nell. "You know, maybe that's not such a bad idea. I could make up a poster and stick it on the village community board outside the post office."

"You could also get some leaflets printed and drop them directly into people's homes and offices," Nell suggested. "You just need to walk around the village and stick them into post boxes."

"Yes, I'll do that!" said Poppy, her enthusiasm growing. "And maybe I'll donate some arrangements to places where lots of people can see them, as a form of free advertising..." She hugged her friend impulsively. "Oh Nell, I think it could work!"

"Of course it will work," said Nell placidly, leading the way back to the kitchen. "Now, before I forget—I wanted you to taste these Chelsea buns and tell me what you think. Too much cinnamon? Or lemon zest?"

Poppy realised belatedly that there was a wonderful, delicious smell of fresh baking wafting through the kitchen and, as she watched Nell take a large baking tray out of the oven, she realised that her friend had been busy. Her eyes widened, though, when she saw the number of buns on the tray.

"My goodness, Nell—we're never going to eat all that!" she protested.

"They'll keep for a few days," said Nell. Then she added nonchalantly, "Besides, I thought that Dr Noble next door might like to have some."

Poppy tried to hide her surprise. Nell and Bertie's first meeting hadn't got off to a great start (she still wasn't sure if Nell had forgiven Bertie for bringing his pet laboratory rat along when he'd come over for tea)—and she thought that Nell had remained suspicious and hostile towards the eccentric inventor. So the last thing she'd expected was for Nell to offer him some home baking! Some of what Poppy was thinking must have shown on her face because Nell said defensively:

"Well, he *is* all alone in that ramshackle house next door, with no one to take care of him, and I'm sure—left to his own devices—he would never eat properly. Since I was baking anyway, I thought... well, it was easy just to make a bit more."

Poppy smiled and gave her old friend another hug. "That's really sweet of you, Nell—I'm sure Bertie will appreciate it. You're right, he gets so engrossed when he's deep in one of his experiments that he probably completely forgets about his meals. It will be lovely for him to have some ready-baked goodies to munch on."

Poppy reached for one of the Chelsea buns and bit into the soft, chewy roll embedded with juicy raisins and sultanas, and scented with cinnamon and mixed spices. The sweet, sugary glaze on the bun was offset by the tangy tartness of the lemon zest rolled into the dough, and the whole combination was absolutely delicious.

"Mind that little dog of his doesn't get hold of any, though," Nell added as she transferred several buns onto a separate plate. "There are raisins and sultanas in these and they're poisonous to dogs."

"Mm-hmm... okay," said Poppy with her mouth full. "I'll pop over and take these to Bertie now."

A few minutes later, Poppy stepped out of the garden gate and into the lane outside Hollyhock Cottage. To her left, the lane ran past Nick's large Georgian-style house and continued on towards the village green and the high street where the shops were congregated. Poppy turned in the opposite direction—to her right—where the lane ended in a cul-de-sac and where a small property beyond Hollyhock Cottage held a shabby house and garden. That was where Bertie lived and, in fact, Poppy usually took the shortcut through a large gap in the stone wall between the two properties, but today, as she was carrying a plate heaped with buns, she decided to take the orthodox route.

Pushing the garden gate open, Poppy hurried down the short path to the front door and rang the bell. Normally Einstein would have barked to sound the alarm as soon as he heard anyone on the front porch, but today the house was strangely silent.

She wondered if Bertie might have gone out and was just turning away when the door was opened by the inventor himself.

"Poppy! How lovely to see you, my dear. You weren't leaving already?"

"Oh... I thought you weren't at home," said Poppy, stepping into the house. "Normally Einstein barks—" She broke off as she caught sight of the scruffy black terrier on the floor in the sitting room. He looked nothing like his usual perky self, though. He didn't dance on his hind legs or beg for a biscuit or do any of his other usual antics. Instead, he lay with his chin on the floor, his eyes dull and his ears drooping, and barely even twitched his tail when Poppy went over to say hello.

"Einstein just hasn't been himself since we got back from the fête yesterday," said Bertie, scratching his head. "I don't know what is wrong with him. He won't eat or play or do any of the things he's normally interested in. Perhaps I ought to take him to the vet tomorrow. I wonder if he's sickening for something..."

Poppy eyed the terrier. Poor thing... She suspected that he was suffering from a broken heart.

"I think Einstein's ailment started when he fell head over paws for a certain white toy poodle," she said with a laugh.

"Yes, well, that *was* terribly naughty of him to rush up to that lady and her poodle like that," said

Bertie, tutting. "He was really not himself yesterday. He doesn't normally run off all the time. He was even doing it before we arrived at the fête."

"What do you mean?"

"Well, he chewed a hole in his leash and ran off as we were on our way to Duxton House. We took the shortcut, you see, which comes out near the woods at the back of the estate. I would never have caught Einstein if that nice young man with the red sports car hadn't helped me." He inhaled suddenly. "My dear! What is that wonderful smell?"

"Oh, I nearly forgot—I brought these for you, Bertie. Nell made them," Poppy explained, holding up the plate of buns.

The old inventor's eyes lit up. "Chelsea buns! How delightful! I was just about to have some tea— would you like a cup?"

"Thanks, that sounds great."

Left alone, Poppy was about to sit on the sofa when she heard a familiar feline voice and, a minute later, an orange-striped head popped around the side of the still-open front door. It was Oren. Poppy was surprised to see the ginger tomcat. There had been an ongoing battle between cat and dog ever since she'd first arrived in Bunnington—in fact, Oren and Einstein seemed to have a new round of skirmishes at least once a day. Usually Oren got the upper hand but, like a typical terrier, Einstein refused to admit defeat and launched himself into combat with fresh fervour every time he saw his feline neighbour.

Their fights usually took place in the Hollyhock Cottage gardens, though, which were conveniently sandwiched between their respective houses, and Poppy had never seen Oren on Bertie's property before. The ginger tom looked like he was searching for something. His whiskers quivered, scenting the air, as he prowled cautiously down the hallway and into the sitting room. Then his eyes lit up as he saw Einstein and he puffed up to twice his size, all his fur standing on end.

"*N-OW!*" he said gleefully, eyeing his old foe.

Einstein glanced up, then sighed and put his chin down on his paws again.

Oren stopped, confused. He tried again, hissing and puffing himself up even bigger than before. "*N-OW?*"

No response.

The ginger tom stalked over and glared at Einstein. "*N-owwww?*" he demanded.

Nothing.

Oren strutted back and forth, lashing his tail and flexing his claws. He even went up and prodded the terrier with a paw.

"*N-ow? N-OW?*" said Oren, starting to sound desperate.

Einstein sighed deeply and turned his head the other way.

"*H-ow? H-ow?*" said Oren, looking bewildered.

Poppy laughed. "Oren... I think you've got

competition. And it's a glamorous female no less."

The ginger tom stomped off and jumped up onto the windowsill, where he curled up with his front paws tucked under his chest and fixed Einstein with a baleful glare. Poppy chuckled again, then, wondering if Bertie needed a hand, went to the kitchen to find him. She found the old inventor busily preparing two mugs on the kitchen counter, whilst the kettle whistled on the stove behind him.

"Here, I'll get the hot water," Poppy offered, starting towards the stove. Then she stopped and nearly tripped, trying to avoid stepping on the slimy brown pile on the floor.

"*Eeuw!* Bertie, I think Einstein had an accident indoors," she cried.

He glanced down. "Oh no—that's my Dog Poo Transmitter."

Poppy gaped at him. "Your what?"

He smiled widely. "It's one of my latest inventions. I've been commissioned by the British government, you see, to develop an arsenal of espionage tools with superior—"

"*You* work for the British government?" Poppy said, looking at him incredulously.

"Oh, for many years now... just as a consultant, of course. MI6 usually, although I occasionally consult on projects for MI5. I like working with the spooks better, though," Bertie added in a confidential tone. "Nothing like knowing your invention is helping British intelligence abroad!"

More like wreaking havoc abroad, thought Poppy. She was amazed that any government agency would let Bertie near their equipment, but perhaps the old inventor had a serious side that she didn't know of. After all, he had once been a professor and head of a department at Oxford University...

She realised that Bertie was still speaking and hurriedly turned her attention back to him:

"...most common spy cameras and audio bug devices are far too easily detected and recognised, so MI6 have tasked me with designing some innovative upgrades."

Poppy glanced down again. "And you've come up with dog poo."

"Ah, well, you see, the brilliant thing about canine faeces is that they are a global phenomenon," said Bertie enthusiastically. "You find dog poo everywhere, in every country and every society." He paused, his forehead puckering. "Well, except for Japan, perhaps—that country is disturbingly clean and orderly... hmm... yes, I will have to come up with an alternative for the Far East agents..." He brightened again. "But almost everywhere else, dog poo is something that no one would look twice at. Nor is it something that people would want to touch or handle if they can help it, so it really is the perfect disguise for an audio transmitter or even a micro camera..." He reached down and scooped up the pile of turds, shoving it proudly towards Poppy. "Isn't the detail marvellous?

Oh, don't worry—it is perfectly fine to handle. It is all plastic polymers. I am most impressed with the advances they have made in 3D printing. It looks remarkably realistic, doesn't it?"

Poppy leaned back, wrinkling her nose. "Yeah… it smells remarkably realistic too."

Bertie beamed and picked up a small atomiser from the counter. "Yes, that was the final touch! I invented a top-up spray which an agent can use to refresh the turds from time to time. It is a carefully balanced mix of volatile sulphur compounds, to create an authentic 'poo' smell. Would you like a sample?"

"NO! No, thanks," said Poppy, taking a hasty step back. "Um… shall I help you carry the tea back to the sitting room?"

CHAPTER NINE

Poppy let herself out of Bertie's house fifteen minutes later and started back home. She had barely gone a few steps, however, when a movement caught her eye, and a second later she saw a familiar scruffy black shape emerge from the undergrowth around the side of the house. It was Einstein. Poppy was pleased to see that the little dog seemed to have stopped moping and come outside. She was about to call him when she noticed that he seemed to be moving in a very purposeful fashion. He made a beeline for a clump of bushes and began scrabbling at the base of it.

He's digging, she realised, as she saw clods of earth flying through the air. A few minutes later, the little terrier backed out from beneath the bush, his face covered in soil and an enormous marrowbone clamped in his mouth. He gave himself a good shake, then picked up the marrowbone again and trotted towards the gate.

Where on earth is he going? wondered Poppy. She watched with surprise and admiration as Einstein reached the gate, set the bone down temporarily, and jumped up so that he could push the latch with his nose. A moment later, the gate swung open and the terrier trotted through, carrying the bone once more. Poppy stared blankly after him for a few seconds, then rushed to the gate herself and peered out into the lane.

Einstein was disappearing rapidly up the lane, in the direction of the village green. Poppy hovered uncertainly by the gate, wondering if she should alert Bertie. After all, Einstein wasn't her dog. On the other hand, she had left the old inventor immersed in one of his experiments and by the time she got his attention, explained the situation to him, and got him outside to chase after his dog, Einstein would probably be gone from sight.

Deciding to go after the terrier herself, she stepped out and hurried up the lane. When she reached the corner where it joined the larger street which led to the village green, however, she was surprised to see no sign of Einstein in that direction. Where had he gone? How could he have disappeared so quickly?

She turned and looked down the street in the opposite direction. She was just in time to see a little black tuft of a tail disappearing around a corner farther down the street. Quickly, she followed and found herself in a meandering lane that wound between various cottages as it led to the outskirts of the village. It opened at last into a narrow country road which encircled a small country estate and Poppy was surprised to realise that this was in fact the grounds of Duxton House, where the fête had been held yesterday. Muriel's home was much closer to her cottage than she had thought—probably because yesterday, she had entered the estate via the front gate, which was approached from the village green. But the route she had just taken was a shortcut which brought her to the rear of the large property. In fact, she recalled Bertie mentioning that they had used a shortcut to get to the fête, and so Einstein must have simply retraced the route from the day before.

There was a tall hedge around the perimeter of Duxton House estate, but this petered out at the rear where the grounds merged with the nearby woods. The leaves and branches were sparse and straggly there, perhaps because the trees blocked out too much light for the hedge to grow properly. Poppy was just in time to see Einstein burrowing through the hedge, and when she hurried over, she found herself staring at a large gap in the thinning foliage. Through it, she could see Einstein's scruffy black shape in the distance, trotting purposefully towards the house, the marrowbone protruding from either side of his muzzle.

She debated for a moment what to do. She could make her way around to the front of the estate and go in the main gates, but that would take several minutes and she was worried about what Einstein might get up to in that time. She had a sneaking suspicion of where he was heading: to find Flopsy and woo his new love with a nice smelly marrowbone. She had to catch him before he got into trouble.

Ducking down, she crawled through the gap in the hedge and stood up on the other side. She cast a quick look around, wondering how to explain herself if any of the estate gardeners or other staff saw her, but thankfully the area around her seemed to be empty. She started at a light jog towards the house, but she hadn't gone several yards when a male voice shouted:

"*OY!* What are you doing there?"

Poppy froze and looked frantically around. Then she realised that the shout wasn't directed at her. A man in green overalls—obviously one of the estate gardeners—was shouting and chasing a group of teenage boys near the rear perimeter of the property. They raced towards the hedge and scrambled over, all while laughing and taunting the gardener. For a moment, it looked like the youngest in the group—a boy who couldn't have been older than twelve—might not make it as he tripped and fell. Then he picked himself up and dived through the gap in the hedge, just before the gardener reached him. More jeers and taunts came from the other side of the hedge as the gardener shook his fist and yelled at the boys.

Poppy hastily took advantage of the diversion to continue on towards the house unseen. She ran past the carefully clipped topiary and perfectly geometric beds alongside the manicured lawns, past the empty stalls and marquee tent which was leftover from the fête, until she arrived at last at the rear of the manor. There, she skulked past the tall shrubs beside the house, slowly circling around it as she searched for any sign of a scruffy black terrier. She was rewarded at last when she came around the south corner and found Einstein outside a set of French doors which led onto the terrace. His little tuft of a tail was wagging madly and he was making excited whining sounds as he stared through the glass door. On the other side of the door, Poppy saw Flopsy the poodle with one dainty paw raised and her head cocked to one side.

Einstein dropped into a play bow and wagged his tail at the poodle. Then he nosed the marrowbone closer to the glass door and looked expectantly at her. Flopsy lowered her head, as if trying to sniff through the glass, and she stared at the bone in fascination.

Then Poppy heard voices. She ducked instinctively before she realised that they were coming from an open window a bit farther along the side of the house. She crept a bit closer and saw that the room Flopsy was in—a sort of antechamber leading out onto the terrace—was connected to a larger room beyond. From the sound of the voices, Muriel Farnsworth was in the bigger room, talking to someone.

"...ohhh... what am I going to do without her?" came Muriel's loud, tearful voice. "Ursula always took care of everything—she always knew what to do... And Flopsy!" She gasped. "Who is going to look after Flopsy now if something happens to me?"

A man's voice answered—too low to hear clearly. Poppy hesitated, then crept closer, until she was right underneath the window. There was a large camellia bush growing in a pot beside the window, its bushy branches with glossy, dark green leaves arching out to form a convenient cover on one side. Carefully, Poppy raised herself so that she could look over the windowsill into the room but still be camouflaged by the camellia bush.

She saw Muriel sitting on an overstuffed sofa, in a lavishly furnished drawing room with a formal marble fireplace and oil portraits on the walls. There was a man in the room with her and, as he shifted position and came into view, Poppy saw that it was Kirby the pet nanny. He leaned over Muriel and said:

"I know you're upset, ma'am, and Ursula's death is a tragic, tragic loss..." Kirby paused and fumbled with his eye, as if wiping away a tear, then added silkily, "But don't forget—you have *me* here with you. I know I've only been at Duxton House for a year, but I already see this place as my home and you as my family... and Flopsy—well, I love her as if she's my own child!" His voice vibrated with emotion.

"Oh Kirby!" cried Muriel, sniffing into a handkerchief and looking up at him warmly.

"And you know, although Ursula did run the household and take care of many things, she didn't *really* spend much time with Flopsy," he continued smoothly. "I mean, *I'm* the one who understands Flopsy's needs and who takes care of her every day. I'm the one who—"

Kirby broke off, an expression of frustration and annoyance crossing his face as a girl stepped into the room. She was not in uniform, but somehow Poppy was sure that she was a member of the household staff, and this was confirmed a moment later when she inclined her head respectfully to Muriel and said:

"I beg your pardon, ma'am, but there's a Detective Sergeant Lee of the South Oxfordshire CID here to see you."

Yikes! Poppy ducked back down beneath the windowsill as she saw the sergeant being ushered into the room. The last thing she needed was for the police to find her skulking under the window! She started to back away, then stopped as curiosity got the better of her. She could hear Sergeant Lee mention Ursula's murder and she wondered what was happening with the investigation. Moving as quietly as possible, she raised herself once more so that her eyes were level with the windowsill and she could peer into the room, through the leaves of the camellia bush.

Sergeant Lee was seated next to Muriel, tapping on a slim tablet with exaggerated flourish. Obviously, the traditional pencil and notepad of the classic detective were not good enough for him. He cleared his throat importantly and said:

"This is just a formality, madam, as we are well on the way to closing this case, but I just needed to check a few things... You said that Ursula wasn't with you when you went to watch the Terrier Racing?"

"Well, Flopsy and I were supposed to present the trophy to the winner, you see, so we went to sit at the trophy table, at the end of the track. I just assumed that Ursula had gone with Mrs Peabody to watch the race. The crowds were very rowdy, you know," she said, glaring at Sergeant Lee as if it was his fault. "Flopsy is very sensitive to loud noises. They hurt her ears. And then there was that *dreadful* dog!" She clutched her chest. "A common mongrel, and he had the temerity to sniff Flopsy's bum! Can you believe it?"

"Er..." The sergeant shifted in his seat, looking like he didn't quite know how to respond.

"And then the next thing, I heard this awful

screaming and I saw that Sonia woman come rushing from the marquee. And then I heard... I heard..." Suddenly, Muriel's composure deserted her. Her face puckered. "Ursula was dead! I couldn't believe it! How could she be dead? She was only forty-eight... she always ate so sensibly and was kind to everyone... How can she have been killed? Oh... ohhh... what am I going to do now? What am I going to do?"

Muriel plunged her face into her handkerchief and began to sob loudly, her shoulders shaking. Sergeant Lee looked alarmed and glanced nervously around.

"Perhaps I'd better get her a brandy, sir," Kirby spoke up, fussing around Muriel.

"Oh... er... yes, go ahead..." said the sergeant, looking very uncomfortable. "And while you're doing that, can you give me an account of your movements during the fête too?"

The pet nanny paused on his way to the drinks cabinet and stiffened. He turned back to face the sergeant and said loftily, "I was with Mrs Farnsworth all the time. My main duty is to see to Flopsy's needs, you see, so I'm required to be on standby at all times. Oh, except once when I had to return to the house to fetch some mineral water."

"Yes, you were gone for ages!" Muriel complained, surfacing from the soggy depths of her handkerchief.

"We were out of Perrier in the kitchen, so I had to

go down to the cellar," said Kirby quickly.

"Hmph. You shouldn't have had the wrong brand in the first place," Muriel grumbled.

For a second, Poppy saw a look of irritation flash across Kirby's face, then it was quickly wiped clean and he said: "Yes, of course, you're right, ma'am— I'm very sorry. It won't happen again."

He returned from the drinks cabinet with a goblet of amber liquid for Muriel, but he had barely handed it to her when they heard high-pitched yapping coming from the next room.

Muriel gasped. "That's Flopsy! Where is she?" She sprang up and looked around. "Flopsy? Flopsy-pooh... where are you?"

More yapping came from the adjoining antechamber, echoed by a rush of different barking from outside. Poppy jerked around in horror. It was Einstein! The scruffy black terrier was dancing around on his hind legs in front of the French doors, obviously showing off, and on the other side of the glass, Flopsy was scratching the door and barking with excitement.

"Shush, Einstein! Stop that!" Poppy hissed, diving for him.

She managed to grab him and put a hand over his muzzle, silencing him, then hunch down against the base of the wall. She held the terrier's squirming body tightly against her as she crouched behind a large bush, praying that nobody would think of looking outside. There was a rumble of voices in the antechamber, and someone rattled the handle of the French doors, but, to her relief, no one came out onto the terrace, and a minute later she heard the voices drift back into the drawing room, including Muriel saying loudly:

"Come and sit on Mummy's lap, Flopsy-pooh... There, there... Nothing to be afraid of... Kirby, shut the windows! Something outside is upsetting poor Flopsy."

There was a protesting yap from Flopsy and Einstein squirmed harder, but Poppy kept a firm grip on him. She waited until she heard the click of the window closing and the sound of conversation being muted, before she relaxed slightly. The minute her hold loosened, however, Einstein wriggled free and sprang away from her.

"Einstein!" hissed Poppy, lunging after him.

She missed, and he scampered away, disappearing around the side of the house. *Bugger!* thought Poppy, creeping slowly out from behind the bush. *How am I going to find the little monkey now? I need to catch him and get off the property before anyone spots us—*

A hand clamped down on her shoulder and a male voice behind her said:

"What are you doing there?"

CHAPTER TEN

Poppy whirled around and found herself looking up at a young man. He was very good-looking, with blond hair that was carefully cut so that it flopped boyishly over his brow, half-covering one of his eyes. His tall frame was carelessly dressed in a designer blazer teamed with tailored shorts, and the tanned length of his calves ended in a pair of expensive Italian loafers. He looked almost like a male model who had just stepped out of a photoshoot for *GQ* or *Esquire* magazine—even his teeth, when he smiled at her, were dazzling white.

And yes, he was smiling rather than frowning, Poppy noted quickly. It was a rather quizzical smile but at least it was a friendly expression. She took heart from this and from the fact that he had deliberately kept his voice down, so as not to alert those in the drawing room.

"Er... um... I was... um..." Poppy stammered, then said the first thing that came to mind. "Muriel—I mean, Mrs Farnsworth hired me to work on a garden project. I've... um... I've come to check out the site where I'll be planting."

The stranger grinned and raised his eyebrows. "Underneath the drawing room window?"

Poppy flushed. "No, I... er... was walking past and thought I saw some weeds... I just can't stand weeds, you know," she babbled. "You have to get on top of them right away otherwise they spread so quickly... so... um... I thought I'd just yank them out while I saw them."

The young man leaned sideways to look over her shoulder and raised his eyebrows again. Poppy flushed an even brighter red as she followed his gaze and saw that the area beneath the drawing room window was an extension of the terrace and was beautifully paved, with no chance of a weed or anything else growing there. It was obvious that she was lying—and making a bad job of it too—and she expected the stranger the challenge her on this. But to her surprise, he merely grinned again and said with a wink:

"Well, I'm glad to see that Auntie Muriel has hired someone who is so thorough."

"Muriel is your aunt?"

"Great-aunt, actually. Muriel's husband was my grandfather's brother. My parents passed away last year and I don't have any other family, so I came to live with Muriel at Duxton House. It was quite handy, actually—I was just starting my first year at Oxford, which is only about twenty-minutes' drive away." He flashed her another brilliant smile. "Ten, actually, in my Porsche, if the roads are empty and it's late enough that you can ignore the speed limit..." He held out a hand. "We haven't been properly introduced. My name's Henry. Henry Farnsworth. And you are?"

"Poppy Lancaster." Poppy shook his hand, eyeing him curiously. As far as she knew, most students started university at seventeen or eighteen, but Henry looked to be about her age—somewhere in the mid-twenties. "Did you say you've just started at university?"

"Yes, I deferred entry—decided to go travelling around Europe for a bit first," he said carelessly. "Hired a car, drove through Italy, Germany, France... ended up in Monte Carlo and stayed on for a while... It was a bit of a bummer returning to England, to be honest, and then having to leave the house in London to come and live in the country. I stay in college during the term, of course, but Oxford terms are very short and so, for the rest of the time, I'm stuck here. Still, I always thought village life would be a total bore..." His smile widened as he let his gaze travel admiringly over her. "But now I see that maybe I haven't been exposed to the right company."

Poppy realised he was flirting with her and felt

herself blushing. She said in a prim voice: "Yes, the people are very nice in Bunnington. I only moved here a little over a month ago myself and everyone has been very welcoming."

"Ah, you live in Bunnington too?"

She nodded. "At Hollyhock Cottage. I inherited my grandmother's cottage garden nursery."

"Oh, I see—that's why you're doing some gardening work for Auntie Muriel."

"Yes, Ursula introduced me to her at the fête yesterday." At the mention of the murdered woman, the mood sobered. Poppy paused and added, "I'm very sorry about what happened."

Henry assumed a sombre expression. "Yes. Bloody awful tragedy. I wasn't related to Ursula, of course—she was Muriel's own sister's daughter—but I'd got to know her quite well because she lived at Duxton House too. It was a pretty big shock when I got back yesterday evening and heard what had happened."

"Oh? Weren't you at the fête then?"

"Oh no... I was in Oxford. Stuck in the college library all day, actually," he said with a rueful face.

"Isn't it the summer holidays at the moment?" said Poppy in surprise. "I would have thought that the new term doesn't begin until September."

"October, actually. But I let things slip quite a bit last year on the academic front so I thought I'd better do some extra studying, to make up for lost time before the new year begins," he said smoothly.

"Darby College is officially closed out of term, but we members can always gain access—in fact, some of the overseas students stay on during the holidays rather than return to their home countries."

He came a bit closer and said with a winsome smile, "Hey, listen... I don't usually move so fast but—would you like to have dinner with me?"

Poppy was taken aback. "Dinner? T-tonight?" she said stupidly.

Henry shrugged, smiling. "Tonight, tomorrow night—any time that would suit you." His voice lowered suggestively. "I'm all yours."

Poppy hesitated. She had to admit that she was incredibly flattered to be pursued by such a charming, good-looking man. She had never thought of herself as much of a beauty—her clear blue eyes, which stood out vividly against a milky complexion that was prone to freckling in the sun, were probably her prettiest feature. Much to her regret, she hadn't inherited her mother's beautiful honey-blonde hair; instead, hers was a more boring dark brown, which she normally wore pulled back in a functional ponytail. And her figure, while decent, wasn't curvy enough to be called voluptuous nor toned enough to be called athletic—it was a sort of non-descript "in-between", which was pretty much how she'd always seen herself: average height, average figure, average looks.

And yet here was a handsome, wealthy young man looking at her as if she wasn't "average" at all.

Poppy would have been less than human if she hadn't been flattered. Nevertheless, she reminded herself that aside from anything else, Henry was a client's relative and the last thing she wanted was to complicate a professional relationship. So she gave him a regretful smile and said:

"Thanks for the invite, but I think I'd better not. I mean... well, I'm really here to work for your great-aunt."

"That doesn't mean we can't have a bit of fun on the side," he said, arching one eyebrow and giving her a suggestive grin.

His gaiety was infectious and she couldn't help chuckling in response, but no matter how much he tried to persuade her to change her mind, she laughingly declined.

"Well, you must come in for a cup of tea at least," he said at last, obviously keen to have her company for a bit longer in any way possible. "I insist!"

Poppy couldn't see any way to refuse without making a scene and she decided that she could always give Muriel the same excuse about coming to check out the site first.

"All right, thank you," she said, allowing him to take her elbow and gently lead her around to the front of the house.

As they came out onto the wide circular driveway in front of the manor, Poppy saw a gleaming red sports car parked by the door.

"Wow—is this yours?" she asked, going over to

lay an admiring hand on the bonnet. "It's gorgeous!"

Henry beamed with pride. "Yes—I sweet-talked Auntie Muriel into buying it for my birthday last year. It's a limited edition Porsche 911, with custom interiors and personalised plates."

Poppy glanced down at the number plate, which read: "SQZ 9970", and frowned in puzzlement. The sequence didn't look very personalised to her.

Henry laughed. "Yes, well, they *will* be personalised. I'm still working on that—there's a chap who has the plate I want—it spells 'HEN 12Y'—but he's a tough negotiator... In the meantime, though, I've got a custom border and 3D effect on the letters." He gestured to the plates, which did look very striking.

Poppy walked around the car once more, admiring the beautiful lines and feeling a slight pang of envy that she didn't have a rich great-aunt who could give her expensive birthday gifts like this. *I did have an estranged grandmother who gave me a cottage garden nursery, though—complete with two eccentric neighbours, a cat who thinks he knows everything, and a dead body in the flowerbed*, she thought with a wry smile to herself.

"Poppy...?"

She snapped out of her thoughts to see that Henry was standing on the front steps, waiting for her. She started to join him, then paused as she saw a scruffy black shape loitering around the rear bumper of the car. It was Einstein! She swooped down and grabbed the terrier before he could get away. This time she kept a firm hold on him with one hand while reaching into her pocket with the other. She was grateful that she happened to be wearing her work trousers—the pair used to do things around the garden—and in the pocket was some leftover garden twine. It wasn't very long but it was just enough to fashion a makeshift leash which she tied to one end of Einstein's collar.

"Is that your dog? Great little character, isn't he?" said Henry with a smile as he watched from the front steps. "Why don't you bring him in with us? Auntie Muriel is dog mad anyway. I'm sure she won't mind."

Actually, she would probably mind very much! thought Poppy. After the fiasco at the fête yesterday, she didn't think that Muriel would take kindly to her bringing that "common mongrel" in for tea. But she couldn't leave Einstein loose to roam around the estate either.

"Do you think there's somewhere I could keep him, just while I'm having tea with you and your great-aunt?" she asked Henry.

"Oh, certainly." Henry ushered her into the foyer, then pointed down the hallway. "You should be able to leave him in the utility room, by the kitchen. Betsy, one of the maids, is usually in there. Down the hall, last left, then through the big double doors." He gave her a wink. "I'll go on to the drawing room first, but I'll be waiting for you!"

CHAPTER ELEVEN

The manor kitchen was a vast room with high ceilings, an enormous Aga cooker in one corner, and country-style wooden cabinetry spanning the walls. Old-fashioned copper pans hung from a rack above the kitchen island and beautiful matching sets of china were displayed in a large traditional dresser.

Poppy paused in the doorway, unsure whether to go in. The kitchen seemed empty. She could see a large tray on the central island, neatly arranged with teapot, teacups, milk jug, and sugar bowl, and a kettle on the stove with steam rising from its spout. It was as if someone had been in the middle of preparing tea and had suddenly been called away. Then she heard a bang and, a minute later, a girl rushed into the kitchen from a door on the other side of the room.

It was the girl Poppy had seen earlier, announcing Sergeant Lee's arrival, and she guessed that this was Betsy the maid. Her hair was coming loose, with stray wisps escaping from its bun, and she was panting like someone who had been running. She hadn't seen Poppy—the view of the kitchen doorway was partially blocked by the large dresser—and she rushed over to the sink where she hurriedly washed her hands, then grabbed the kettle and returned to the tray and frantically began filling the teapot with hot water.

"Er... excuse me?" said Poppy, stepping forwards.

"*OH!*" The girl jumped so hard that she sloshed hot water from the kettle all over the tray.

"Sorry—I didn't mean to startle you," cried Poppy. "Did you scald yourself?"

"No, no... it's fine... you didn't startle me," said the girl, nervously wiping her hands on her apron. "Can I help you, miss?"

Poppy looked at her curiously. The girl seemed incredibly jumpy. And she had patently been lying when she said she hadn't been startled.

"Um... yes, I've been invited to join Mrs Farnsworth and her great-nephew for tea, and I was wondering if there was somewhere I could leave my dog?" Poppy indicated Einstein. "It's just for twenty minutes or so. Perhaps you have a laundry room where I could shut him in?"

"Oh, sure… over here…"

The girl led Poppy to the door that she had come through a few minutes ago and showed the way to a large utility room. They settled Einstein comfortably—although Poppy did feel slightly guilty as she saw his forlorn face watching her leave—and then returned to the kitchen, where the girl mopped up the spilt water and finished loading the tray. Poppy followed her back through the manor house to a large drawing room with low, wide windows that looked out onto the landscaped grounds of the estate. She saw the glossy, dark green leaves of a camellia bush waving just outside the window and realised that it was the plant that had provided her with the convenient cover when she had been eavesdropping earlier.

The room looked very different viewed from this angle, although Muriel was still sitting on the sofa. Instead of Kirby, however, it was Henry who hovered next to her now—the pet nanny seemed to have disappeared with Flopsy. And across from them sat Sergeant Lee. He was talking as they entered, saying:

"…believe we've got our man, ma'am. We still have to get a confession, of course—right now, the man is denying everything—but rest assured, it's only a matter of time."

"And are you sure this is the man who killed Ursula?" asked Muriel in a quavering voice. "He's a complete stranger! I just don't understand why he would want to harm her."

"Well, as I explained, ma'am, the man is a convicted ex-robber and has been known to have a special interest in mobile phones and similar electronic gadgets. It's obvious that he must have seen Ursula talking on her device and decided to take it by force. It was quite an expensive model, wasn't it—her phone?"

"Yes, well, I don't really understand these things…" said Muriel, looking lost. She glanced at her great-nephew. "Henry would know."

"Yes, Sergeant, it *was* the latest model iPhone, in a limited-edition custom case," said Henry. He gestured to something on the coffee table next to them. "Ursula had a matching cover for her iPad as well."

"Hmm… yes…" The sergeant leaned over and looked at the iPad, then made some notes on his own tablet. "Yes… rose-gold… embellished with Swarovski crystals, it looks like… Yes, something like that would be very eye-catching and very tempting to a petty criminal."

Henry glanced up, seeing Poppy and the maid in the doorway, and sprang up with a smile.

"Poppy! I was just wondering where you'd got to."

"*Poppy?*" Muriel turned around to look at the doorway in surprise.

"Yes, I bumped into her outside and invited her in for tea," said Henry. He winked at Poppy and added, "She was checking out the site where she is going to be working. So diligent of her."

Poppy tried not to flush. "I... um... thought it would be a good idea to familiarise myself with the area... the... um... soil type and things like that..."

Muriel nodded approvingly. "Yes, very good idea. I like your initiative, young lady. Well, do come in and sit down."

Sergeant Lee frowned slightly, obviously not liking the interruption, but since it wasn't a formal interview, he didn't object as Poppy came over to join them. Betsy came into the room too, carrying the tray to the central coffee table. She began carefully pouring the tea and handing out teacups. As she placed a cup in front of Muriel, however, the old lady gave a gasp of outrage.

"What on earth have you been doing, Betsy? Your hands are filthy—I cannot abide dirty nails!"

"Oh!" The maid jerked her hands back, but not before Poppy saw dirt under her fingernails. She darted a frightened look at the sergeant. "I... I'm terribly s-sorry, ma'am..." she stammered. "I just... it was... I... I did wash 'em but—"

"Well, see that it doesn't happen again," said Muriel.

"Yes, ma'am," murmured the girl.

Quickly, she passed around the rest of the teacups, and then, with a last nervous glance at the sergeant, she picked up the tray and hurried out. Sergeant Lee didn't seem to notice her tense behaviour; he was busy talking about the ex-robber once more and congratulating himself on a quick arrest.

"...we should have a confession by the end of the week, with the man in court facing the charges before the end of the month—which will be setting a new record in how fast an investigation is solved, if I do say so myself," he said, rubbing his hands and grinning. "Even my guv'nor—that's Detective Inspector Suzanne Whittaker—hasn't ever wrapped up a murder enquiry in under a week."

It's no use being fast if you're wrong, thought Poppy sourly. She'd met Sergeant Lee a couple of times before and had never liked him. Arrogant and smug, Lee was quick to jump to conclusions and seemed more keen to make arrests and wrap up a case quickly—just to "score points"—than to put in the proper detective work to make sure that the right person was brought to justice. She couldn't help remembering what Nell had said and found herself agreeing with her old friend: something about Ursula's murder just didn't feel like a straightforward "mugging-gone-wrong".

When the sergeant took his leave a few minutes later, Poppy hesitated, then sprang up impulsively and—throwing a hasty "Excuse me, I just need to ask Sergeant Lee something!" at Henry and Muriel— she rushed out after the detective. She caught up with him just as he was walking down the front steps of Duxton House.

"Sergeant Lee! Sergeant Lee! Can I have a word

with you, please?"

He turned around and looked at her impatiently. "Yes?"

Poppy paused, wondering how to broach the subject. "Um... it's about this murder investigation. I just wondered if you might have any other suspects?"

His brows drew together. "Other suspects? Why would we need other suspects? We've got our man."

"Yes, but just in case you're wrong—"

He bristled. "Wrong? Of course I'm not wrong! Are you questioning my professional judgement?"

"No, no, of course not—it's just... well... don't you think it's a bit far-fetched?" Poppy blurted out. "I mean, why would this ex-robber suddenly decide to attack a random woman when he's out on parole? Why would he threaten his own chances of freedom?"

"Because he's a criminal!" Lee said in a patronising tone. "These thugs can't help themselves. He probably walked past and saw Ursula with her phone and decided to take his chances. Got cocky, probably. Thought it would be an easy steal."

"But why didn't he just snatch the phone and run? Why did he kill her?"

Sergeant Lee gave an exaggerated sigh of patience and said in the voice of someone talking to a very stupid person: "Be-cause... Ursula put up a fight! It's obvious what happened: he tried to grab her phone, she resisted, they struggled, and he lost it and clobbered her."

"Did you find Ursula's phone on him?" asked Poppy.

"No, but that doesn't mean anything. The man could have got rid of it before we arrested him."

"What about the murder weapon? What did he stab her with?"

Lee scowled. "That hasn't been found yet, but I'm sure it will turn up in due course. These are just loose ends—the important thing is, we've got our man, he's in custody, and, with a bit more time, I'm sure we'll get a confession out of him."

"But they aren't just loose ends!" Poppy protested. "They're all important leads that could change the direction of an investigation. Shouldn't you at least dig a bit deeper, not just jump on the first convenient suspect? I know that Suzanne—I mean Inspector Whittaker—wouldn't have just made assumptions like that."

As soon as the words were out, Poppy realised that she'd said the wrong thing. No one likes being compared to their superiors and found wanting. Sergeant Lee's face darkened, and he said through clenched teeth:

"I am perfectly capable of running a murder investigation on my own! It's clear here who the culprit is. Mrs Farnsworth is already very upset—I'm not going to cause the family of the deceased any more distress by dragging things out unnecessarily."

"They'd be more upset if you arrested the wrong person and the real killer went free," Poppy retorted.

"All right, then, Miss Smarty-Pants—who do you think it is, then? Eh? You seem to have all the answers," he sneered. "Give me some names, then! What other suspects do you want me to investigate? Do you have proof of anyone's guilt?"

"I..."

Put on the spot, Poppy hesitated. She didn't have any concrete evidence of guilt, just some vague, uneasy feelings about things she had observed: Kirby's slimy manner... the maid's nervous manner... Nell's melodramatic theories about Norman killing Ursula in a fit of passion...

"No, nothing," she admitted.

"Well then, in that case, I suggest that you stop sticking your nose where it doesn't belong and let the *professionals* get on with their work," said Sergeant Lee, putting heavy emphasis on the word "*professionals*". He gave her a curt nod. "Good day."

CHAPTER TWELVE

Poppy made her way slowly back to the drawing room, feeling humiliated and frustrated. She knew that Lee was right in a way—it *was* none of her business, she *was* just a civilian, and she should forget about Ursula's murder investigation and get on with her own life. But it was so hard to stand by and do nothing when you could see things that might make a difference!

She arrived at the drawing room doorway and was just about to step in when she heard Henry's voice saying in a wheedling tone:

"...it would be just a little loan, Auntie Muriel— just a few hundred quid to get me out of a spot of bother."

"Didn't I give you two hundred pounds last week, Henry?"

"Oh... no, you must be remembering wrong, Auntie. Perhaps you intended to give me the money but then you forgot."

"But I was sure..." Muriel sounded confused.

"In fact, I think that's probably what happened," said Henry smoothly. "You know how forgetful you are these days."

Muriel sighed. "I suppose so. Although Ursula did warn me... she said—"

"Yes? What did Ursula say?" Henry's voice was suddenly sharp.

"She thought that I was spoiling you. She said that you get a very good allowance as it is and it should be more than ample to cover your needs, so there was no need to give you more money."

"Ah..." Henry's voice softened and relaxed again, taking on a playful tone. "Well, I *am* your only nephew, Auntie Muriel—in fact, I'm your only family now. Who else can you spoil, if not me? Anyway, this is for some extra textbooks. They're not on the official syllabus but one of the other students told me that they're fantastic—he's sure they helped him get a First in his final exams."

"Oh... well, certainly, if it's something to help your studies, my dear boy. If you bring me my chequebook later, I'll write you a cheque... two hundred pounds, did you say?"

"Well... actually, if you can spare a bit more, Auntie Muriel—"

The sound of nails clicking on the stone tiles

made Poppy turn around and look up the hallway; she saw Flopsy approaching. She shifted uneasily as the toy poodle trotted past, remembering those sharp teeth from the meeting at the fête, but thankfully the little dog showed no interest in her. She went straight into the drawing room, and a second later Poppy heard Muriel cry:

"Flopsy! There you are! Mummy has been missing you! Come... come and give Mummy a kiss, Flopsy-pooh..."

Deciding to follow the dog's cue, Poppy stepped into the room and returned to her seat. She saw a look of annoyance flash across Henry's face as he eyed the dog, then it was wiped clean, to be replaced by his familiar charming smile as he turned to her and said something flirtatious. Poppy picked up her teacup and sipped the now-cold brew, nodding and making polite conversation, and wishing that the whole thing could be over. Still, she was very pleased when Muriel mentioned the scent garden and learned that the old lady still wanted her to go ahead. In fact, she wanted Poppy to start work the next morning.

"You can ask the estate gardeners to help you with any heavy lifting or digging," instructed Muriel. "There are quite a few large rocks in those beds which you might want to remove."

"Oh, I might be able to just plant around them," said Poppy. "I've been doing some reading and a lot of the herbs and scented plants like dry, well-draining soil—things like lavender and thyme—so an old rock garden is actually an ideal spot to plant them in." She smiled at the old lady. "Actually, I wanted to ask you: have you noticed Flopsy gravitating towards certain plants when she's out in the grounds? I read that dogs often self-medicate when they're given the chance to do so and it would be good to know what sort of plants Flopsy likes, so I can make sure that I include those."

"Well, let me see... Flopsy does like lavender, but I don't know about thyme... Hmm... I've noticed that she loves marigolds—she's always running up to sniff them when she sees them... And chamomile," Muriel added. "We have some growing in the vegetable patch behind the kitchen and Betsy tells me that Flopsy is always sniffing and rubbing herself on the chamomile leaves."

Poppy took out her phone and consulted the list she had made. "Yes, apparently dogs with skin irritations or stomach upsets will often be attracted to chamomile."

Muriel gasped. "Skin irritation? Stomach upset? Does that mean Flopsy needs to see the vet?"

Poppy glanced at the poodle sitting on the old woman's lap. With her bright black eyes and thick woolly coat, Flopsy looked the picture of health.

"I'm sure Flopsy is fine," she reassured Muriel. "Perhaps it was just a small thing—you know, like we sometimes get a bit of indigestion after a big meal and have a cup of peppermint tea to settle the stomach? Maybe Flopsy was doing the same with the chamomile. I'm sure it's nothing to worry about."

"Oh... and she loves that plant with the tall stalks of little white flowers...oh, dear, what is it called?" Muriel furrowed her brow for a moment. "Ah yes—valerian."

"Oh, *Valerian officinalis*! You know, in medieval times, it was known as 'all-heal' because it was used to treat so many things, like headaches and insomnia, and it's supposed to calm nervous animals too. Although... it's supposed to smell awful when it's dried, like old socks or the sewer," added Poppy, laughing. She sat up. "Hey, you know—I've just had a thought: Hollyhock Cottage has several scented plants growing there already. Would you like to bring Flopsy down to have a wander around and see how she reacts to them? Because we don't want to pick something that she might absolutely hate."

Muriel nodded approvingly. "Ooh yes, wonderful idea! I'm afraid I'm busy tomorrow—I need to see my solicitor in Oxford and I also have a meeting with the undertakers regarding Ursula's funeral..." Her voice shook for a moment, then she steadied herself. "But the day after that, perhaps?"

Ten minutes later, Poppy finally managed to excuse herself, retrieve Einstein, and leave Duxton House. She walked slowly back to Hollyhock Cottage, trailing Einstein behind her. The terrier had not wanted to leave the estate and she'd had to practically drag him off the property. Trying to get a terrier to do something he didn't want to do was a challenge at the best of times and Poppy found her patience wearing thin as Einstein alternately lay down and refused to walk, or braced his hind legs and pulled backwards. She had to resort to a mixture of cajoling and stern reprimands to finally get him moving again. Even when they were no longer within sight of Duxton House, he kept looking backwards and whining, straining on his leash and wanting to return.

"Oh Einstein—I'm afraid Flopsy's out of your league," said Poppy, giving him a sympathetic look. "You have to give up this hopeless romance of yours."

"*Ruff! Ruff-ruff!*" barked Einstein indignantly. Obviously "give up" was not in any self-respecting terrier's vocabulary.

Poppy sighed and gave him another gentle tug to encourage him forwards. They made slow progress across the village and, as she chivvied Einstein along, her thoughts returned to Ursula's murder and her experiences at Duxton House that morning. She couldn't quite put her finger on it, but something bothered her. And she was positive that the murder wasn't as straightforward as Sergeant Lee believed.

***

Bertie looked slightly bemused when Poppy turned up on his doorstep with Einstein in tow. She had a feeling that he hadn't even noticed that his dog had been gone.

"Oh, that was very good of you to go after him, my dear." Bertie tutted and shook his head. "I really do not know what has got into Einstein! He has been misbehaving dreadfully these few days. First running off into the woods yesterday and bothering that nice young man with the sportscar, then breaking out of the terrier racing, and now this—"

"Wait, Bertie..." Poppy caught his arm as his words made her think of something. "This young man with the sportscar that you're talking about—what kind of car was it?"

Bertie frowned. "It was a Porsche, I believe."

"And it was red, you said?"

"Oh yes, lovely colour."

"And I don't suppose you remember the number plate?" asked Poppy without much hope.

"Well, as a matter of fact, I do. It was SQZ 9970. I noticed it, you see, because it reminded me of the square root of two—also known as Pythagoras's constant—which is expressed as $\sqrt{2} = 99/70$. Isn't that a marvellous coincidence?"

Poppy chuckled. How lucky—or unlucky for him—that Henry's number plate should happen to resemble a famous mathematical constant.

"What did the young man look like?"

"Oh…" Bertie seemed a bit nonplussed. "Like a nice young man."

"What colour was his hair? Was it quite long? Did it fall over his eyes like this?" Poppy demonstrated.

Bertie looked at her in surprise. "How did you know? Yes, that was exactly how he had his hair."

"And was he very good-looking?"

"Yes, I suppose he was. He certainly looked like a gentleman. He was dressed very smartly. In fact, I was quite mortified that Einstein got muddy pawprints all over his nice cream trousers."

Poppy frowned and said, half to herself, "I wonder what he was doing in the woods…"

"Oh, he was talking on his phone," said Bertie. "Although I did wonder why he wanted to speak there—woods and forests are notorious for having dreadful mobile phone coverage as the dense foliage blocks cellular signals. In fact, it has been shown that most homes and offices receive much better reception in autumn, simply because many trees have dropped their leaves." He held up a forefinger and said excitedly: "I did have an idea once for a portable mobile phone signal booster—like the kind used by forestry technicians—which would amplify 3G and 4G signals, although my invention would not need to rely on an existing mobile phone signal in a separate location…"

Poppy was hardly listening. Instead, she was recalling, with a quickening of excitement, that

Ursula had received a phone call just before she was murdered. In fact, it was because of that call that Ursula had gone back to the marquee alone.

"Bertie!" She interrupted his rambling (he was still going on about boosting phone signals) and asked eagerly: "Do you have any idea who Henry—I mean, who this young man might have been talking to?"

Bertie frowned. "I couldn't hear very well—he had a hand over his mouth, you see, and was keeping his voice low. I think he might have been arranging to meet someone—I did hear him say: 'I'll see you soon.'"

"That's all he said? He didn't mention a name?"

"No, well, you see, Einstein ran up to him then and he ended the call."

A few minutes later, Poppy let herself out of Bertie's garden and walked back to Hollyhock Cottage, mulling over what the old inventor had told her. She was sure the young man that he had seen was Henry Farnsworth. It was just too much of a coincidence otherwise to think that some other young man, with similar hairstyle, dress sense, and looks, could have been driving his red sports car. But if it was Henry in the woods behind Duxton House estate yesterday, then he had been lying when he told her that he'd spent the whole day in Oxford. So why had he lied?

CHAPTER THIRTEEN

When Poppy arrived back at Hollyhock Cottage, she was delighted to find a man in green overalls at the back of the cottage. He was carefully painting over the ugly graffiti that had been spray-painted on the wall and Poppy realised that Nell must have lost the battle with soap and water, and decided to call in reinforcements.

"Joe! How nice to see you," she cried, smiling at the spry old handyman.

With his grey hair tied back in a low ponytail, and his stern, weather-beaten face and laconic manner, Joe Fabbri came across as intimidating, even frightening when you first met him. But Poppy had quickly realised that the old handyman was wise and kind, with a wealth of knowledge that he was happy to share—providing you could decipher his one-word answers!

"I've been deadheading all the roses and other flowers like you said," she told him proudly. "It's really helped to keep everything blooming. And you know those bushes that you cut back? It's amazing how much new growth has appeared already! Thanks for doing those. I would never have known how to prune them."

Joe nodded approvingly, then he jerked his head at the gravel path and said, "Lop."

Poppy followed the direction of his gaze in puzzlement. What on earth was he talking about? Then her eyes alighted on the clumps of lavender lining the path. They were just coming to the end of their flowering, their purple flower spikes fading and drying now, and she made a guess.

"You mean the lavender? They need to be cut back too?"

"Summer prune. Woody and leggy else."

"Oh..." Poppy walked over to one of the clumps and crouched down next to it, putting out a hand to touch the grey-green stems. A wonderful fragrance was released as she rubbed the soft, feathery foliage, filling the air with a sweet, woody aroma that was somehow soothing and yet invigorating at the same time. Poppy breathed deeply. She loved the smell of lavender. All the store-bought essential oils in the world couldn't compete with the smell of freshly crushed lavender sprigs.

"Hidcote. English lavender," Joe said, watching

her. "Best perfume. Hardy."

"Do you just trim the flower stalks?" asked Poppy, fingering one long, slender stem.

"Naw, bush too. One third." He motioned with his hands. "Round."

Poppy thought of the front door of the cottage. There was a terracotta pot there, with another lavender growing in it. "What about the one by the door? You know, with the tufts on each flower spike, like little rabbit ears?"

"Naw. French," Joe said dismissively, then he returned to his painting without another word.

French? Poppy frowned in confusion. It wasn't until she had gone inside the cottage and fired up her ancient laptop to research "lavender pruning" that she realised what Joe had meant. The clumps of lavender by the path were *Lavandula angustifolia*, known as "English lavender" (although they came originally from the Mediterranean), and they were the easiest to grow, although they did need annual pruning to keep them in good shape and flowering well. The one in the pot, though, was a different variety—*Lavandula stoechas*, otherwise known as "French lavender" (Strangely enough, this plant actually originated in Spain! Early lavender growers obviously needed geography lessons.)—and this one didn't need anything more than deadheading because it flowered right through the summer.

"I've just been reading all about lavender," she told Nell excitedly as she collected her secateurs from the greenhouse. "I'm going out to prune them."

"Don't you think you should wait for Joe?" asked Nell, looking doubtful. "You haven't done any proper pruning yourself yet and everyone says lavender can be quite tricky. Maybe you should let Joe do it once, so you can watch? He's gone now but I'm sure he can pop back round tomorrow."

"No, no, I want to do it myself. Don't worry—I've read all about it online. I even watched some YouTube videos," said Poppy, grinning. "I'm a lavender expert now!"

She spent the next hour happily tackling the lavender clumps along the side of the path, humming to herself and falling into a relaxing rhythm of cutting, snipping, collecting, and stacking the cuttings in little piles. The perfume that wafted from the trimmed foliage was glorious and Poppy was surprised to find that she really enjoyed pruning. There was something incredibly therapeutic and satisfying about the act of cutting away the old brown stems and removing shrivelled, dry sections.

As she worked, her mind wandered back to the murder and, in particular, to Henry Farnsworth. Once again, she wondered why had he lied about his whereabouts that day. Well, one reason could have been to provide himself with an alibi. By approaching the estate from the rear, it would have been easy for Henry to slip onto the property unnoticed. She had done it herself that morning via the gap in the hedge without being seen by anyone—and she guessed that those teenage boys had used the same route. Things would have been even more chaotic during the fête yesterday, with so many strangers milling about and all the attention centred on the main lawn at the front of the house. Henry could have quietly made his way to the marquee where he'd arranged to meet Ursula, killed her, then sneaked back out. Then he could have "arrived" at the main gate later that evening pretending to have just come back from Oxford.

But what motive could Henry have for wanting to murder Ursula? *Money*, thought Poppy. One could see at a glance that Henry Farnsworth was used to a lavish lifestyle, with his designer clothing, his luxury sports car, and his carefree travels at the expense of his studies. Then there was the conversation she'd overheard... it sounded like Henry made a habit of asking Muriel for extra funds. Money was obviously something that the handsome young student craved and needed.

But we all want and need more money, thought Poppy with a frown. *We don't all go around murdering people! Besides, why should Ursula's death make a difference? It's not as if—*

"POPPY!"

Poppy came out of her thoughts and looked up in surprise to find Nell standing beside her, staring aghast at something. Poppy followed her gaze and her heart gave a lurch of dismay. Where billowing mounds of lavender had once lined the side of the path, there was now a row of bare twiggy stems.

"What have you done to the lavender?" gasped Nell.

"Er... well, I might have taken off a *bit* more than I planned to—"

"A bit? You've hacked them all down to nothing!" cried Nell.

Poppy winced. "I... um... was having such a good time, I sort of got carried away. But they'll grow back... won't they?" She looked at Nell hopefully.

"I don't know. They look pretty awful," said Nell, examining the barren stumps.

Poppy swallowed as she looked at them as well. Oh God, the more she looked at them, the worse they seemed. Nell was right—the woody stems looked stiff and dead. She couldn't imagine anything growing from them again.

"But... but I saw Joe pruning other things in the garden," Poppy said. "He cut them right down to the ground too and they all bounced back! Within a couple of days, they all had lots of fresh green shoots and leaves popping out."

"Well, maybe they're different. I mean, not every plant behaves the same way. You probably have to use different pruning methods for different things."

"Oh Nell, what am I going to do?" wailed Poppy. "This was such a beautiful part of the cottage garden and it's the path leading up to the front door too, so it's the first thing people see. And now it's ruined!"

Nell sighed. "Well, I did tell you to wait for Joe, dear. He would have shown you the correct way to do it."

"I know—but I wanted to surprise him," said Poppy miserably. "I want him to be proud of me when he comes back and sees what I'd done."

"Well, he'll certainly get a surprise all right," said Nell dryly. She patted Poppy's hand. "Never mind, dear. You can always plant new lavender bushes if these die. I suppose you have to make mistakes to learn." She bent and picked up a pile of lavender flower spikes which had been trimmed from the bushes. She sniffed them appreciatively. "These are lovely though! They still smell gorgeous, even though they're faded. You could use these in dried flower arrangements, you know. I'll take them in and sort them into bunches."

Left alone in the garden, Poppy glanced guiltily at the row of scraggly wooden stems once more and felt like kicking herself. Then she sighed and turned to look around at the rest of the garden. Somehow, seeing all the riotous flowerbeds bursting with colour cheered her up a bit. Nell's comment about flower arrangements reminded her of her new business idea and she decided impulsively to make up a sample bouquet. Then she could take some photos on her phone and design a simple leaflet on her computer later that night. And tomorrow morning, she would head to the village post office shop, which offered a simple printing service, and get some material printed. She could also donate the arrangement to the postmistress, she decided; the whole village passed through the post office shop regularly and her flowers would be prominently displayed to all those who came in.

Poppy hurried through the beds, selecting various blooms at random. There were still some sweet peas twining their way up through old wooden supports, with ruffled blooms of soft pink, cream, and lilac; there were billowing white cosmos on slender stalks and stately snapdragons with columns of opulent flowers. At the front of the beds, pretty calendula in shades of coral and burnt orange vied for attention with bright zinnia blooms. And finally, she picked some dainty sprays of cow parsley together with aromatic stems of rosemary to provide fillers and foliage around the flowers.

She found an old metal jug and arranged the flowers in a loose, informal fashion, making sure to balance the colours and keep a nice shape overall. When at last she was done and stepped back to look at the beautiful arrangement, she felt her spirits lifting in spite of herself. She might have been a lousy gardener, but at least she was good at picking and arranging flowers!

Smiling with satisfaction, Poppy got hold of her phone and began snapping some photos. With her phone being an older model, the camera wasn't the most powerful, but somehow the warm afternoon sunlight filtering through the trees and the slightly grainy quality of the photos combined to give them a soft vintage effect which looked very attractive—almost as if she had created the illusion on purpose!

Pleased with her efforts, Poppy took the arrangement into the cottage and left it in a cool corner of the sitting room. Nell heard her and called from the kitchen:

"Have you had lunch, dear? No? Well, you must eat something now! It's terrible to skip meals, especially with all this hard gardening work you're doing—you'll wear yourself down to skin and bones! And then how are you ever going to find a man? Men don't like scrawny women, you know, no matter what the magazines say. They appreciate a girl with a healthy appetite and some curves to fill out a dress..."

Poppy rolled her eyes, but she submitted to Nell's fussing with good-natured grace. She wolfed the food down and, as soon as the last bite was gone, sprang up to head back out to the garden again.

"Where are you rushing off to now?" complained Nell. "You've barely let your food go down!"

"I just thought—since I can't work at Duxton House—today's a good day to catch up on a lot of stuff I still need to do in the garden," explained Poppy. "I'm a bit worried about the stone wall between us and Nick Forrest, you know. The section with the huge stand of ivy growing on it."

"Oh, yes, that's a terrible mess," said Nell, making a face. "It's a huge tangle with dead leaves and old birds' nests and spiders' webs—"

"Yes, it looks awful, doesn't it? It's one of the last things I need to tackle, but I've been putting it off..." Poppy took a deep breath. "I'm going to sort it out this afternoon."

"But I thought Joe said the other day that you should prune most things in late winter or early spring?"

"Yes, but he also said that if the ivy is getting out of hand, then you can trim it any time to reduce the size. This one is *horribly* overgrown and it's really top-heavy too. There are parts where you can see it pulling away from the wall and hanging down. And that wall is already old and crumbling—what if the ivy pulls it down?"

"My lordy Lord, yes, the last thing you need is the expense of replacing a stone wall," Nell agreed. "It's a shame Joe's gone now—you could have asked him to help you."

"It's okay. I know what to do—"

"That's what you said about the lavender," said Nell, pursing her lips.

"No, no, this is different," Poppy insisted. "This doesn't need any special pruning technique. This is just cutting away overgrown stuff."

"Well... he's left the ladder out by the back door," said Nell grudgingly. "But make sure you're careful on it, dear. I watched this programme on telly about accidents in the home and workplace, and did you know that nearly half of all falls are from a ladder? It's because people don't use them properly. They're impatient and careless, and they don't make sure that the ladder is stable before they climb up."

Poppy assured Nell that she would take care and lugged the ladder over to the section of the wall with the ivy. The ground beneath the wall was soft and uneven, and it was impossible to have the legs of the ladder evenly balanced, so she propped it against the wall. She gave it an experimental shake. It seemed secure enough. She climbed to the top and looked curiously around. Everything looked different from this higher vantage point—she could see across the entire cottage garden, all the way to the rear of the property.

And on the other side of the wall, she could see Nick's garden. It was an elegantly landscaped area of low maintenance hedges and shrubs, combined with a well-tended lawn. It looked calm and inviting—nothing like the riotous mix of colours, shapes, and textures that dominated her own cottage garden—and for a moment, Poppy had the treacherous thought that something like Nick's green haven would be so much less work and hassle.

Then she remembered how the crime author loved coming over to Hollyhock Cottage, because it seemed to magically help his writing. So much so, in fact, that her grandmother had invited him to visit whenever he was struggling with writer's block—an arrangement that Poppy continued to honour. Nick's garden might have been neat and low-maintenance, but it was the wild, colourful wonderland on her side of the wall that helped to get the creative juices flowing!

She began clipping back the rampant new growth on the ivy, carefully making sure that she cut each stem just above a leaf bud. It was strange how she had never paid much attention to the architecture of a plant before, but ever since Joe had shown her how new growth would appear from the little nodes at the base of each leaf, she had been excited to spot it happening on plants all over the garden.

Humming to herself once more, Poppy was just settling into a comfortable rhythm of untangling and clipping when she heard a roar from inside the house on the other side of the wall.

"YOU BLOODY CAT! I'm going to kill you!"

CHAPTER FOURTEEN

Poppy looked across the wall and saw a commotion in the open upstairs window opposite her. A large orange cat sprang up onto the windowsill. *Oren!* He was followed a second later by Nick Forrest himself, looking absolutely livid. He lunged for the cat, but Oren was too quick for him. The ginger tom sprang off the windowsill, sailed through the air, and landed nimbly on top of the wall next to Poppy.

"ARRRRGGHH!" fumed Nick. He leaned out of the window and saw her. Pointing a finger at Oren, he snarled, "Hold him—don't let him get away! I'm going to wring his neck!"

"*N-ow?*" said Oren cheekily.

Poppy suppressed a laugh. "What did he do?" she asked, refraining from adding "this time".

"He's destroyed a book I borrowed from one of the Oxford college libraries!" snapped Nick. "It's a valuable old edition that would normally never be allowed out of the library doors, but I managed to sweet-talk the librarian into letting me borrow it for book research and bring it home for a few days. I *promised* her I would take very good care of it..." He disappeared from the window, then returned a second later holding up a book for Poppy to see. "Look! Look what the bloody cat has done!"

Poppy flinched as she saw that the beautiful leatherbound cover had been shredded, with long claw marks raking in parallel lines across the embossed calf's hide surface. Oren had obviously decided to use the priceless old book as a new scratching pad. Even now, the ginger tom looked unrepentant, licking a paw nonchalantly as if he hadn't done anything wrong. Nick growled again as he eyed his cat and looked ready to make good his threat to come and strangle Oren. Poppy hastened to distract him.

"Can't you just get a new binding for the book?" she asked. "I mean, isn't the content the really valuable thing? So as long as Oren hasn't damaged the pages—"

"It's a rare edition! The value isn't just in the printed pages but also in the aged leather covers and the marbled binding and tooling on the spine... I can't just have a new cover stuck on! Besides, the point is—I gave the librarian my word that it would not be damaged." Nick groaned and ran a hand through his unruly hair, making it look even wilder. "How am I going to explain this to her now?"

Poppy gave him a helpless smile. "Maybe she's a cat-lover too and she'll be understanding?"

Nick sighed, calming down slightly. "Well, I'd better head back to Darby College library tomorrow and face the music."

Poppy pricked up her ears. "Did you say Darby College?"

"Yes, why?"

It was the same college that Henry had said he belonged to. In fact, he had said that he was in the college library all day yesterday, instead of being at the fête—and yet Bertie had claimed to see someone very like Henry with a red sportscar that carried Henry's number plate...

"Is the college library very big?" Poppy asked.

"No, Darby is one of the smaller Oxford colleges. The library is really just one long room covering the south side of the main quad. Why?"

Poppy ignored his question, asking instead: "If it's just one room, would you have been able to see everyone who came in or out?"

Nick raised an eyebrow. "That sounds a bit pointed. Is there someone in particular that you had in mind?"

"Henry Farnsworth—Muriel Farnsworth's great-nephew," said Poppy. She described him and looked hopefully at Nick. "Did you see him?"

"No. I was in the library most of the day before I came to the fête and I didn't see anyone of that description."

"So he *was* lying!" said Poppy triumphantly. She saw Nick looking at her quizzically and explained: "I met Henry at Duxton House this morning. He's a student at Oxford—at Darby College—and he told me that he was studying in the college library all day yesterday. He said that he didn't return to Bunnington until the evening—but Bertie says that he saw Henry and his red sportscar when he was walking to the fête."

Nick's face darkened at the mention of Bertie and he growled, "Are you sure you can trust that old codger? It might have been another young man with a red sportscar."

"No, I'm sure it was Henry. Bertie remembered the number plate on the car—because it resembled the value for the square root of two," she added as she saw him start to protest again. Nick paused, then gave a wry nod, obviously knowing his father well enough to realise that was enough confirmation.

"So Henry lied about his whereabouts on the day of the murder," Nick stated.

Poppy nodded. "It looks that way. But why?"

"Well, the obvious answer is to provide himself with an alibi. But does Henry have a motive to kill Ursula? Does he stand to gain in any way from her death?"

Poppy shrugged. "I don't know. The only thing I could think of is that with Ursula gone, he's Muriel Farnsworth's only remaining relative now and I assume that he would get the lion's share of her estate."

"I wouldn't assume anything," said Nick with a cynical smile. "People can be funny in their wills. For all you know, she could leave everything to that poodle of hers. In any case, even if that were true, it seems a bit strange for Henry to suddenly decide to kill Ursula now. Muriel is only in her seventies and she's in good health—it's not as if she's on her deathbed. Why would Henry go to the trouble of murdering Ursula now, just for the *chance* of more money—which he won't receive until several years into the future anyway? Unless they're homicidal psychopaths, people need a good reason to embark on something as serious as murder."

"It's so hard to imagine him as a murderer, anyway," said Poppy with a sigh. "I mean, I can't imagine why Henry would need to kill anyone. He seems to have everything: he's rich, good-looking, educated, charming—"

"Lots of murderers are charming," said Nick with a grim smile. "Take it from me. I met several during my time in the CID."

"I suppose it's just as well, then, that I didn't accept Henry's dinner invitation."

Nick raised his eyebrows. "He asked you out to dinner?"

Poppy felt her cheeks reddening. "Yes, he asked me out on a date. Not that I would have accepted anyway. For professional reasons," she added primly.

Nick looked amused and was about to reply when he was interrupted by a loud yowl from Oren:

"*N-owwww!*"

The ginger tom was obviously bored with their conversation and peeved at being ignored. He walked along the top of the wall until he was level with Poppy's shoulder, then peered down at the ladder. Before she could stop him, Oren sprang from the wall, aiming for one of the lower rungs. He missed his target, making the ladder shudder as he hit the metal frame, then it swayed precariously as Oren scrambled to climb back onto one of the rungs. Without stable footing on the ground, the ladder began to teeter as the cat's weight rocked it.

"Whoa—*Oren!*" gasped Poppy. She clutched at the wall as the ladder swung away and her feet slipped from the rungs.

"Careful!" shouted Nick.

Oren gave a petulant *"N-ow!"* and jumped off the ladder, landing nimbly in the undergrowth. Poppy tried to do the same but she was too high and the ladder tangled with her legs as it fell away from the wall. She cried out, groping wildly for a handhold, and fell against the ivy covering the wall. Leaves and stems tore away from the stone and, for a moment, Poppy thought the whole vine was going to collapse with her buried underneath! Then, to her relief, she felt the sturdier, older branches break her fall and found herself hanging against the side of the wall, her face pressed into the thick carpet of ivy leaves.

"*Poppy!* Are you all right?" came Nick's voice from the other side of the wall.

"Yes..." she mumbled. "Yes, I'm fine. The ivy saved me."

Slowly, using the ivy branches as handholds, she climbed down and lowered herself to the ground. Stepping back from the wall, she dusted herself off and shot a dirty look at Oren who was sitting nearby, once more nonchalantly washing a paw. She was beginning to see why Nick found the feline so infuriating!

She paused as she turned back to the wall and something caught her eye. A section of the ivy had torn away, exposing the stone slabs behind it. She frowned, going closer and reaching out to push the ivy leaves aside for a better look. She could see a little alcove in the wall—a small recess where the mortar between the slabs had worn away, leaving a gap. Not deep enough to open through to the other side, but enough to form a sort of cubbyhole, the kind of place you might hide your secret treasures and belongings...

There was a tin wedged in the hole—a biscuit tin, with faded pictures and rusty edges showing that it had been there a long time. Poppy reached for it and carefully eased it out. Someone had stuck a home-made label across the top. Time and the elements had faded the ink, but Poppy could just make out the words written in a childish hand:

Private Property of Holly Lancaster
Do Not Open Without Permission!

She caught her breath, her heart pounding. This had belonged to her mother! Then she realised that she could hear Nick's voice from the other side of the wall, sounding very concerned.

"Poppy? Poppy, are you all right?"

"Yes, I'm fine," she called. "I'm down now. And I... I think I found something."

"What? Hang on—I'm coming over."

A few minutes later, the front gate of the cottage garden creaked open and Nick hurried in, his long legs carrying him quickly over to the section of the wall where Poppy was standing. She was still staring down at the box, her mind whirling with a mass of thoughts and questions.

"What's that?" asked Nick, coming to a stop next to her.

"I think this belonged to my mother," murmured Poppy. "It was in a hole in the wall. I think she must have put it in there when she was a child or teenager. The ivy wouldn't have been as overgrown then and a lot more of the wall would have been exposed. Maybe she found the hole and used it as a secret hiding place."

"What's inside?"

"I don't know—I haven't looked." Poppy hesitated, then gave him an embarrassed smile. "I know she's dead and this was from a long time ago but... it felt a bit wrong opening it without her permission, you know?"

Nick smiled with unexpected gentleness. "Yes, I know what you mean. But I'm sure your mother wouldn't mind."

Poppy took a deep breath and carefully prised the lid off the round metal tin. They both peered inside. There was an assortment of odds and ends, the kind of keepsakes that a young girl would treasure. There were several blank greeting cards and stickers portraying unicorns and rainbows, a keyring in the shape of a shamrock, a half-filled notebook that looked like it could have been a diary, several hair ribbons, a little bottle of nail polish with the remnants of pink enamel paint clinging to the sides, a home-made bracelet made of pretty glass beads, a few dried flower heads, and—at the top of the pile—a yellowed photograph.

Poppy pounced on the last item and held it up to the light. It showed a group of girls of about sixteen or seventeen, sitting in a row, some smiling self-consciously at the camera, others hunched over shyly. Poppy recognised her mother immediately: even in the old, faded image, Holly Lancaster stood out as the prettiest girl in the group, with her honey-blonde hair tossed over her shoulders and her blue eyes bright and intelligent. She had an arm around one of the other girls and her lips were spread in a wide smile.

Behind the girls stood several young men, some holding guitars, and all looking handsome and moody. Poppy felt her pulse quicken as she peered closer at the photograph, scanning the faces of each of the men and searching for any sign of familiar resemblance. But the picture was too dark and the quality too poor to make out much detail.

"Is that your mother?" asked Nick quietly.

Poppy nodded, pointing Holly Lancaster out in the photo. "I'm guessing the other girls are the groupies she used to hang out with."

"And the men behind them? Are those the rock musicians they followed around?"

"I don't know. Maybe." Poppy hesitated, then added in a small voice, "One of them might be my father."

She half expected Nick to make a mocking comment, like he usually did, but to her surprise, he said nothing. Instead, he reached out to take the photo gently from her and look more closely at it.

"I would have been able to pick your mother out even if you hadn't told me," he said with the ghost of a smile. "You look like her."

"*Me?*" Poppy stared at him in astonishment.

"Your hair is dark and you have more freckles," Nick conceded, looking from Poppy down to the photograph and then back up again. "But otherwise, you have the same eyes and that pert nose and generous mouth—"

"Don't be silly! My mother was *beautiful* whereas I'm very ordi—" Poppy broke off, flushing.

Nick looked amused. "Oh, I doubt Henry Farnsworth would have been so keen to ask an *ordinary* girl out on a dinner date."

Poppy looked down, not knowing how to reply. She didn't know why but the thought of Nick noticing her looks suddenly made her feel very flustered.

"I have a friend who restores old photographs. If you like, I can ask him to work on this and see if he can produce a cleaner copy, one that might give you more details," said Nick.

"Oh... thanks," said Poppy, surprised again. "That's... that's really kind of you."

"*N-o-o-ow...*" came a familiar petulant cry behind them.

Poppy glanced at Oren, then back to Nick, and said with a rueful laugh: "You know, I almost have to thank Oren. I would never have found this box without his antics. You could say he's a hero."

Nick looked at the ginger tom and scowled. "Don't give him any ideas. That cat has too great an opinion of himself already!"

CHAPTER FIFTEEN

Poppy was up early the next morning, partly because she was keen to pop into the village post office shop before she went to Duxton House, but also partly because she was still excited by the discovery she'd made behind the ivy. It had taken her a long time to fall asleep last night as she tossed and turned, and thought about her parents. She had given Nick the precious photo, but she had carried the tin with the rest of her mother's teenage belongings back to her room, eager to pore over them once again.

After the photo, the most exciting thing was the notebook filled with Holly Lancaster's handwriting. She had started to read it with eager expectation before she realised that it was not so much a diary as a place where her mother had written down all sorts of random things, from song lyrics she liked to fragments of poetry that she was composing, from drawings of dresses she admired to doodles of flowers and plants in the cottage garden. There was no coherent chronology to the entries—it was as if her mother had simply chosen a blank page at random whenever she felt like recording something; plus she seemed to have added to and written over older entries with careless abandon. Which meant that it was all very confusing. At last, Poppy had rubbed her tired eyes and switched off the lights. She could see that deciphering her mother's notebook was not going to be a quick job. She would have to take her time and go through it slowly.

Poppy arrived at the village shop to find it already buzzing with activity. Like many similar institutions in small English villages, the post office shop wasn't just a place to buy stamps and send a parcel—it was also where you could pick up newspapers, everyday groceries, stationery, over-the-counter medicines, local baking, fresh farm produce, and—most importantly of all—the daily gossip.

There was a large group of village ladies congregating by the counter and Poppy was conscious of them all listening avidly as she handed over the USB drive with the leaflet she had designed and asked the postmistress to print out several copies. They also all watched with admiration and envy as she presented the postmistress with the bouquet that she had picked from the garden the day before.

"Ooh, ta, dear—that's lovely! They'll look beautiful here on the counter. And I'll be sure to let everyone know where they're from," added the postmistress with a big smile.

"Thanks, that's really kind of you," said Poppy, delighted.

"So you're offering fresh flowers, are you?" said the postmistress, taking the first leaflet from the printer and eyeing it with interest.

"I saw your arrangement at the fête," one of the ladies by the counter spoke up. "It was absolutely gorgeous! And this one too... Where did you learn to arrange flowers like this?"

"Um... nowhere, really," said Poppy with an embarrassed laugh. "I just sort of follow my instincts."

"Well, they are fabulous instincts, dear."

"Thank you," said Poppy, blushing. "My mother had an amazing way with flowers. She could pick a bunch of weeds from the roadside, stick it in a jam jar, and somehow make it look a million pounds," she said with a laugh.

"Well, now, I always think flowers in a jam jar look delightful," said another lady.

A third lady nodded emphatically. "Oh yes, I've never liked those fancy arrangements from the florists nowadays, with bits of twisted wires sticking up everywhere and strange seed pods and things from Australia—"

"Quite right," her friend agreed with a superior sniff. "A nice, simple bunch of English country flowers is what I want, looking like they were just cut from the garden."

"Oh, that's exactly what I'm offering!" said Poppy. "My arrangements will all be sourced from the Hollyhock Cottage garden, picked fresh and delivered straight to you."

"Do we get to choose the type of flowers?" a new woman spoke up from the back of the group.

Poppy turned a regretful face to her. "Um... well, not really, I'm afraid. I'll just be working with a seasonal selection of what's in the garden. That way, you get the freshest flowers... But if you tell me your colour preference, I'll do my best to accommodate that," she added brightly.

"That sounds great. I'm having a birthday party for my little girl tomorrow and I've invited several of her friends and their mothers, and it will probably be mayhem with a house full of under-fives," she said, rolling her eyes and laughing. "I know I won't have much time to make the house look nice, but it would be lovely to at least have a big bunch of fresh flowers on the table." The woman reached into her handbag and pulled out a chequebook. "So how do I put in an order? Do you take cheques?"

"Oh... er..." Poppy fumbled. She hadn't expected to be getting orders so quickly! "Um... yes, of course."

"And can you make it mostly pink flowers? My little girl loves pink," said the lady with a fond smile. She held a hand out. "I'm Moira, by the way. I live in that big Tudor house at the edge of the village."

"I'll do the best I can," Poppy promised, shaking the woman's hand and giving her a smile.

"How much are the arrangements?" asked another lady with interest. "And do you do smaller posies too? I don't need a big bouquet, but I'd like to have a small posy to take when I'm visiting my mother at the nursing home tomorrow. She loves fresh flowers and she's missing her garden."

"Oh... of course, yes, I can do smaller posies," said Poppy.

She did some rapid mental calculations in her head and named some prices with trepidation. When she saw how happily everyone accepted them, she wished she'd dared to quote higher! By the time all the leaflets had been printed, Poppy already had a list of orders tucked into her pocket and a busy time of picking and arranging ahead.

She was just paying the postmistress for the printing when the bells attached to the door chimed. Conversation ceased as suddenly as if someone had hit a mute button. Poppy turned in surprise to see the thin, angular woman with wispy orange hair who had just come in the door. It was Sonia, and she looked nervously around as everyone stared at her.

"Hello, Sonia!" called the postmistress with forced cheerfulness. "How are you today?"

"I'm... I'm fine..." said the woman, coming hesitantly forwards. The group by the counter parted to let her through. "I'm just on my way to Duxton House to help Mrs Peabody with the take-down of the fête stalls, but I wanted to post this first."

The postmistress took the envelope and looked at the address with nosy interest, then said: "Another job application, Sonia? Was the last one not successful then?"

"N-no," said Sonia, flushing dark red.

"But I thought you said they were considering offering you the job and were just checking references?"

"They... they changed their mind," Sonia mumbled, looking down. "Anyway, I'm not sure I'd like to live in a city."

"Yes, I totally agree," said the postmistress heartily. "My niece wanted to get a job in Oxford, but I told her a nice secretarial position in one of the local offices would do her just as well. Oxford's not that big a city but it's busy enough."

"Oh, village life is much better," one of the other ladies piped up. Then she exchanged glances with the other women in the group and said in an affected voice: "I do hope you've got over your traumatic experience at the fête, Sonia. It must have been such a shock finding a dead body like that!"

"Yes, I don't know what I would have done," chimed in another lady.

"Did you realise it was Ursula straightaway?" a third lady asked.

"Er... no... I mean, yes... I... I..." Sonia looked around helplessly. "I... I don't remember much about what happened... It was all a blur..."

"Well, I can't blame you for wanting to put the whole thing out of your mind," said the postmistress. "That's the kind of thing that could give you nightmares for life!"

"I heard that Ursula had been stabbed in the chest," said the first lady who had spoken.

"No, I heard that it was in the back," said her friend.

"In her heart—definitely in her heart," said the third lady.

"Was there a lot of blood?" asked another lady in the group, a ghoulish gleam in her eye.

Sonia swallowed. "Y-yes, there... there was blood everywhere... I never realised there would be so much blood..." She shuddered and squeezed her eyes shut, as if trying to blot out the memory of the day. "It was that knife—that dreadful knife! If it hadn't been there, none of this would have happened."

"What do you mean?" asked the postmistress, looking confused.

"That knife was bad luck!"

The group of ladies tittered. Obviously, the village residents were used to Sonia's hysterical outbursts and superstitious paranoia, and didn't take her seriously at all. She flushed again and wrung her hands, her eyes going around the room and alighting at last on Poppy. "You were there! You heard me tell Mrs Peabody that the knife would be bad luck, didn't you? I knew it the moment Ursula dropped it and it landed sticking into the ground. It was a death omen! You saw it too, didn't you?"

"Well, I... er..." Poppy didn't know what to say, especially as the other ladies in the group were rolling their eyes and looking unimpressed. "I don't know if it really meant anything—"

Sonia made a sound of anguish, like someone who had been terribly betrayed, and pushed roughly past Poppy, rushing out of the shop. They heard the sound of sobbing before the door swung shut behind her. Poppy stumbled backwards and regained her balance, startled by the woman's vehemence.

"Don't mind Sonia," said one of the ladies in the group, making a twirling motion with one finger by the side of her head. "She's completely batty."

"Oh yes, one sandwich short of a picnic," declared a second lady.

"*One*? I'd say more than three!" shouted another lady

They all burst into malicious laughter and began

making fun of Sonia, mimicking her words and copying her mannerisms. Poppy felt slightly uncomfortable; she had been startled by Sonia's abrupt behaviour, but she didn't really mind it. It had reminded her of a frightened animal lashing out, like a horse kicking or a cat scratching—a reflexive action, with no genuine ill intent behind it. Besides, she felt a certain compassion for the neurotic woman. She knew what it was like to be poor, with no job prospects or financial security. That would be enough to make anyone anxious and insecure, without the added stress of fearful superstitions. And then to be shunned and ridiculed everywhere you went in the village…

Poppy noticed that the postmistress wasn't joining in with the group; in fact, the woman seemed to share her compassionate thoughts.

"Ah… poor Sonia," she said quietly to Poppy. "I do feel sorry for her. It must be very disheartening to keep getting rejections. She's been applying for months now, you know, and I don't think she has much savings, poor thing, so she's getting quite desperate." She glanced at the group of gossiping ladies and made a face. "She does bring it on herself, though, you know, with her ridiculous babbling about death omens and things like that… it's just not the way to make friends in the village."

"Does she have *any* friends?" asked Poppy.

"Ursula was her only friend, really. I mean, I think Ursula just felt sorry for her, but Sonia was completely dependent on her." The postmistress sighed and shook her head. "I don't know what she's going to do now that Ursula is gone."

Poppy started to reply, then overheard something the other ladies were saying:

"...do you think there really *was* a knife or it was just Sonia's imagination going loopy again?" one of them was asking.

"No, there really was a knife," Poppy spoke up. "I brought it myself—I mean, I fetched the box that it was in. It was with a collection of things that Norman Smalle had donated for the raffle."

"Ah... *Norman...*"

"Norman... *of course...*"

Poppy saw several of the women exchange meaningful looks. The postmistress, however, made an impatient noise in her throat and said to the group:

"Oh for goodness' sake, you're not still thinking that Norman could have anything to do with the murder, are you? The police have already arrested a man."

"That ex-robber fellow?" said one of the other ladies scornfully. "He's not the murderer! The police have got it completely wrong."

"Yes!" Another lady nodded. "Everyone knows that most people are murdered by someone they know."

"And Norman was always following Ursula around like a sad puppy, wasn't he?"

"Ooh, yes, almost a bit creepy."

"Obsessed, that's what he was."

"I heard that Norman got arrested for stalking once!"

They all turned to see a younger woman standing at the back of the group. She looked a bit embarrassed to suddenly have all the attention on her and fidgeted self-consciously.

"What d'you mean?"

"Heavens—really?"

"*Arrested!*"

"Well, I'm not sure if he was actually arrested," admitted the young woman, backtracking slightly. "But he was definitely reported to the police and then he got served with one of those legal things— you know, when you can't go near someone or talk to them—"

"A restraining order?" said Poppy.

"Yes, that's right!" said the young woman, nodding. "A restraining order, so he couldn't go near the girl."

"How do you know all this?" asked one of the older ladies.

"My hubby had a job at the technology park up in Cowley and he met this chap who used to work with Norman at one of the big academic publishers. He said Norman got in trouble for stalking this girl who also worked there."

"The same Norman?" asked the postmistress sceptically.

The young woman nodded. "My hubby remembered it when we passed the antique shop yesterday and he saw the name 'Smalle'—it's not a very common name, is it? I mean, with that spelling. And we were just chatting about the murder and I was telling him all the talk about Norman having a crush on Ursula—"

"And what did he do? Norman, I mean. What did he do to that girl he was stalking?" asked one of the other ladies eagerly.

The rest of the group gathered closer, their faces avid.

"Did he get violent with her?"

"Did he try to force himself on her?"

The young woman frowned. "No-o, I don't think so... I think he just kept sending her love letters and cards and flowers... and making all sorts of excuses to pass by her desk or be hanging around just as she was leaving the office, so he could walk her home..."

Poppy thought it all sounded rather sweet and pathetic, rather than sinister and dangerous, and the postmistress obviously shared her thoughts because she waved a hand and said dismissively:

"That just sounds like a bit of old-fashioned courtship to me."

The young woman shook her head. "Yeah, but he wouldn't stop! Even when the girl told him that she didn't like him that way, Norman still wouldn't give up. He just kept sending her even more cards and flowers... until she got frightened and reported him to the police."

"That's how it always starts with these stalkers," said one of the other ladies, nodding knowledgeably. "You see it in movies all the time. They start out being sweet and harmless and then they turn into psychopaths. Just look at that film—the one with Glenn Close—"

"Oooh! *Fatal Attraction!*" several of the other ladies chorused.

"Yes, I saw that!"

"Ugh—horrible! I couldn't bear to watch the part with the bunny boiling in the pot."

"Me too! I'll never forget that film"

"Yes, but that's just the point—it was a film," said the postmistress impatiently. "Real people don't behave like that. Besides, I saw Norman yesterday, you know, and he's absolutely heartbroken about Ursula's death. He looks as if his world has ended. I just can't believe that a man who is so devastated could have killed—"

"Ah! But you can never tell with people, can you?" said one of the other ladies. "He could be putting on an act."

The postmistress shook her head firmly. "This wasn't an act. You should have seen him—he looked dreadful."

The other ladies didn't look convinced. Poppy found herself wondering which side was right. It was true that people could fake emotions to cover up their real feelings. Still, she found it hard to imagine the timid antique dealer as a vicious psychopath...

CHAPTER SIXTEEN

The scene at the post office shop left Poppy very troubled. As she walked over to Duxton House, she couldn't help wondering if Nell and all the village gossips might be right after all. Could Norman Smalle have been the murderer? She wondered what his alibi was. The last time she'd seen him had been in the marquee, just before she left to fetch his box of donated items, and she remembered Ursula persuading him to go to the manor house to lie down and rest. Was that where he had been at the time of the murder? With everyone busy at the fête, no one would have known if Norman had sneaked out of the house and returned to the marquee—where he could have met Ursula and killed her.

But why would he want to kill the woman he loved? Poppy still struggled to believe the stalker-turned-psychopath theory. Norman seemed like such a mild-mannered man. And while any kind of obsessive, repetitive behaviour was a bit creepy, Norman's actions seemed more like those of a shy, pleading lover than the kind of aggressive homicidal maniac who could stab someone as viciously as Ursula had been attacked.

When she arrived at Duxton House estate, Poppy found the place heaving with activity as a team of people dismantled the stalls, marquee, and other structures from the fête. It was a job that had been delayed because of the murder investigation, and now staff and hired workers were hurrying to and fro as they restored the grounds to their original state.

Poppy saw Mrs Peabody standing in the middle, bossily giving orders, and she paused to say hello. She wanted to thank the older woman again for her encouragement and to tell her about the great response from the villagers to the flower arrangements idea.

"Ah, good, good," said Mrs Peabody, nodding with satisfaction. "Things will spread by word of mouth, I'm sure, and you'll soon be inundated with orders."

"That would be amazing, but I hope I'll be able to keep up with the supply," said Poppy worriedly. "I mean, I'm not really a flower farm and I haven't got a proper cutting garden—so I don't know realistically how many arrangements I'm going to be able to provide from what's currently growing in the beds."

"You can cross that bridge when you come to it," said Mrs Peabody calmly. "People like the idea of 'seasonal' things—look how popular the local farmers' markets are. You never quite know what's going to be available week to week but that's part of the fun: to see what's fresh and growing at the time."

"Yes, I suppose in my case, 'this week's special' really *will* be special, since I'm unlikely to get the exact same flowers in the garden again," said Poppy with a laugh.

"And that's just like a *real* garden," said Mrs Peabody. "Which is what makes your arrangements different and charming. If people want to get the standard roses or carnations on order, they can just buy them from the big chain florists. With you, they're getting something interesting and unique."

Poppy looked at the older woman, impressed. She was beginning to think that Mrs Peabody had missed her calling—she could probably have had a high-flying career as a marketing executive in the city!

"I saw your friend, Mrs Hopkins, in the village yesterday," said Mrs Peabody, changing the subject. "She was looking for Joe the handyman... something about painting over graffiti on a wall?"

Poppy pulled a face. "Yes, someone spray-painted offensive pictures on the back wall of the cottage. We think it was probably that gang of teenage boys—"

"Ah! Those boys are getting worse by the day," said Mrs Peabody, her mouth tightening. "Did you know that one of the shops in the village high street had fresh sheep manure smeared all over its windows? It was absolutely disgusting. That section of the street stank to high heaven! Everyone was so upset, especially the ladies at the tourist information office. They work so hard to promote Bunnington as a great place to visit and this kind of thing completely ruins their efforts."

Poppy grimaced. "I'm surprised the police haven't done anything."

"I've called the police several times but they just don't seem to treat it as a serious problem," said Mrs Peabody angrily.

"Well, I suppose compared to murders and assaults, it probably isn't—"

"And where do they think those murderers and violent criminals come from?" demanded Mrs Peabody. "It's boys like these—ooh, yes, you mark my words. They might start with malicious pranks but if no one stops them, they'll soon move on to more serious crime."

"What about the parents? Can't you speak to them?"

"They're not from the village. No one has been able to identify those boys. I imagine they're from one of the nearby towns. They seem to come to

Bunnington and sneak onto properties during the night. What we need to do is catch them red-handed! Anyway, I hope Mrs Hopkins was able to find Joe to sort out your graffiti?"

"Oh yes, he came over yesterday afternoon and painted over it in a jiffy. He was so kind—he said it was just a small job and refused to take any money for it. Nell insisted that he take some of her Chelsea buns, though—"

"Ah, Mrs Hopkins bakes, does she?" said Mrs Peabody with grudging approval.

"Yes, she really enjoys it. When we lived in London, her cleaning jobs were usually in the evenings, so she was free in the daytime and used to do a lot of her baking then."

"And I understand she'll be working for your cousin, Hubert Leach, and cleaning his office, as well as all the rental properties that his company manages?"

Poppy blinked. How did this woman know everything? "Er... yes, that's right."

She didn't add that she was still dreading the day Hubert would demand his "pound of flesh". When Nell had lost her cleaning contract in London, it had seemed logical to approach her cousin and ask if he could help find work opportunities for her friend. And when Hubert had offered a permanent cleaning job that Nell could walk into as soon as she moved to Oxfordshire, it had seemed a small price to pay to agree to an unnamed "favour" for the future. Still, although Hubert hadn't contacted her yet, Poppy had been wondering uneasily what it might be.

"Well, perhaps when your friend has settled in more, she might like to consider joining the church committee," said Mrs Peabody. "We often hold fundraising events and someone who can bake well would be very helpful. In fact, she could even—" Mrs Peabody broke off as her eyes alighted on a couple of men dismantling the bunting strung across the stalls. She raised her voice and said in exasperation: "No, no, no—you need to concertina the flags so that they lie on top of one another! If you just dump them in a pile, it will take forever to untangle them!" She rushed over and snatched the tangled bundle from the men.

"Where is Sonia?" Mrs Peabody asked, looking irritably around. "She was supposed to be here to help and me supervise those men!"

"I just saw her in the village post shop," said Poppy. "Perhaps she's still on the way?"

"Oh, no, she was here—she was ranting and raving about that knife again, and saying something about finding Ursula's real killer... To be honest with you, I stop paying attention when she becomes like that. I asked her to fetch something from my car, but she should have come back by now." Mrs Peabody heaved an exasperated sigh. "I only asked her to come help me with the take-down because all other members of the committee were busy, but now I'm wishing I hadn't bothered! Really, I don't know what to do with that woman. She is completely unstable. Did you know, last month she nearly made us stop a committee meeting because Greg—that's the treasurer—accidentally broke the hall mirror in my house? It was loose anyway, you see; I'd been meaning to fix the hook for ages... Anyway, Sonia started wailing about seven years' bad luck and insisting that we drop everything to pick up the broken pieces and break the curse."

"Is there actually a way to counteract the curse?" asked Poppy, curious in spite of herself.

Mrs Peabody rolled her eyes. "Oh, several apparently. According to Sonia, you can bury the pieces in the moonlight or throw them into running water or pound them up so that they can't reflect anything again... Frankly, it's all a load of twaddle if you ask me! I refused to stop the meeting just to humour her ridiculous superstitions and Sonia stormed out." Her mouth twisted. "If it had been up to me, I would never have had her on the committee, but Ursula felt sorry for her, you see. Sonia has been out of work for a long time and hasn't been able to get another job yet. I suppose Ursula felt that it would help her self-esteem to have some kind of official role on the board of SOAR. We're all volunteers, of course, so it's unpaid, but it was supposed to give her some sense of purpose and identity."

"That was really considerate of her."

"Yes, Ursula was always so kind and thoughtful that way." Mrs Peabody shook her head sadly. "I just don't understand why anyone would want to kill her!"

CHAPTER SEVENTEEN

There was no sign of Muriel anywhere when Poppy finally left Mrs Peabody and went into the house. As she walked farther down the hallway, however, she heard the sound of a dog whining. It sounded like Flopsy and it was coming from the end of the hallway. Thinking that Muriel might be in a room at the other end with her pet, Poppy made her way down the hallway, following the sound until she came to a door that was slightly ajar. She was about to knock when she heard a yelp from inside the room, followed by the sound of a man cursing viciously. She froze with her hand in mid-air, then leaned slowly forwards so that she could peer around the corner of the partially open door.

Through the gap, she saw a room that had probably once been an elegant morning parlour but had been converted into a combination of a dog-themed playroom and a canine grooming parlour. Framed portraits of Flopsy decorated the walls and a luxurious dog bed in the shape of an overstuffed bone occupied the centre of the room, surrounded by piles of dog toys, rubber chews, treat balls, cushions, and blankets. Beside the window was a raised table and a rack filled with an assortment of scissors, grooming brushes, nail clippers, conditioning sprays, and even a hair dryer.

The toy poodle herself was standing on the table, being groomed by Kirby. She didn't look like she was enjoying it, squirming and wriggling and then letting out another yelp as he ran the grooming brush roughly down her back.

"Oh, shut up!" Kirby snarled, yanking the brush even more viciously.

Flopsy growled and jerked her head around, as if to bite him, but Kirby clamped a hand around her neck and grabbed her by the scruff. He gave her a shake, leaning down and sneering:

"Don't try anything with me, you little bitch! Your '*Mummy*' isn't here now—it's just you and me—and I'm going to show you who's boss!" He gave her another shake.

Flopsy whined again and writhed in his hands, but Kirby tightened his cruel grip, forcibly holding her squirming body down on the table.

"Stop that! Stop that or I swear I'm going to teach you a lesson you'll never forget!"

He grabbed a pair of scissors from the rack and Poppy gasped as she saw the light glinting off the sharp edges. The sound made Kirby freeze and look up.

"Who's there?" he asked sharply.

Poppy stepped into the room. The pet nanny hastily dropped the scissors and let Flopsy go.

"Oh... it's you." He relaxed slightly, then gave a forced laugh. "You probably heard darling Flopsy and me having a little spat. I was just giving her a groom—her coat gets horribly tangled, you know, and needs constant attention to maintain it at salon perfection. But Flopsy and I love our grooming sessions together... don't we?"

He gave the poodle an exaggerated look of affection, then reached out a hand to pat her head. Flopsy bared her teeth at him and backed away.

"Ah... haha—look at her playing games with me," said Kirby quickly, giving another high-pitched laugh. "She can be so naughty sometimes... but, of course, I do love her and all her little antics."

The poodle growled at him and lifted her lips, showing tiny gleaming white teeth.

Kirby cleared his throat, then turned back to Poppy and said: "Was there anything I can help you with?"

"I was just looking for Muriel," she replied. "I wanted to ask if she had any final instructions for me before I started digging up the old rock garden."

"She's gone to Oxford," said Kirby.

Poppy was surprised that the old lady hadn't taken her precious poodle with her. Kirby must have guessed her thoughts because he added smoothly:

"She was going to see her solicitor and then have lunch with some friends at one of the posh restaurants, but they don't accept animals, so she decided to leave Flopsy at home. In any case, she knew that Flopsy would be in good hands, here with me... don't you agree, Flopsy-pooh?" he cooed, puckering his lips and blowing a kiss at the poodle.

Poppy turned away, disgusted by his hypocrisy. "Oh, right... thanks. I'll just head out and get started then," she said shortly, not wanting to stay in the man's company for any longer than necessary.

Outside, she headed for the secluded area around the side of the house, away from all the activity at the front, and surveyed the old rock garden. From her pocket, she pulled out the paper with the list of scented herbs and plants that she'd made. Poppy had been determined not to make the same mistake from her first gardening job a couple of weeks ago—where she had done no research, naively assuming that all that was required to produce a beautiful garden was to dig a hole, pop the plant in, then add some water. She had paid for her naivete and newbie arrogance, and had nearly lost the whole flowerbed, not to mention her good name. This time she had made a great effort to not only research the plants but also note down their growing requirements, such as what kind of soil they preferred and how much sunshine they needed.

Now, armed with this knowledge and feeling much more confident, Poppy walked around the area, consulting her notes and mentally placing plants in different positions. *I'll plant lavender here, along the side of the path, just like at Hollyhock Cottage—that way you can smell their gorgeous fragrance when you walk along the path and brush against them*, she thought, following the route where she intended to lay the gravel. *And over here, where the ground slopes upwards, I'll plant clary sage and thyme together, since they both like really well-draining soil. The little pink flowers of the thyme will look really pretty with the spikes of purple flowers on the clary sage...* Poppy smiled as she imagined the scene. She turned around to survey the opposite side of the path. *And I'll plant some marigolds here, beside these rocks—their bright orange and yellow flowers should really pop against the dark grey rock... Oh, and this spot would be perfect for a chamomile lawn—oh wait, maybe it's too shady—maybe that area instead? I could put some marsh mallow here instead—they're supposed to be happy in some light shade... Hmm... what about the valerian? It's supposed to grow to a metre and a half tall, so it needs to go somewhere at the back... maybe next to those rocks there?*

She paused and scanned the area again, wondering what to do about all the rocks and boulders scattered around the area. It would be much easier to work with the existing landscape, instead of trying to change too much, but there were definitely some rocks that needed to be shifted and rearranged. She would need the help of the estate gardeners to move the larger boulders but she could probably shift many of the smaller rocks herself. She bent down and began to experimentally move a few. Most of them came fairly easily, but there was one in particular which—despite not being that large—seemed to be deeply embedded in the ground. Poppy knew that she should probably leave it for the estate gardeners to handle as well, but once she'd started it became like a personal challenge for her to loosen it and get it out.

Perhaps if I dig a trench underneath it, then I can get a spade in and lever it up, she thought, dropping to her hands and knees and starting to scrabble in the soil around the rock. She was surprised to find that the earth was quite loose—almost as if it had recently been dug up and then pushed back. And she had barely started scraping the earth away when her fingers touched something hard.

Poppy paused, then went a bit more slowly. She groped with her fingers, finding a slim object buried in the earth. She wiggled it and pulled it out from underneath the rock, brushing aside the loose soil to reveal a dark brown wood handle, with a hinge on one side and the edge of a metal blade showing through a slot in the wood.

It's the pruning knife, she realised suddenly. The one that had been in the box of items donated from Norman's antique shop; the one that Sonia had had a screaming fit about and insisted would bring bad luck. The last time Poppy had seen it was when Ursula had picked it up and removed it from the raffle donations, to soothe the hysterical woman. In her mind, Poppy heard Mrs Peabody's voice again, saying: *"Oh yes, it's very sharp. Cuts through most things..."*

Her fingers trembling slightly, Poppy turned the knife over and carefully flicked it open. Then she froze, her heart pounding as she stared at the blade. It gleamed dully, its cutting edge marked by a rusty brown stain.

The police would have to test it to confirm, but Poppy knew that it was blood. The knife dropped from her nerveless fingers.

She had just found the murder weapon.

CHAPTER EIGHTEEN

Poppy stared at the knife, wondering what to do. The obvious thing, of course, was to call the police and report it. Surely, now that Sergeant Lee had new evidence in the case, he would be willing to consider alternative theories? Then her mouth tightened as she remembered the way Lee had brushed her off. Somehow, she had a bad feeling that the arrogant sergeant would still insist on sticking to his original theory. He would simply say that the ex-robber had managed to bury the murder weapon in the old rock garden before he was arrested, or something similarly ridiculous. Poppy had seen before how the sergeant massaged facts to support his theories, instead of the other way around.

I should just bypass Lee and go straight to

Suzanne, she thought. She had hesitated to do that so far because it seemed petty to challenge the sergeant's authority on the case and it made her feel like she was telling tales to his superiors. After all, if Suzanne trusted her sergeant to handle the case, then who was Poppy to question that? *Except that he's not handling the case properly!* fumed Poppy. *He's not considering all the alternative scenarios, the other potential suspects...*

She stared down at the knife again. *Perhaps there will be fingerprints that can be lifted*, she thought, looking down at the rough, porous surface of the wooden handle. *Or perhaps DNA fragments or some other kind of marker. The forensic technology available nowadays is amazing, and even if the murderer just brushes things with their bare fingers—*

The thought of "fingers" brought the image of dirty fingernails suddenly to her mind. *Betsy the maid... and her fingernails with soil embedded underneath...* Poppy recalled the girl's pale, frightened face and the way she had seemed so nervous and jumpy yesterday. And then she remembered the way Betsy had come running breathlessly into the kitchen. *Where had she been?* Poppy glanced down at the knife again. *Outside burying the incriminating murder weapon?*

On an impulse, she sprang up and hurried back to the manor with the knife carefully wrapped in her gardening gloves. She approached via the rear of the building and was pleased when she found the utility room door open, with Betsy just backing out, carrying a basket of laundry.

"Betsy?"

The girl jumped and whirled around. "Yes?" She relaxed slightly as she saw Poppy. "Oh, it's you."

Poppy said without preamble: "I was digging in the old rock garden and I found something strange..." She held up the knife for the girl to see. Betsy's eyes widened and her face drained of all colour.

"It was you, wasn't it?" Poppy said, taking a step forwards. "You buried the pruning knife under that rock. That's why you had soil under your fingernails yesterday. You were trying to get rid of the murder weapon—"

"*NO!*" cried Betsy, her face horrified. "I would never—I didn't kill Miss Ursula! I couldn't murder anyone—"

"But you *did* bury the knife?" insisted Poppy.

The girl hesitated for a moment, looking as if she was going to deny it, then she crumpled and nodded. "Yeah... I did... but I didn't murder Miss Ursula—I didn't! You have to believe me!"

"Then why were you burying the knife? Why did you have it in the first place?"

"I just found it—okay? It was pushed under my mattress. I dunno how it got there. On the day Miss Ursula got murdered, when I got back to my room that night, I found the door open. Someone had come in and shoved the knife under my mattress!"

"Are you saying that someone planted it there?"

The girl nodded vehemently. "Yeah, I think someone is tryin' to frame me!"

Poppy frowned. "But... why would anyone want to do that?"

"'Cos I'm an easy target!" cried the girl. "I'm the maid, aren't I? People always suspect maids; they always think we're stealin' or things like that. Plus, Miss Ursula managed the household—she was, like, my boss. People are goin' to say we had a fight and I was holdin' a grudge against her or somethin'..." She paused, then gave Poppy a pointed look. "I'll tell you who really had a fight with Miss Ursula: Henry!"

"Henry Farnsworth? Muriel's great-nephew?"

Betsy nodded. "Real nasty it was too. He was furious, callin' her all sorts of names, and then he stormed out and drove off."

"When was that?"

"The night before the fête. He didn't come back until the next afternoon, after... after it all happened."

"What was the fight about?" asked Poppy.

"I was listenin' through a door so it was muffled; I only got bits and pieces." Betsy paused, thinking. "It was somethin' about money... I heard Miss Ursula say: 'I've been too soft with you, Henry—I should've told Muriel about this long ago, when I got that call from London, but I was feeling sorry for you—' and Henry cut her off; he was beggin' her not to say anythin', but Miss Ursula kept insistin' that Mrs Farnsworth deserved to know, as it was her money... and then Henry started gettin' nasty and swearin' and callin' her names... Then he told Miss Ursula that if she said a word to Mrs Farnsworth, he'd make her sorry."

Poppy stared at the other girl. The whole thing sounded almost too perfect to be true—like scripted dialogue for a movie. Was Betsy telling the truth? Or was *she* the one who was trying to frame someone else—namely Henry? After all, if she had been found out, the logical thing was to think on her feet and push the blame onto someone else as fast as she could.

"You don't believe me, do you?" Betsy looked at her tearfully. "You think I'm lyin'! You think I'm makin' it up!"

"I... well, you have to admit, it sounds a bit too pat. I mean, do people actually say 'I'll make you sorry' in real life?"

"That's what I heard!" cried Betsy. "Honest! That's what I heard through the door."

"So why didn't you tell this to the police?"

"I was goin' to! But then when I found the knife, I panicked, right? I mean... it's the murder weapon, isn't it? And on telly and things, they always arrest the person who has the murder weapon... I didn't know what to do! When that detective sergeant arrived yesterday mornin', I was so scared. What if he decided to search the house?"

"So as soon as you'd shown him to the drawing room, you ran back to get the knife and bury it outside," guessed Poppy, remembering the gap between the time she'd seen Betsy escort Sergeant Lee in and the time she met Betsy herself in the kitchen.

The girl nodded miserably. "Yeah... I thought I'd better get it out of my room fast. I was just plannin' to stash it somewhere safe until I decided what to do with it—like, whether to turn it in... or... or get rid of it..." She heaved a shuddering breath at the memory. "Oh God, when Mrs Farnsworth mentioned the dirt under my fingernails, I nearly died! I thought the sergeant was sure to suspect somethin' then!"

No such luck, thought Poppy sourly. Sergeant Lee wouldn't know a clue if it came up and danced topless on his lap.

"I was so thankful to get out without him sayin' anythin'." Betsy heaved a sigh of relief in memory. "But I stayed outside the door to listen and see if you were all talkin' about me, and I heard that sergeant say the police already arrested somebody— some bloke who used to be a criminal. So they were goin' to wrap up the case anyway and I thought... well, I thought: why make trouble for myself? So I just decided to keep quiet and say nothin' about the knife."

"But in the meantime, Ursula's real killer would

have got away," said Poppy accusingly.

Betsy gave her a sullen look. "Look, I know it was wrong, okay? But it's easy for you! You can be all sanctimonious, 'cos you're not the one who was a murder suspect! You didn't have a murder weapon in your room! And you know, I picked up that knife before I realised what it was. Then I opened the blade and I saw the brown stains..." She shuddered. "But you see? It's got my prints all over it now and that'll make me look guilty too!" She reached out to clutch Poppy's arm. "Please, miss... don't say anythin' to the police! It doesn't matter if they have the murder weapon or not; they've already got their man—"

"But they haven't!" protested Poppy. "That's just it. Sergeant Lee is wrong. I'm sure Ursula wasn't murdered by that ex-robber they arrested... and the fact that the pruning knife was found in your bedroom proves it."

"But... but that ex-con could have put it there—"

"Aww, come on! Not you too!" said Poppy in exasperation. "That is so far-fetched that it's ridiculous. A man who is out on parole for good behaviour suddenly decides to viciously attack a random woman he never met while out at a busy public event—just for a mobile phone in a fancy cover? And then he takes the time to run into the manor house and find the maid's room to hide the murder weapon under her bed? And then... he stays on at the fête, remaining in the crowd while the police arrive—just so they can easily arrest him?"

Betsy bowed her head. She looked so miserable that suddenly Poppy felt bad. In her zeal to find Ursula's killer, she hadn't really thought about the girl's position. It was true that seeking justice was easy when you weren't personally affected by it. She softened her voice and said:

"I'm sorry, Betsy; we can't hide this from the police. They *have* to know about the murder weapon—it's just too important to the investigation. But don't worry—I'm sure they'll be reasonable. In fact, I'm going to call Inspector Suzanne Whittaker—she's Sergeant Lee's superior and I know she won't jump to conclusions. And I'll vouch for you and support your story."

"It won't help," said the girl bitterly.

CHAPTER NINETEEN

Poppy swallowed her misgivings and went to call Suzanne. The detective inspector didn't answer so she left a message and returned to work on the scent garden. She pulled out her notes again and tried to immerse herself once more in the planning of the new garden, but she found it hard to concentrate, and she pounced on her phone when it rang a few minutes later.

"Hello, Suzanne?" she said excitedly.

To her dismay, a familiar nasal voice came across the line. "No, it's Sergeant Lee here. The guv'nor asked me to return your call."

"Oh... I was really hoping to speak to her," said Poppy.

"Well, you can't," said Lee shortly. "She's at Scotland Yard, down in London, for an important conference."

"Will she be back tomorrow?"

"No, it's running all week. Now, what did you want to speak to her about? You can talk to me. I'm in charge of everything while she's away," he said importantly.

Poppy hesitated. It would be petty and childish—and downright wrong—to refuse to tell the police about her discovery just because she couldn't speak directly to Suzanne.

"I think I've found the murder weapon," she blurted out. "The weapon that was used to kill Ursula Philips."

"What? What do you mean?" demanded Sergeant Lee.

She told him about her grisly discovery in the old rock garden, then reluctantly added her hunch regarding Betsy's dirty nails and the maid's subsequent confession. She was pleased when Lee seemed to take her very seriously, saying that he was coming to Duxton House straightaway. He arrived a short while later, with several constables and a Forensics team in tow, and Poppy quickly went to meet him. She was anxious to put in a good word for Betsy before he went into the house and got the maid's statement. Before she could speak, however, one of the estate gardeners came rushing up to them.

"Sir! Sir! Thank God you're here! 'Bout time the police took this seriously."

"Eh?" Sergeant Lee looked at the man in confusion.

"Those vandals, sir—that's what you're here for, isn't it? Come an' see what those little blighters have done this time!"

Without waiting for him to reply, the man grabbed Lee's arm and hustled him around the east side of the manor house. They rounded the corner and Poppy gasped in dismay. Someone had taken a pair of pruning shears to the beautifully clipped topiary decorating the formal flowerbeds and hacked at them brutally. Tall, elegant spires had been chopped in half, perfectly rounded domes were now sporting ragged holes, and the centrepiece, which had been clipped in the shape of a graceful swan, had been attacked with such aggression that the swan's head had been completely hacked off and lay on the ground, amid a pile of broken twigs and scattered leaves. Nearby, Poppy could see a pair of shears lying on the ground, as if someone had been interrupted in the act, tossed it there, and run away.

"It's them bloody boys! Going around the village, spray painting things an' damaging property. I caught 'em on the estate yesterday an' I chased 'em off—but they must've come back sometime this morning. It looked fine when I walked past an hour ago!" The gardener stared at the damaged plants, his chest heaving. "How could they do this? Do they have no heart? It's taken me years..." He broke off and choked, looking near to tears.

Poppy felt a surge of pity. It must have taken years of careful growing and training and pruning to produce these magnificent topiary specimens. Besides, even if it hadn't, the sheer senseless destruction of beautiful, healthy plants was enough to disgust her. This seemed to be going beyond boyish mischief and into cruel vandalism.

"Aren't you going to do something?" the gardener demanded of Sergeant Lee. "You need to find these boys an' lock 'em up!"

"I am CID—we don't deal with petty crime like vandalism," said Lee disdainfully. "But I'll send one of the boys from Uniform to come and take your statement. If we can get an ID or catch them in the act, then we'll arrest them."

"But—"

"Now, if you'll excuse me, I have a *murder enquiry* to attend to," said Sergeant Lee importantly. He turned and marched away.

Poppy gave the gardener a sympathetic smile, then hurried after the sergeant. He had taken the alternative route back round the manor house, going via the rear rather than the front, and she caught up with him just as they were passing through the courtyard behind the manor.

"Sergeant! Sergeant Lee!" she shouted.

He swung around impatiently to face her. "Yes, Miss Lancaster?"

"It's about Betsy—" Poppy broke off as she

caught sight of something beyond Lee's shoulder.

On the far side of the courtyard was an old stone outhouse, with a roof that was partially covered by the spreading branches of an oak tree. She realised that she could see figures through the leafy branches: teenage boys crouched on the roof, scrambling to climb over the courtyard wall and drop down the other side.

There were three of them on the roof... and struggling to climb up and join them was the same young boy she had seen trip and fall yesterday. He was lunging up, desperately trying to reach the edge of the roof and swing himself up, like the older boys had done, but he just wasn't tall enough or strong enough, and the older boys weren't helping him. They were too busy saving themselves, getting over the wall as fast as they could. In a minute, they all dropped over the other side and disappeared from sight.

The abandoned boy whirled around, his eyes wide with fright as he saw Poppy and Sergeant Lee. He stood looking scared and helpless, with his back to the outhouse and his hands splayed out on either side of him, pressing against the wall as if for support. He was trapped and if Lee turned his head in that direction, the detective sergeant was bound to see him. In fact, all Poppy had to do was call his attention and point. The police were on site. They could probably chase and still catch the older boys and they could certainly take the youngest one into custody...

Poppy met the boy's eyes, pleading mutely with her, and she hesitated.

"Yes, Miss Lancaster?" said Sergeant Lee again, even more impatiently. Then he noticed her looking over his shoulder. "What are you staring at?" He frowned and began to turn around.

"Uh—nothing! Nothing!" said Poppy brightly, grabbing his arm and yanking him back to face her. "Er... my mind wandered for a moment... Listen... um... I wanted to ask you about... about Betsy. It's really just one of those circumstantial evidence situations, isn't it? I mean, it doesn't have to mean she's guilty. In fact, her being honest about burying the knife should count in her favour, right?"

As she was talking, Poppy purposefully led the sergeant back the way they had come, retracing their steps around the house. She darted a quick look over her shoulder just as they rounded the corner and saw the young boy sagging with relief against the side of the outhouse. Then she turned her head back hastily as she realised that Lee was responding to her:

"...connection to the murder weapon is always suspicious, and in this case the subject has even confessed to trying to conceal the weapon. I shall be arresting her and taking her down to the station—"

"What?" Poppy stared at him, aghast. She was horrified to discover that Betsy had been right about the police's reaction "No, you can't do that!"

Sergeant Lee bristled. "I can do what I like. I'm the investigating officer in this case."

"No, I mean... don't you think you're jumping to conclusions again?"

"It's not jumping to conclusions when the suspect has confessed to burying the murder weapon and to having her prints on it too."

"But she could have been framed!" Poppy protested.

"What—that story about someone planting the knife under her mattress?" scoffed Lee. "Do me a favour! A kid wouldn't believe that story!"

"But it *could* be true," Poppy insisted. "You need to give her the benefit of the doubt and start new lines of investigation—"

"Don't tell me how to do my job," snapped Sergeant Lee.

No amount of arguing would change his mind, and finally Poppy had to follow him back into the house, where she stood and watched miserably as Betsy was arrested and escorted to the police car. She felt racked with guilt. Had it actually been the right decision for her to call the police? Should she have made more of an effort to speak directly to Suzanne? *An innocent girl could end up going to jail now—and it could be all my fault.*

CHAPTER TWENTY

The police had cordoned off most of the rock garden—especially the area where the knife had been found—with crime-scene tape, which meant that Poppy would have been unable to continue work on her new project even if she had wanted to. But in any case, she felt too miserable to concentrate and was only too glad to have an excuse to leave Duxton House and return home.

As she walked down the lane leading to the cul-de-sac where Hollyhock Cottage was situated, she passed Nick Forrest's large, elegant property and looked hopefully towards the wrought-iron gates. Oren always managed to bring a smile to her face and she had a sudden longing to see the demanding, talkative feline. He was often waiting by the gate for her, but today there was no sign of the ginger tomcat.

Poppy hesitated for a moment outside the iron gates, and then, on an impulse, pushed them open and went up the path to the front door. She rang the bell and waited for several moments before the door was flung open and a glowering Nick Forrest stood on the threshold.

"WHAT?" he snapped.

For a moment, Poppy had a sense of déjà vu as she flashed back to the first night they'd met here in Bunnington. She had brought the wandering Oren back to his owner and Nick had opened the door with a similarly grumpy demeanour. Since then, she had got to know the crime writer a lot better, and knew that his moods were usually tied to his books. When his writing was going well, he could be the most affable, charming man in the world—and when it wasn't, he was worse than a T-Rex with a toothache.

"What do you want?" he growled.

"I..." Poppy paused. She wasn't sure herself why she had suddenly come to see Nick. Perhaps she had hoped to find someone to talk to—someone to soothe her troubled conscience about Betsy's arrest. Well, it didn't look like she was going to find a sympathetic ear. She hesitated, eyeing his scowling countenance, then mumbled:

"Er... um... never mind. It's nothing."

She started to turn away, but Nick put out a hand to stop her, saying irritably:

"Hang on, hang on—you interrupt my writing, make me come out here... just to tell me it's *nothing*?"

"Well, all right... it's *not* nothing. I just... A girl's been arrested—one of the maids at Duxton House—and, well, it might be my fault," said Poppy in a rush. "I mean, I *had* to tell the police about the murder weapon—I couldn't *not* say anything—but I honestly didn't think they would jump on Betsy like that!"

"*What?*" Nick looked even more irritable. "What are you rabbiting on about?"

Quickly, Poppy told him everything that had happened. He listened, then shrugged and said:

"You did what was right. It's a shame about this girl but, if she's really innocent, I'm sure it'll sort itself out."

"But what if it doesn't?" asked Poppy. "I mean, people have been wrongly convicted before, haven't they? Put away for a crime they didn't commit? What if that happens to Betsy? I'll feel awful. I already do." She shook her head in frustration. "If only Sergeant Lee would consider investigating other suspects!"

"Like who?"

"Like... like Henry Farnsworth!" said Poppy. "Betsy told me that she heard him having a fight with Ursula the night before she was killed. He even threatened her. *And* he lied and gave a false alibi for the day of the murder: Bertie saw him in the woods behind the Duxton House estate, when Henry said he was in Oxford. *Plus*," she added excitedly, "Henry was making a phone call just around the same time that Ursula got her call!"

"Well, the answer's obvious then, isn't it?" said Nick. "You need to find out if Henry was the person calling Ursula. If you can establish that, even Lee won't be able to ignore this new lead."

Poppy frowned. "Ursula's phone is still missing—– the police haven't been able to find it—so we don't know who her last caller was."

"Then check Henry's phone," said Nick impatiently. "See who he was ringing that day around the time of the murder."

Poppy stared at him. "But... but how would I do that? How would I even get a chance to look at his phone?"

"Well, one way could be if you accept his dinner invitation."

"What? Go out to dinner with Henry?"

"Don't look so scandalised. It's not as if I'm suggesting that you sleep with him."

"I... I didn't think you were," said Poppy huffily. "Anyway, I don't see how—even if I were to go out to dinner with him—I could get into his phone. Most people have a passcode or something to unlock their devices. How would I get past that?"

Nick heaved a sigh. "I don't know! Use your imagination. Do you need me to do everything for you? Figure it out yourself."

Poppy stepped back, stung. She muttered a curt "Thanks" and was just turning away to leave when Nick added quietly:

"My father would know."

Poppy whirled back, her eyes wide. She had never heard Nick voluntarily mention Bertie and had certainly never expected him to acknowledge the father-son relationship.

"You mean Bertie?" she said.

Nick gave her an ironic look. "He could figure out how to hack Henry's phone. Something like that would be child's play to him." He paused, then added, "Don't forget, though, if you don't find Ursula's number, that might not mean anything. Henry could have simply deleted—"

"That's a great idea about asking Bertie!" Poppy cried. "Thanks, I'll go and ask him now." She gave him a hesitant smile. "Um... would you like to come with me?"

"What? No, I've got to get back to the book. I've already wasted enough time discussing this bloody murder as it is!"

With another scowl, Nick retreated into the house, slamming the door behind him. Poppy stared speechlessly at the shut door for a moment, then turned and stomped back to Hollyhock Cottage. Half of her was seething, furious and indignant at Nick's offhand manner, but the other half of her was reluctantly grateful for his help and ideas. She also found, to her surprise, that although she hadn't got the sympathetic ear she had hoped for, her encounter with Nick *had* left her feeling in better spirits. She might not have been able to help Betsy directly, but just having a plan and being proactive, rather than watching helplessly from the sidelines and waiting for the police to act, made her feel a lot better.

Then the sound of a loud engine broke the peace. Poppy paused halfway to her own gate and turned to see a grey Bentley roar into the cul-de-sac and pull up beside her. A man in a chauffeur's uniform jumped out of the driver's seat and ran around to the rear passenger door on the other side. A minute later, the top of Muriel Farnsworth's head emerged.

Poppy stepped forwards, a polite smile on her face, thinking that perhaps her client had come to see her—then her smile faded as Muriel rounded the side of the car and Poppy saw that she was holding a black terrier by the scruff of his neck. It was Einstein! The terrier was squirming and wriggling, trying to get free, and whining indignantly.

"Oh no, you don't," said Muriel, tightening her hold on him. She glared down at the dog. "Thought you could sneak into Duxton House when nobody was looking, eh? Trying to get your filthy paws on Flopsy, are you? Well, you won't succeed—you mangy little beast!"

"*Ruff!*" said Einstein, giving her a defiant look. "*Ruff-ruff!*"

Muriel looked up and saw Poppy. "Look who I caught trying to get in the front gates when I arrived back from Oxford?" she said indignantly. "Where is the man who owns this dog?"

"Oh, that's Bertie—I mean, Dr Bertram Noble. He lives there." Poppy pointed to the garden gate several yards down from hers.

She followed anxiously as Muriel marched up to Bertie's door and jabbed her finger on the doorbell. A minute later, the door was opened and Bertie shuffled out, wearing nothing but a pair of baggy boxer shorts and a scuba mask. Muriel gave a scandalised gasp.

Bertie hurriedly removed his mask. "Oh, I do beg your pardon!" he said. "Please excuse my state of undress—I was just cleaning my fish tank... Goodness gracious me! You've got Einstein!" he exclaimed as he saw his dog.

Muriel shoved the terrier at him. "Your *mongrel*, Dr Noble, was found trespassing at Duxton House."

"Really?" Bertie scratched his head and glanced back towards his own house. "But... I could have sworn that he was sleeping in the sitting room..."

"He's a menace!" snapped Muriel. She wagged a finger at him. "And if you don't control him, then I will be forced to take drastic measures. I will *not* have him besmirching Flopsy's pure breeding with his flea-ridden—"

"Oh no, Einstein doesn't have any fleas," said Bertie brightly. "I dose him every month myself with my special formula. Would you like to try some?"

"*Me?*" said Muriel, looking outraged. "Are you suggesting that I might have fleas?"

"Oh no, not fleas—but you most definitely have mites."

"How dare you!" gasped Muriel.

"I wasn't passing judgement on your standard of personal hygiene," said Bertie earnestly. "I was referring to demodex mites. We all have them in our eyelashes. They eat our dead skin—which is a lot more in your case, of course, because of your advanced age."

Poppy groaned inwardly as she saw Muriel go very red in the face and start to splutter angrily. One of the things she found the most charming about Bertie was his childlike candour and the way he would voice the things so many people thought but were too afraid to say. Still, there were times when she wished the old inventor would learn a bit of tact and diplomacy... like now. She hurried to intervene as Bertie leaned forwards, peering at Muriel's heavily made-up face, and said:

"You probably have a larger population of mites than normal, you know, due to your excessive mascara usage. They love to breed in mascara—"

"Er... hadn't you better go and check on your experiments, Bertie?" Poppy cut in hastily as she stepped between him and Muriel Farnsworth.

The old lady looked like she was going to spontaneously combust at any moment, if her livid colour was anything to go by. Poppy was relieved that Bertie trotted back into the house, taking Einstein with him, without further argument.

"Really! I have never been more insulted in my life!" Muriel seethed, her bosom heaving. She wagged a finger in Poppy's face. "I will not abide any more nonsense from that man or his dog! If I find that mongrel at Duxton House again, I will tell my gardeners to shoot him!"

CHAPTER TWENTY-ONE

Poppy was up early again the next morning. She was eager to get into the cottage garden and pick the flowers for her first order—the posy for the lady who was visiting her mother in the nursing home— but first she went to check on her new plant arrivals in the greenhouse. As she surveyed the trays of plug plants laid out on the central bench, she found it strange to think that these seedlings were going to provide the first sales for her fledgling nursery business. Despite being bigger than the ones she'd grown herself from seed, these baby plants still looked so small, so insubstantial—she could hardly believe that they would grow into flowering plants that people would want to buy.

And yet just seeing all the trays laid out on the bench like that suddenly made her feel a lot more grown up and professional. When she'd just had that one batch of seeds she'd sown herself, it hadn't felt very "real" yet—but now that she'd invested in all these trays of plug plants, it was really beginning to hit her: she was going to open a plant nursery!

Poppy bent over each tray to check the tiny plants individually. She would have to spend some time transplanting each one into small individual pots to grow on, but there was no rush. According to the instructions she had been given by the wholesale growers, she could wait a couple of days as long as she kept them moist and in a cool, bright, and airy place.

She used a finger to feel the compost that they were growing in; they had been watered yesterday, straight after they'd arrived, but they seemed to have dried out a bit, so she watered them again, careful not to get any water on the leaves and to make sure that there was ample drainage. Then she left them spread out across the bench, so that there would be good airflow between them, and headed outside to create her first official customer order.

For several minutes, Poppy wandered through the flowerbeds, carrying a bucket of cold water and a pair of secateurs, and selecting flowers as they caught her eye. She cut several long stems of delicate white cosmos, some velvety snapdragons in a blend of peach and lemon colours, clusters of sweet Williams in a pretty pink, and finally a couple of penstemon stalks with bells of lavender flowers that contrasted beautifully with the other colours. She placed these all into her bucket, then added some stems from plants which didn't have big colourful blooms but which provided beautiful foliage to surround the flowers.

With her bucket brimming, Poppy returned to the cottage and took everything into the greenhouse extension at the back. She set the flowers on the bench, then hesitated for a moment as she wondered how to arrange them. She knew that a bouquet of flowers was traditionally tied in a symmetrical bunch, with spiralling stems, and then wrapped in decorative tissue paper or cellophane, but she wasn't confident that she had the skills to produce a professionally hand-tied bouquet. Besides, she felt that the whole difference of what she was offering was that her flowers looked as if they had been freshly cut from your own garden, naturally arranged in any convenient container—a simple, home-grown look, not a slick, commercial product. She also thought her client might appreciate something that could be placed immediately by her mother's bedside, without the need to hunt for a vase and transfer things into water.

So Poppy decided to follow her instincts. Instead of tying the flowers into a traditional bouquet, she arranged them loosely in a jam jar, which she decorated with a length of straw ribbon around its neck for a country look. As a final touch, she cut a square of brown paper and carefully wrote "Hollyhock Cottage Flowers" on one side, with little doodles of leaves and flowers surrounding the words, and the cottage's address and telephone number on the other. Then she punched a hole in one corner and strung the label into the ribbon round the neck of the jam jar. When she'd finished, she stood back to admire the effect and felt pleased.

"My—that looks lovely, Poppy!" exclaimed Nell as she came into the greenhouse. "Very professional, and yet somehow simple and home-made too."

"Do you think so?" said Poppy, delighted. "I hope you're right. Well, I'd better get these flowers to my first customer while they're still fresh." She picked up the jam jar and laughed. "'My first customer'— oh, that sounds so official!"

"Well, I'm off to work; I've got a couple of houses in Oxford to do, so I won't be back until this evening," said Nell, turning to go. "I might see you, though, before your dinner tonight?"

Poppy nodded. "I'll be here most of the day. I've just got this posy to deliver this morning, and then another flower order for a birthday party—"

"Aren't you going over to work on the scent garden in Duxton House today?"

"I'm not sure if the police are finished with the place yet. They put up crime-scene tape all round the rock garden yesterday and it sounded like they're going to be doing a thorough search of Betsy's room, plus the rest of the house and the grounds today. But anyway, it doesn't matter because I'd arranged for Muriel to bring Flopsy over today just before lunch... you know, to check out some of the scented plants here. So I'll still be sort of working on the new garden."

Twenty minutes later, Poppy arrived at the house of the lady who had ordered the posy and nervously rang the doorbell. But her apprehension evaporated when the door was opened and she saw the smile of delight on the other woman's face.

"Oh! That is absolutely gorgeous!" cried the lady, reaching out to take the flowers. "And how clever of you to put them in a jam jar. That will be so much easier for me to carry to the nursing home, and I can put it by my mother's bedside right away. Thank you so much!"

"You're welcome," said Poppy, smiling. "I'm so happy you like it."

"You know, you should really charge a bit more if you're going to provide your flowers in containers," said the lady. "Otherwise you'll be losing the cost of the materials."

"Oh... well, I thought I'd just use recycled glass jars," Poppy explained. "I could collect unwanted ones from the houses in the village."

"Yes, but there's still your time and energy spent collecting them." The lady smiled and patted her hand. "Trust me, dear—people don't value things they don't have to pay for. You're offering a wonderful product so don't be afraid to charge for it."

As she walked away a few minutes later, with her first payment safely tucked in her pocket, Poppy reflected ruefully that there was still an awful lot she had to learn about running a business. She hadn't even thought about "cost" and "profit" but the lady was right—it might have been fine to ignore those things with one order, but she couldn't afford to keep doing that if she hoped to make money from her venture.

As she retraced her steps along the high street, the window of a shop on the other side of the road caught her eye. Poppy crossed over to take a closer look. There was a collection of assorted old jars and bottles in beautiful vintage shades of green and brown. *I wonder how much they are*, she mused. *They'd be perfect for my flower arrangements!*

She glanced absently upwards at the shop sign, then did a double take. It was Norman Smalle's shop. She turned back to peer through the large display window. Through the various shelves of antique curios and vintage furniture stacked beside the aisles, she could see a balding middle-aged man sitting at a desk at the back of the store. He seemed to be busily polishing something. She couldn't see any other customers in the shop, and for a moment she hesitated, recalling the gossip in the post office shop yesterday morning and wondering if it was wise to go in by herself. *Don't be silly!* she berated herself. It was broad daylight, after all, and besides, no matter what the village gossips said, she just couldn't believe that Norman could be Ursula's killer.

She pushed the door open and stepped inside. A tinkling bell announced her arrival and Norman looked up from his job as she approached him. She eyed him curiously, wondering if she would see the changes that the postmistress had mentioned. He did look haggard, his hair greyer and his shoulders drooping, and, for a moment, Poppy felt her heart go out to him. Then she reminded herself that he might've looked strained because he was worried about the ongoing investigation into Ursula's murder. Guilt could make you lose sleep at night, just as much as grief did.

"Hello... can I help you?" Norman asked politely.

Poppy gave him a perfunctory smile. "Yes, I wanted to ask about the old glass jars and bottles in your window. I was wondering—" She broke off suddenly as she caught sight of the item he was polishing.

It was a pruning knife, the long, hooked blade gleaming against the dark wooden handle. It looked almost identical to the one that had been donated to the fête raffle and which she had found buried in the rock garden—the one that had probably been used to kill Ursula.

CHAPTER TWENTY-TWO

Norman followed her gaze and flushed as he guessed where her thoughts were straying. He fumbled with the knife, hastily rotating the blade and slotting it back into the handle, closing it. Then he put it down quickly on the desk, as if it'd burned him.

"I… I'm sorry…" Poppy swallowed. "That looks just like the pruning knife that Ursula—"

"Yes… well…" Norman cleared his throat. "It was part of the same collection of gardening tools that I'd obtained at an auction."

There was an awkward silence, then Poppy said, "I'm sorry about Ursula. I understand that she was a good friend."

Norman looked agonised. He opened his mouth to speak, shut it again, then suddenly burst out:

"Ursula was more than just a friend!"

Poppy hesitated, not knowing how to respond.

Norman gave her a sulky look. "Don't tell me you didn't know. Everyone in the village spends their spare time gossiping about Ursula and me. And they think I murdered her too, don't they?" he demanded. "I see the way they look at me now when I go out and about in the village. They all think I'm some kind of lunatic or psychopath..." His face crumpled. "How could they think that I would kill her? Ursula was my sun, my moon, my stars! We were going to be together forever—"

"I didn't realise that you were together!" said Poppy in surprise.

"Oh... well... we weren't 'together' in the conventional sense," Norman said, fussing with a packet of "sour cream and onion" crisps on his desk and avoiding her eyes. "Ours was a much purer relationship than the usual sordid romances you see. I expressed my love and devotion through poetry and gifts..."

"And Ursula?"

Norman looked shifty. "Ursula was a lady. A lady never shows her emotions in public." He raised his eyes suddenly to her, his face aglow. "But I knew— even though she showed no outward sign of it—that she really loved me. I knew!"

Poppy looked at him askance. It sounded to her like Norman was living completely in his fantasies.

"I still can't really believe that she's gone, you

know," he continued in a sad voice. "I keep thinking the whole thing is a bad dream and that I'm going to wake up and see Ursula walking past my shop." He smiled in reminiscence. "She always pretended to be very busy and hurried past my window, but..." He smiled smugly. "I knew that she must have come past my shop on purpose, just so she could catch a glimpse of me." He patted his balding head, smoothing his comb-over across his forehead. "She was always too shy to say it, of course, but I think she found me quite attractive."

The man's delusional, thought Poppy, eyeing him with a mixture of pity and amusement. She could just imagine how cloying and irritating he had been to Ursula but, as usual, the woman had probably been too kind-hearted to tell him bluntly to his face that she had no feelings for him.

"Um... have the police questioned you about the day of the murder?" she asked, trying to change the subject.

"Well, a constable took my statement at the fête but that was it. No one has spoken to me since."

What is that Sergeant Lee doing? wondered Poppy in annoyance. At the very least, he should have found out the gossip about Ursula and Norman, and come to question the antique dealer himself.

"When was the last time you saw Ursula at the fête?" she asked.

"Oh, it was after the paramedics left. We walked

to the manor together and she showed me to one of the smaller sitting rooms at the back of the house, where there was a *chaise longue* for me to lie down. I knew she was probably secretly hoping that I would ask her to join me—but I was much too much of a gentleman to do that," he added virtuously.

"Er... right," said Poppy, restraining the urge to roll her eyes. "So then she left you there and went back to the fête?"

"Yes, I lay for a while, trying to shut my eyes and rest, but I just couldn't settle. I could hear a lot of shouting and cheering, and I kept wondering what I was missing."

"That must have been the Terrier Racing," said Poppy. "The crowds were really rowdy then."

"Yes, that's right! I could faintly hear this chap speaking on the megaphone... Anyway, I got up in the end and decided to go back to the fête. And then—just as I was leaving the house—I heard a woman screaming. I rushed back and then I saw the crowds around the marquee..." He clenched his fist. "If only I had been there! I could have protected Ursula, grabbed that knife from her attacker, saved her life!"

Maybe in your dreams, thought Poppy, eyeing his weedy form. More likely there would have been *two* dead bodies in the marquee for Sonia to find.

"I don't suppose you saw anyone who could be her attacker?" she asked without much hope.

"When you were coming from the manor house, you must have had a view of the marquee from a distance—did you see anyone running away?"

He took a crisp out of the packet and chewed it thoughtfully. "No, I didn't see anybody. Even the house seemed to be empty—all the staff were helping at the fête, I think... Oh, wait... actually, I did hear someone come in earlier, when I was lying down. I think it was that pet nanny chap—Kirby. I heard him cursing. He uses disgusting language." Norman made a fastidious face.

Poppy thought of the colourful cursing she had overheard yesterday morning, when she had stumbled upon Kirby grooming Flopsy.

"Yes, Kirby did return to the house to get a special brand of mineral water for Flopsy," she recalled. "He was gone for a long time; I remember Muriel complaining about it. Kirby said it was because he'd had to go down to the cellar, as they were out of Perrier in the kitchen—"

Norman frowned. "Down to the cellar? No, I don't think he went there."

"What do you mean?"

"Well, I'm sure I heard his footsteps on the other side, in the wing that houses the old servants' quarters."

Poppy caught her breath. "Servants' quarters—you mean, where the maids' rooms are?"

"Well, only one of the maids lives in. The other one lives in the village—"

"Yes, but Betsy—she's the maid who lives in, isn't she? She has a room at the manor?"

Norman nodded. "I don't understand why Kirby would have been going to her room, though, unless..." He brightened suddenly. "Do you think he might be in love with Betsy? Perhaps he is suffering from a secret, hopeless passion too—er, I mean, *unlike* me..." He coughed and cleared his throat. "I do so sympathise with those who haven't found their soulmate."

Poppy was barely listening. *No, Kirby isn't secretly in love with Betsy,* she thought grimly. *I can think of a different reason why he would have gone to her room: to hide the murder weapon...*

"Listen, Norman—did Ursula ever say anything to you about Kirby? Did she like him?"

"That man is a snake," spat Norman. "Muriel should never have hired him. In fact, he wouldn't have got the job except that Ursula felt sorry for him and put in a good word with Muriel. Kirby used to work at a dog groomers' salon in London, you know, but he was fired."

"Why was he fired?" asked Poppy quickly. "Did he get violent with the customers or something?"

Norman shrugged and ate another crisp, chewing noisily. "I don't know... I don't think so. He told Ursula that the salon's owner had a grudge against him."

"And she *believed* him?" said Poppy. She was beginning to think that Ursula's propensity to always see the good in others and feel sorry for everyone was less a virtue and more a weakness.

Norman shrugged again. "Flopsy's last pet nanny had just resigned, you see, and Ursula knew that Muriel was looking for a replacement, so she recommended Kirby for the position." He gave her an indignant look. "But you know what? The minute he was settled at Duxton House, that arrogant sod began taking advantage. He should have been grateful to Ursula, you know, for helping him get such a cushy position, but he was always giving her lip and saying things to the other staff behind her back. And he would fawn and grovel in front of Muriel, but then show a totally different face to everyone else. He was abominably rude to me whenever I went up to the manor!"

Poppy thought back to the scene she had witnessed when she was eavesdropping through the drawing room window and her distaste at the pet nanny's smooth, insinuating manner.

"Did you tell Ursula?" she asked.

"That Kirby was rude to me?"

Poppy rolled her eyes. "No, that he was trying to undermine her authority and maybe even badmouth her behind her back."

"I didn't want to spend my precious time with Ursula speaking about Kirby. We had other, more important things to talk about," said Norman peevishly. "Anyway, I doubt she would have listened. Ursula always thought everyone was just misunderstood and—" He broke off suddenly and stared at her. "Do you think *Kirby* could have killed her?" he asked in hushed tones.

"Do you?"

"I wouldn't be surprised! I told you the man was a snake—he's a greedy, two-faced liar who's out to get whatever he can for himself—"

"But why would he want to kill Ursula? Does he benefit from her death?" asked Poppy.

"Well, I suppose not," said Norman grudgingly. "It's not as if he would get a pay rise if Ursula was dead."

No, but perhaps his eye was on a bigger fish, thought Poppy, remembering once again the man's creepy pandering and suggestive words to Muriel. *Perhaps he wasn't thinking of his job but of his future. Undermining Ursula was one step towards replacing her—especially in the affections of a wealthy old lady who had a large estate to bequeath...*

CHAPTER TWENTY-THREE

Her chat with Norman had delayed her and, as she left the antique store, Poppy cast a worried glance at her watch and realised that she would have to hurry if she was to deliver her second order to the birthday party in time. Remembering Moira's special request for pink flowers, she set off once more around the cottage garden with a bucket and pair of secateurs, and picked everything in every shade of pink she could find, from salmon to fuchsia, blush to magenta. She was delighted to see several dahlias already in flower, with their striking pompom blooms almost as big as dinner plates, and a few stands of sweet peas still producing lovely ruffled flowers as well. There were also wallflowers in a deep mauve and phlox in a bright bubblegum pink, and even dainty daisies with pretty pink and white flowers and yellow centres.

When she passed the rose bushes, Poppy hesitated. Several were flowering again and their pink cupped blooms, filled with petals, looked so beautiful. But she remembered that it was a children's party and decided not to include anything with prickles. Likewise, she avoided the tall spires of foxgloves, despite their lovely magenta flowers, and also the delphiniums, remembering from her recent brush with another murder case that both were plants that contained poisonous alkaloids.

At last, she stood back and examined her bucket. Because this was going to be a table centrepiece, she wanted a very full arrangement. She had a lot of different flowers, but somehow, something seemed missing. She realised it was because they were all mostly small blooms—aside from the dahlias, there was nothing really big and dramatic, to make a strong impact. Then her gaze strayed to the patch of the border closer to the stone wall, where several large hydrangea bushes were growing under the shade of the trees. Their enormous mophead flowers looked like cheerleaders' pompoms and lit up that corner with romantic spheres of soft pink and mauve.

Of course! She could include some hydrangea blooms! Eagerly, Poppy went over to cut several stalks. She found some blooms that were still fresh and vivid, and others which had started to fade, the pink blending into a beautiful mix of soft bronze and green. They were the perfect last addition to her collection, and when she had returned to the greenhouse and arranged everything into an old metal milk jug, she was really pleased with the result.

The trip across the village took longer this time—the jug filled with water and flowers was heavy—and Poppy arrived at the big Tudor house slightly late. But her apologies were waved aside as she was met by another big smile from another delighted client.

"Oh, don't worry—people have only just started arriving. The party hasn't officially started. My goodness, this looks fabulous!" Moira gasped as she took the jug. "And you've done all pink flowers too! Look, Emma—the nice lady has picked these especially for you, because pink is your favourite colour, isn't it?"

The little girl who was clutching her mother's skirts nodded and eyed Poppy shyly. She looked no older than three and still had a thumb in her mouth. Beyond her, Poppy could see the hallway opening into a large living area which already seemed to be filled with screaming babies and toddlers.

Moira caught her expression and gave a laugh. "I know—everyone told me I was mad to organise a birthday party for three-year-olds and then invite all their baby sisters and brothers too. What was I thinking!"

Poppy left a few minutes later, after having met several of the other mothers, who *oohed* and *ahhed* over the arrangement, and asked for her details. As she walked slowly back to Hollyhock Cottage, she felt flushed with pride and happiness. For the first time since leaving her old life in London and moving to the countryside, she felt like things were finally on track. She had found something she loved and could do well, and was a great solution for bringing in extra income too!

It was nearly lunchtime by the time she got back to the cottage and she wondered suddenly if Muriel might have arrived already. It would be terribly bad form to keep the old lady waiting. When she walked through the garden gate, however, she was surprised to see that Flopsy was not accompanied by her elderly owner but by Kirby. The pet nanny was smoking and busily texting on his phone, completely ignoring the toy poodle who stood straining at the end of her leash.

Poppy eyed the man warily, her conversation with Norman that morning still fresh in her mind. *Could Kirby be Ursula's killer?* She'd never liked his insincere, two-faced manner and she had certainly seen the vicious streak in him when she spied him mistreating Flopsy yesterday. But did he really have a motive for killing Ursula? The idea that he'd done it on the off-chance that he might benefit from Muriel's will in the distant future seemed so far-fetched, even ludicrous.

Still, there was what Norman had said: about hearing Kirby in the old servants' quarters... if he *hadn't* been planting the murder weapon in Betsy's room, then what had he been doing there?

Poppy realised that Kirby had looked up and seen her.

"Oh... there you are," he said ungraciously. "I've been waiting ages."

Poppy hesitated, then plastered on a polite smile and approached him. He might have been a suspect but he also represented her client and, until she had proof, she had to treat him as normal.

"Where's Muriel—I mean, Mrs Farnsworth?" Poppy asked.

"Oh, she had to go down to London unexpectedly. She won't be back until tomorrow evening, so she asked me to bring Flopsy over," said Kirby, lazily stubbing out his cigarette in a nearby plant pot.

Poppy felt a flicker of irritation. "That's not an ashtray," she said.

"Oh? Well, it's all organic, isn't it? It'll break down," said Kirby, giving her an insolent smile.

Poppy felt her irritation growing but she took a deep breath and said, as coolly as possible, "Why don't you walk Flopsy around so she can sniff the plants?"

Kirby moved off in a bored fashion, dragging the toy poodle behind him. It was obvious that Flopsy didn't like him and didn't want to go anywhere with him, and Poppy felt slightly sorry for the dog. She watched askance as Kirby made a half-hearted attempt to wander around the flowerbeds, barely paying any attention to the dog that he was pulling behind him.

"Look... you're going too fast," she called out. "You're not giving her any chance to sniff anything! You should be following her, not the other way around. I want to see which plants she picks out on her own."

Kirby heaved an exaggerated sigh and followed her instructions with bad grace, but Poppy was pleased to see that, after a few moments, Flopsy seemed to relax and begin to show some interest in the surrounding plants. The poodle wandered over to a large clump of yarrow and sniffed it with interest, then turned her attention briefly to a patch of chamomile, before trotting towards a small shrub which she seemed to become very excited by. She rubbed her face against its clusters of hairy, grey-green leaves.

Poppy frowned, trying to recognise the plant. It looked a bit like mint, although she knew it definitely wasn't that herb. It had a few spikes of dirty pale-pink flowers, and overall wasn't a very attractive plant. But whatever it was, Flopsy obviously loved it. Poppy hurried into the cottage and grabbed one of her grandmother's plant books—a handy pocket guide with well-thumbed pages that suggested Mary Lancaster had often used it too. She flipped through the book as she walked back outside, searching for a plant that resembled the one Flopsy was nuzzling. *No... not this... nor this one... hmm... it could be this but the leaves look different... or how about—*

Poppy stopped in her tracks, her heart skipping a beat, as the page fell open to a photo of flowering hydrangeas. Underneath the image were the usual sections of information on the plant's origins, ideal location, and watering needs, as well as other things to watch out for, such as pests, diseases, and toxicity. It was the last section that Poppy stared at. Her heart began to pound as she read the words:

"Many people know about infamous poisonous plants, like Datura and deadly nightshade, but few know that the common Hydrangea macrophylla*, found in many home gardens, can be toxic to pets and humans as well. All parts of the plant contain cyanogenic glycosides—a poisonous compound which causes nausea and vomiting, stomach pain, sweating, diarrhoea, lethargy, and, in severe cases, convulsions and coma..."*

"OH MY GOD!" Poppy gasped.

She dropped the book and ran past a puzzled-looking Kirby and Flopsy as she rushed out of the cottage garden. She raced across the village, running faster than she'd ever done in her life. Her stomach churned as her imagination conjured up images of sick and dying children sprawled around her flower arrangement, and distraught mothers wailing with grief.

No... no... no... how could I have missed that? I thought I was safe with all the flowers I'd picked... Oh God, what if a child ate one of the flowers? What if they all did? How am I going to face the mothers? How am I going to live with myself?

She arrived at Moira's house gasping and panting, and had to support herself against the door jamb as she rang the bell. Her chest hurt and she felt as if she could hardly draw a breath, although she didn't know if this was due to the gruelling run or to the panic swamping her. Moira opened the door and stared in surprise.

"Poppy! What on earth—"

"The... the flower arrangement..." Poppy gasped. "The hydrangeas... mustn't let any child... poison..."

"Poppy, slow down—I can't understand what you're saying," said Moira. "Here, would you like to come in and have a glass of water—"

She was interrupted by the sound of a scream and then a child wailing, followed by several cries of alarm coming from the end of the hallway.

Poppy's heart leapt into her throat. She stumbled after Moira as the woman hurried into the living room, then froze as she stared in horror at the scene in front of her.

A little girl was clutching her stomach and hunched over, vomiting onto the carpet, which was covered with red stains. A woman was bent over her, trying to hold her up, whilst the other mothers were trying to soothe the rest of the children, who were crying and wailing as well.

"*Oh God!*" Poppy rushed over to the little girl and grabbed the mother's arm. "What happened? Did she eat the leaves? Or the flowers?"

The woman looked at her. "I'm... I'm sorry?"

"The hydrangea!" cried Poppy, almost wild with panic. "Which part did she eat?"

"N-none of them," said the woman, looking baffled. "She just had too much jelly."

"*J-jelly?*" Poppy sagged backwards and stared at her. "You... you mean..."

"Oh dear—is it the food colouring?" asked Moira, coming to join them. "I did try to choose the one that had the least artificial ingredients but—"

"Oh, don't worry," said the mother, smiling. "Sarah always gets over-excited and eats too much jelly too quickly and then she's sick everywhere... I probably shouldn't let her have any, but she does love it so much..."

Their voices seemed to fade away into the distance. Poppy groped for somewhere to sit down. Her legs felt like jelly themselves and she thought she was going to vomit too. She lowered herself trembling onto a nearby sofa and took several deep breaths.

A little girl came up to her and looked at her curiously. "Did you eat too much jelly too?"

Poppy didn't know whether to laugh or cry.

Before she could answer, Moira appeared beside her and eyed her with concern.

"Are you all right, Poppy? You look a bit green around the gills yourself."

Poppy stood up again with an effort and gave the woman a weak smile. "I'm... I'm fine... I just had a bit of a scare." She took a deep breath, then looked around the room. "Er... where did you put the flower arrangement?"

"Oh, it's over there," said Moira, pointing to the dining table on the other side of the room.

Poppy saw her flowers having pride of place in the centre of the table, surrounded by several buffet-style dishes.

"I thought I'd keep it up, out of the way of little fingers. I didn't want any of the children spoiling the flowers," Moira explained.

"Oh... oh, thank goodness!" said Poppy, heaving a shuddering sigh of relief. "I'm terribly sorry—I chose the flowers so carefully this morning and I didn't realise until after I got back home that hydrangea are poisonous. I was terrified some of the children might have eaten them or something—"

To her astonishment, Moira burst out laughing. "And you rushed back here because of that? Well, let me put your mind at rest..." She pointed to the large bifold doors on one side of the living room, which looked out onto the back garden. "We have hydrangea all over the garden ourselves! See?"

Poppy followed the direction of her finger and

saw that there were indeed several large hydrangea bushes in the borders. "But... but aren't you worried about Emma getting poisoned?"

Moira shrugged. "I suppose she could, in theory... but we had hydrangea in the garden growing up, and me and my sisters never had any problems. We had loads of other plants that were supposed to be dangerous too—things like daffodils and irises and poinsettia and, yes, even foxgloves," she said, chuckling. "My parents just explained to us about plants being poisonous and taught us not to eat any leaves or flowers or berries, and to always wash our hands after we'd been in the garden. I'm doing the same with Emma."

Another mother, who had been listening, leaned over and added, "Almost every common plant out there is poisonous if you eat it—you'd end up with nothing but grass in the garden if you tried to avoid everything!"

"Yes, and then your kids would probably get poisoned when they went out to the park or to a friend's house or something," a third woman chimed in.

Moira nodded. "Much better that you show them and teach them in your own garden." She smiled at Poppy. "But it was sweet of you to be so worried. I'm sorry you had a scare, though."

"No, it's okay... I'm just glad that I was worried for nothing," said Poppy, feeling her heart rate finally beginning to return to normal.

"Would you like a cup of tea? Or something to eat?" Moira gestured to the buffet.

"No, thank you. I've got to get back. I've actually got a... a sort of client waiting for me back at Hollyhock Cottage. But thanks very much for the offer," she said with a grateful smile.

Still feeling weak with relief, Poppy walked slowly back home. She would make herself a strong cup of tea when she got back, she decided. With lots of sugar. *And maybe some brandy too*, she thought with a sheepish smile.

Arriving back at the cottage, she looked across the flowerbeds as she entered through the gate, searching for Kirby amongst the shrubs and flowers. She didn't like the man, but politeness dictated that she offer him tea too if she was making a cup for herself. She couldn't see him anywhere though... Poppy scanned the area twice. Perhaps he had taken Flopsy to the back of the property?

Then, as she walked farther up the path, she caught sight of the pet nanny. He was stretched out on the stone bench set against the far wall, smoking a cigarette, with his eyes closed and his face turned up to the sun. Poppy felt that familiar flicker of irritation. The lazy git was supposed to be taking Flopsy around the garden, not enjoying a spot of sunbathing!

She marched up to him and started to say something, then paused and looked around, frowning.

"Kirby—where's Flopsy?"

"Eh?" He opened his eyes and blinked sleepily, then hastily sat up. "Oh... erm... she's just over there."

Poppy turned to look in the direction he was pointing. "Where? I don't see her." She flashed him an accusatory look. "You were supposed to be watching her."

"Oh, don't worry—she can't wander off. I tied her leash to the sundial there."

Poppy bit back the sharp words she wanted to say and stomped over to the sundial. But when she got there, she stared in dismay.

"She's not here!" she cried.

Kirby got up and hurried over, looking annoyed. "What do you mean—she's not there? I tell you, she was tied up—"

He broke off and stared as well. The leash *was* still securely tied to the sundial... but the other end lay limply on the ground, the jagged edges showing where the nylon had been chewed through. Kirby let out an expletive.

Flopsy was gone.

CHAPTER TWENTY-FOUR

Poppy stood self-consciously outside the garden gate of Hollyhock Cottage, waiting for Henry Farnsworth's red Porsche to arrive. After the day she'd just had, the last thing she felt like doing was going out for a romantic dinner—but it would have been too rude to cancel at the last minute. Besides, she needed to go ahead with her plan to check Henry's phone records and see if he was the one who'd called Ursula on the day of the murder. It would be nice to feel like she was in control of *something* and making progress *somewhere*, after the disastrous events of the day.

She thought of her happy mood that morning as she had walked back from Moira's house (the first time!)—how confident and content she'd been, feeling like everything was finally starting to go her way at last... and how quickly that had all changed. First that horrendous scare with the hydrangea in her flower arrangement—she still couldn't think of it without shuddering—and then the horror of finding Flopsy gone.

She and Kirby had searched the whole garden, then the cul-de-sac outside and the surrounding lanes, but there had been no sign of the toy poodle. Of course, Poppy knew that it wasn't technically her fault—after all, *she* wasn't employed to watch the little dog and she hadn't even been around when Flopsy had disappeared. It had been Kirby's responsibility and it was he who would have to face Muriel when the old lady returned tomorrow.

Still, Poppy couldn't shake off the sense of guilt, partly because it had happened on her property and partly because she had an uneasy feeling that she knew who had helped Flopsy escape. She knew one little dog who was smart enough to chew through that leash. In fact, her worst suspicions were confirmed when—after Kirby had left—she popped over to Bertie's house and asked the old inventor where his terrier was.

Bertie had looked up distractedly from the elaborate coil of glass tubes he was heating and said: "Einstein? Isn't he sleeping in the sitting room? He just seems to mope around all the time these days."

But Einstein's bed had been empty and Poppy was sure that the little terrier had somehow realised

217

that his beloved was near, had sneaked into the cottage garden through the gap in the stone wall, and had convinced Flopsy to leave her life of pampering and luxury for one of smelly marrowbones and canine adventure.

Bertie had accompanied her on another search around the area but they had seen no sign of the two dogs. The old inventor had assured her that Einstein would come home of his own accord (apparently it wasn't the first time the little terrier had gone AWOL) and Poppy hoped that he was right.

Well, I can't do anything about it now, she thought with a sigh, trying to push her worries from her mind as she smoothed down the skirt of her dress. *I have to concentrate on tonight.* She looked down and wondered if she had picked the right outfit for the evening. She hadn't wanted to look like she was making too much of an effort—in case that gave Henry the wrong ideas about her feelings for him—but at the same time, she didn't want to be rude by "under-dressing" for the occasion. In the end, she had opted for a cotton dress in a pretty floral print, which had ruffled sleeves, a fitted bodice, and a flared skirt which fell to just above her knees. It was an old dress that she'd bought from Marks & Spencer years ago, but it had lasted well and still looked good.

She had applied minimal make-up—just some mascara to highlight her blue eyes and a touch of pink gloss on her lips—and left her hair down to fall in dark brown waves around her shoulders. Nell had looked at her approvingly as she'd stepped out of the bedroom and had smiled, saying:

"It's so nice to see you dressing up and going out for a date, dear. It's about time you had a bit of fun with a nice young man."

If only Nell knew the real reason I'd accepted Henry's invitation, Poppy thought. She had decided that it was easier not telling her old friend the whole truth. For one thing, she felt uncomfortable admitting her mercenary motives. The idea of being a honey trap had seemed glamorous and exciting when Nick had first suggested it, but now she felt slightly uneasy about the whole thing.

Well, it's too late to back out now, she thought grimly as a red Porsche came down the lane, its engine rumbling. She slipped a hand into the concealed pocket in the skirt of her dress and felt a slim weight press reassuringly into her palm. It was the device Bertie had made to bypass a phone's passcode and she reminded herself that as long as she had this, things should be easy.

"You just have to clamp it over the phone like this, my dear," Bertie had demonstrated eagerly for her. "And it will hack into the phone's system and unlock it for you. It should only take a few seconds."

"It's not going to explode or start singing a song or something, is it?" Poppy had asked. The one thing she'd learned about Bertie's inventions was that they never performed as expected.

"Oh no! Although now that you mention it... hmm... the ability to play music simultaneously would be interesting—"

"Uh... never mind," Poppy had said hastily, snatching the device out of Bertie's hands.

She curled her fingers around the device now, squeezing it once again for reassurance, then withdrew her hand, plastered a smile on her face, and went forwards to greet Henry. He got out of the car and escorted her to the front passenger seat, opening the door with flourish. When she was settled, he returned to the driver's seat, gunned the engine, and swung the car in a wide arc around the end of the cul-de-sac before pulling smoothly out of the lane.

"I say—you look marvellous," he said, eyeing Poppy with open admiration. "I'm going to be the envy of every chap in the restaurant tonight."

"Thanks," said Poppy awkwardly. "Um... where are we going?"

"Oh, to this great place in Jericho," said Henry. "They've got a fantastic wine list—and some pretty good nosh too."

"Jericho?" said Poppy, puzzled.

Henry laughed. "No, I'm not whisking you off to the Middle East. Jericho's a suburb just outside central Oxford. It's sort of hip and bohemian— there's an arthouse cinema and several cocktail bars and some pretty good restaurants with eclectic menus."

"Ah, right... sounds great," said Poppy, trying to look enthusiastic.

All she could think about was that she hoped the restaurant had toilets quite far from the main dining room. Because the only way she could think of getting an opportunity to snoop on Henry's phone was to wait for him to use the Gents (and hope that he left his phone behind on the table). When they arrived at the restaurant, she looked frantically around as they were shown to their table, trying to see the signs for the public toilets.

"Is everything all right?" asked Henry, giving her a quizzical look.

"Oh! Um... yes," said Poppy, hastily jerking her gaze back to him. "Sorry... I... er... haven't been to many fancy places like this," she said, gesturing around the restaurant. "It's all... quite exciting."

Henry looked surprised, glancing around carelessly. "This isn't that fancy, really. I mean, it's not a Michelin-starred restaurant or anything."

"Well, this is probably one of the poshest places I've been to," said Poppy with a laugh. "My mother was a single mum and we never had very much money. Going out to eat was only for special occasions, like birthdays and things like that—and it was usually to the local pub."

"Oh, I see. I'm sorry." Henry gave a rueful smile. "I suppose one forgets that not everyone has a life of privilege. So... did your parents separate then?"

Poppy stiffened slightly. She always dreaded it when the conversation turned to her father. "No. I don't actually know who my father is. My mother never told me. She... she was a bit of a wild child in her teens and she spent some time in the States, following bands around."

"You mean, like a groupie?" asked Henry with interest.

Poppy nodded. "She came back home to England when she got pregnant."

He whistled. "So your father was a musician?"

"I don't know. Yeah... probably."

"Haven't you tried to search for him?"

"Well... Mum never wanted to talk about him when she was alive. And after she died, I did try a bit, but the thing is, I can't afford to go to America, and even if I could, I wouldn't know where to start looking."

"What a fascinating story!" said Henry. "I'll bet you're the daughter of someone really famous—like a big rock star or something. Why not?" he asked as Poppy shook her head, laughing. "You never know! Hey, how about we make a bet right now?" He shoved a hand into his pocket and pulled out a twenty-pound note. "Twenty quid says your dad's a mega star."

Poppy stared at him in confusion. "But... but I might never find out who my father is," she said, frowning. "It seems a bit stupid—"

"Never mind!" said Henry, waving the money in her face. "The point is: if you ever *do* find him and he *is* someone really famous, then I win the bet—right? I can say that I dated his daughter," he said, grinning. "And you'll owe me twenty pounds."

"Er... right..." said Poppy, thinking that by the time she found her father—if she ever found him—she might have no idea of where Henry was and vice versa.

The whole thing seemed like a ludicrous exercise. But Henry seemed to be taking it very seriously—in fact, she didn't think she'd ever seen him so animated. Gone was his usual indolent manner. Instead, his eyes were bright and his whole face was suffused with excitement. *It's funny how any kind of connection to celebrities could excite people so much*, thought Poppy dryly.

"So... um... what about *your* father?" she asked, trying to turn the focus away from herself. "What did he do?"

"Oh, pretty boring, really. He was the son of a wealthy industrialist. Not that I ever knew my grandfather—my grandparents were both dead by the time I was born. I actually knew my great-uncle—Muriel's husband—better. I used to come to Duxton House to stay when I was a boy."

"That must have made it easier when you came here to live last year," commented Poppy. "By the way, I'm really sorry again about your parents. It must have been very hard, losing both of them so suddenly like that."

Henry shrugged. "To be honest with you, I was never that close to them. I suppose I'm a bit of a British upper-class cliché: I was sent to boarding school at a young age and spent most of my childhood and teens there. And when I came home, my parents always seemed more interested in their society parties and the charitable causes they were supporting than in me—which suited me just fine," he added quickly. "I found other ways to amuse myself and I certainly never had to worry about how to afford it." He flashed her a brilliant smile.

Poppy smiled back, although silently she wondered if Henry really didn't mind his lonely childhood as much as he insisted. It was strange to think how different their upbringings were. She'd certainly never had the expensive clothes, endless toys, and luxury lifestyle that Henry had had... but she'd probably enjoyed the one thing he could never get: genuine interest and affection from a parent.

"Anyway, enough talk about family," said Henry suddenly, flipping open the menu. "Let's order some drinks! I'll get a bottle of wine, shall I? What d'you prefer? Red or white? And what about food—what do you fancy?"

Poppy opened her own menu and looked down at the list of items, several of which seemed to be French names.

"Gosh, I don't know... I'm not really familiar with half these dishes." She smiled at him again, fluttering her eyelashes slightly. "Why don't you order for me? I have complete faith in you."

As an attempt at flirtation, it was pretty lame, but Henry seemed to lap it up. When the waiter came, he showed off his fluent French as he ordered their drinks and food, then—when their wine came—delighted in teaching Poppy all about "bouquet" and "body" as he watched her savour the expensive Château Batailley he had ordered. Poppy listened and *oohed* and *ahhed* in all the right places, all whilst looking for a way to bring up the subject of his phone. At last, when there was a lull in the conversation, she saw her chance.

"By the way," she said casually, "what kind of phone do you have, Henry? I really need to replace mine—it's a terribly old model—and I was wondering what would be the best one to get?"

Henry slipped a hand into his pocket and pulled out a slim rectangular device. "Oh, well... I'm an iPhone man," he said with a grin. "Never been tempted to switch to Android. I've got the latest model. Here—you can have a look if you like."

He handed the phone to Poppy, who made a great show of turning it over and looking at it from all angles. Her mind raced, trying to think of a way she could get Henry away from the table, even for a few moments. She came up with nothing, though, and when she couldn't pretend to admire the phone any longer, she handed it reluctantly back. Still, she was relieved to see that instead of slipping it back into his pocket, Henry placed his phone on the table, next to his car keys.

Their first courses arrived, followed by the main dishes. Poppy went through the motions of eating her food and listening to his anecdotes, while her nerves slowly stretched to breaking point as she waited and watched and wished fervently that Henry would feel the call of nature. The man seemed to have a bladder the size of a Zeppelin though, as he guzzled his way through a bottle of wine without showing any sign of needing the bathroom.

Poppy fidgeted in her seat, conscious of the time ticking away. If she didn't make a move soon, dinner would be over and she'd lose any chance of getting her hands on Henry's phone. The whole evening would have been for nothing.

At last, she couldn't bear it any longer. *Perhaps if I go to the Ladies and have a quiet moment to think, I'll come up with a plan*, she thought desperately. Excusing herself, she rose from the table and started to make her way across the room—then stopped short as she suddenly noticed an elderly man with a wild mop of grey hair sitting alone at a table a few feet away.

It was Bertie!

CHAPTER TWENTY-FIVE

Poppy cast a look over her shoulder to make sure that Henry wasn't watching. Thankfully, he was sitting with his back to the room, his head down and his attention engrossed as he tapped on his phone. She darted over to Bertie's table and leaned down next to the old inventor.

"Bertie!" she hissed. "What are you doing here?"

"I followed the signal from my mobile hacking device," said the old man, looking confused. "It incorporates a tracker, you see, which sends out information about its location—"

"No, no, I mean—*what* are you doing here? *Why* did you follow the tracker?"

"Oh, I wanted to watch my invention in action!" said Bertie, beaming like a proud parent.

"Well, you might be waiting a very long time,"

said Poppy with a sigh. "I just can't seem to find a way to get my hands on Henry's phone—without him there watching me, that is."

"Ah... that was the other reason I came," said Bertie. "I had a feeling that you might require my assistance. Never fear! I have devised a method to distract your young man and ensure his absence for a short period. Now let me see... I know I put it in here somewhere..." He picked up the ancient leather case he always carried with him and rummaged inside for a moment before finally pulling something out. "Aha! Here it is, my dear."

Poppy took the glass vial he handed her and peered at it curiously. It seemed to contain several small black specks, each about the size of a grain of rice. At first, she thought they might have been tiny fragments of rock or even seeds, but then she realised that each "speck" had features: six tiny legs, a segmented body, two antennae...

"They look like... ants?" she said quizzically, holding the vial up to the light and rotating it slowly. The black specks seemed strangely inanimate. "Are they dead?"

"Oh no, they are simply inactivated. Once they are triggered by oscillatory motion, they will run on a charge generated by the tiny rotating magnet within their bodies."

"Uh-huh... but Bertie, I still don't understand. How will this help me—"

"They're one of my latest inventions: instant

'Ants In Your Pants'!"

"What?" Poppy wondered if she had heard him right. "*Ants in your pants?*"

Bertie nodded eagerly. "Guaranteed to distract a subject and set them in motion. You simply sprinkle the ants nearby and they will find their way to their target."

"Er... target?"

"Oh, they've been programmed to be attracted to muscle protein and thus they will congregate on the area of highest density—which happens to be the *gluteus maximus*, the largest muscle in the body." He leaned forwards and added in a conspiratorial tone, "Your buttocks."

Poppy blinked at him. "You've... you've invented mechanical ants which are attracted to people's bums?"

Bertie nodded, beaming. "Yes! Isn't it marvellous?"

"Er..." *Marvellous* wasn't the word that she would have chosen. *Still...* Poppy threw a look over her shoulder again at Henry. She didn't have any other ideas. What did she have to lose? She took a deep breath and said: "Okay. Tell me how they work."

"Oh, it's very easy. You simply give the vial a quick, hard shake—that will activate the ants—and then flip the top off and shake them out, perhaps onto the back of your young man's chair. They will start making their way towards their target and reach it within a few minutes."

"And what happens when they get there? They're not going to bite him, are they?"

"Oh no, I did not design them with mouth parts," said Bertie. "That was going to be a future model— but I have not been able to find an investor to develop this prototype yet."

Yeah, I wonder why, thought Poppy.

"In any case, they will only have enough charge to work for a few minutes, after which they will automatically shut off," Bertie added.

"Oh, right. Okay," said Poppy, feeling reassured. "Well, in that case..." She gave him a crooked smile. "Wish me luck!"

She walked slowly back to her table. As she drew level with Henry's chair, she gave the vial a quick, hard shake; then, using her thumb, she flipped the lid off and casually moved her hand to the back of Henry's chair. Quickly, she tapped the contents onto his seat back, then continued on around the table and slipped into her seat opposite him.

Henry looked up from his phone with an expression of mock concern. "You were gone ages. I was just thinking of sending a search party."

"Sorry... queue in the Ladies," Poppy mumbled.

"Would you like some dessert? Or how about a liqueur?" asked Henry. "They do some top-notch brandy and cognac here, as well as—"

He broke off suddenly, a funny look crossing his face.

"Er..." Henry shifted uncomfortably in his seat,

then cleared his throat. "As I was saying, they do fantastic—"

He jerked right. Then left. His hand twitched and reached around behind him, before he remembered himself and hastily drew it away. Beads of sweat appeared on his forehead.

"Er..." Henry's face was getting redder and redder as he tried not to wriggle in his seat. "...the liqueurs..."

Suddenly, he surged to his feet and jiggled on the spot. "I... er... will you excuse me...?"

Turning, he bolted across the room. His usual suave air completely deserted him as he half hobbled, half hopped towards the toilets, while surreptitiously trying to scratch his backside. Poppy felt torn between remorse and laughter. She caught sight of Bertie's gleeful face across the room. The old inventor gave her a wide grin and a thumbs-up sign, and she couldn't help laughing. It had been a mean trick to play on Henry—but it wouldn't really hurt him, and it would give her the time she needed. *Besides, if Henry really is Ursula's murderer, then there's no need to waste sympathy on him*, she thought grimly.

As soon as Henry rounded the corner and disappeared from sight, she dived across the table and pounced on his phone. Somehow, though, she missed and the phone slipped from her fingers. It went over the edge of the table on the other side and fell to the floor.

"Bugger!" cried Poppy.

She dived under the table, furious with herself for her clumsiness. She didn't know how long Henry would take in the bathroom—she might only have minutes—so the last thing she'd needed was to waste precious time retrieving the phone. She crawled under the heavy white tablecloth and peered at the floor. There was not much light under here and the dark, patterned carpet made it even harder to discern any shapes. In fact, she couldn't see Henry's iPhone anywhere.

Poppy cursed as she crawled on her knees, groping frantically with one hand. Then she yelped and jumped, nearly smacking her head on the underside of the table, as a deep male voice suddenly said next to her:

"Having fun?"

She jerked around to see Nick Forrest's face a few inches from hers. He had bent down and lifted a corner of the tablecloth to peer underneath.

"Don't scare me like that!" Poppy snapped. "No, I'm not having fun! I've only got a few minutes to look at Henry's bloody phone and I had to go and drop it. Aaarrghh!"

"Is this it?" asked Nick, reaching forwards to extract something that had slid under the pedestal base of the table.

"Yes!" said Poppy, exhaling in relief and snatching the phone from him.

She crawled back out and stood up, then quickly

whipped Bertie's hacking device out of her pocket. She tried to clamp it on to the phone like the old inventor had shown her, but it wasn't as easy as he'd made it look. Poppy fumbled frantically, getting more and more agitated as she couldn't fit the sensor over the phone in the exact position needed to trigger the automatic decoding system.

"Damn..." she muttered. "Damn... damn... damn!"

A strong male hand closed over hers, steadying her trembling fingers.

"Stop. Relax. Breathe," Nick commanded. "You'll never achieve anything in a panic. Just take a moment to calm down and focus."

Poppy bridled and started to make an indignant reply, then she stopped herself. Nick was right. She closed her eyes and forced herself to take a deep breath, emptying her mind of all thought. Then she opened her eyes again and looked down at the phone once more. She blocked out everything else around her: the buzz of conversation at the other tables, the clink of cutlery, the jazz music issuing from the restaurant speakers, even the tall man next to her... Instead, her world narrowed down to the phone she held in her hands.

Carefully, she clamped Bertie's hacking device over the phone, and this time it slid immediately into place. There was a beep as the device engaged, then she saw a green bar appear on the phone screen. It started on the left and gradually extended across to the right.

15%... 27%... 35%... 58%...

Poppy flicked her eyes towards the other side of the restaurant, at the corridor that led to the toilets. What was Henry doing? How much longer did she have? She looked down again at the green bar which was creeping imperceptibly across the phone screen.

61%... 73%...

Come on... come on... Poppy pleaded silently.

Nick made a sudden movement next to her and she glanced up again. Her heart jumped into her throat.

Henry had just emerged from the corridor on the other side of the room—he was coming back!

CHAPTER TWENTY-SIX

Oh my God, what do I do? Poppy looked desperately back down at the phone, which was still showing "92%" on the green bar. She was almost there. She just needed a few more minutes!

She glanced up again. Henry had paused to speak to one of the waiters but that would only buy her another minute or two at the most. And even when the device unlocked, she would still have to open the phone app and scroll through Henry's call register. She looked frantically towards Bertie's table, hoping for some help from the old inventor, but his seat was empty...

Then she realised that Nick was no longer by her side. Her heart gave a leap as she saw the crime author striding across the room towards Henry. As he approached, Nick did an exaggerated double take and clapped the younger man on the shoulder, crying:

"Stewart! Fancy seeing you here!"

Henry stared at him. "I beg your pardon?"

Nick grinned at him, the picture of amiability. "We met at the last conference, remember?"

Henry frowned. "I think you've got the wrong man."

"Don't you remember me? We were propping up the bar together... stayed up half the night. That hotel had some damned fine whiskys—"

"I'm telling you, I think you've got me mixed up with someone else," said Henry impatiently.

"Aw, come on! I can't believe you've forgotten that night already?" said Nick, still grinning like a buffoon. "We downed a couple and then that tasty little blonde came in—remember? You tried to chat her up." He elbowed Henry and gave him a lewd wink. "You've got pretty good technique, old boy. You must teach me sometime—"

"Look, I'm telling you, I don't know what the hell you're talking about. You've got the wrong man!" said Henry, starting to look really annoyed. "My name's not Stewart and I've never been drinking with you..."

Poppy grinned to herself. She couldn't help being impressed by Nick's impromptu performance: that man could think on his feet! She dragged her attention back to the phone in her hands and was delighted to see that the green bar had disappeared.

Instead, the phone's home screen was displayed, with all of Henry's apps neatly lined up in rows. She tapped the phone icon. The app opened and she navigated quickly to the call history, then began scrolling down through the list of calls, noting the dates, times, and caller IDs.

She frowned. There were several calls around the time of the murder but none listed as "Ursula". Of course, Henry might not have had the murdered woman's number saved as a named contact, although that seemed unlikely—given that they were essentially members of the same extended family, lived in the same household, and had probably contacted each other several times in the past.

So what did this mean? Was Henry not the person who had called Ursula after all? Poppy felt suddenly deflated. She had been so convinced that she would find proof of Henry's connection to the murder. Well, there was no time to ponder it now. She glanced up again to see that the restaurant manager was approaching the arguing men. Quickly, she closed the app, removed Bertie's device, turned off the screen, and slid the phone across the table. And not a moment too soon. She had barely pushed the phone back into place when Henry dropped into his chair.

"What a bloody nutter!" he said irritably. "Kept telling him that he'd got the wrong man but he just wouldn't listen!"

Poppy made an appropriately sympathetic noise while she looked surreptitiously over his shoulder at the other side of the restaurant. Nick was being escorted back to his table by a harassed-looking manager. He caught her eye and lifted an eyebrow. She gave him a faint smile and a nod, feeling a sudden rush of camaraderie as he smiled back. It was strange: despite the tension and fear, a part of her was actually having fun. It was as if suddenly, with Nick there, she felt a part of a team and not like she was dealing with things alone—

An ear-splitting scream rang out across the dining room. A woman sprang up suddenly from a nearby table. She was shaking the folds of her skirt and smacking her bottom with both hands.

"Eeeek!" she screeched, slapping harder. "There's something... in my..."

"WHAT THE—!" Her companion bolted out of his chair as well and looked back down at his seat in bewilderment.

"Sir... Madam... is everything all right?" asked a concerned waiter as the couple began twitching around.

"Hey! What's going on?" demanded the American man at the next table. Then he sprang up as well and began hopping from foot to foot. "Holy sh—" He clutched his behind. "I think... I think I've got ants in my pants!"

"Ants?" screeched a woman at the next table. "Ugh! I hate ants! They make me itch all over!"

"Where are they? Where are they?" cried her friend, looking wildly around.

"Over there! I see one!" shrieked a woman on another table. She pointed a finger at a black speck marching across the white tablecloth. "Oh my God—it's coming straight at me! *HELP!*"

She scrambled backwards, tripped, and fell flat on her face. Other customers also began jumping up from their tables, colliding with each other and sprawling on the floor. Poppy looked around the dining room in horror. It was absolute mayhem. People screamed and shouted as they ran around in a panic, alternately smacking any black spots they saw or scratching themselves furiously. Poppy groaned. She should have known better than to trust one of Bertie's inventions!

Then she caught a glimpse of the old inventor himself suddenly appearing from the corridor on the other side of the dining room. He must have gone to use the Gents and had now returned to a scene of utter chaos. He looked around, then began waving his hands and trying to make himself heard above the uproar: "No... don't worry... they won't hurt you—they don't bite!"

Poppy heard the restaurant manager yelling at a waiter to call the police and her heart sank. Then she saw Bertie rush over to his table and rummage in his leather case. He pulled something out—it looked like a giant red horseshoe magnet, the kind often seen in cartoons. Brandishing it in front of him, he hurried towards the first woman who had screamed and he waved it at her bottom.

Suddenly she stopped screaming. She stood, panting, and looked about her in confusion. "They're... they're gone," she said. She patted her bottom nervously. "They're gone!"

Bertie continued trotting around the room, waving his magnet about, and slowly the screaming abated. People calmed down and began returning to their tables, their expressions bewildered.

"What happened?"

"Dunno—I felt this thing crawling up my bum, and then suddenly it was gone!"

"I thought it was going to get me next!"

"Was it really ants?"

Poppy looked across the dining room to where the restaurant manager and two of the waiters were facing Bertie. *Uh-oh.* She didn't like the expression on their faces.

"It's him! He must have something to do with it!" cried one of the waiters, jabbing a finger at Bertie. "It all stopped after he went around and switched them off!"

"Well, I didn't switch them off, per se—I demagnetised them," Bertie explained, like a patient teacher speaking to a confused student. "You see, the ants are powered by an electric charge created by the tiny magnet in their bodies. I expected them to demagnetise within a short period of time, but for some reason they seemed to become self-recharging—which is marvellous, really, when you think about it—"

"Sir." The restaurant manager crossed his arms and regarded Bertie sternly. "Is this your idea of a prank?"

"Oh no, it's not a prank," said Bertie. "Although I suppose you could use my ants in a jocular situation... but really, you see, I devised them as part of an espionage arsenal, with which one could manipulate subjects to suit one's agenda—"

"Sir!" The manager cut him off. He was starting to breathe heavily and his colour was rising. "This is a serious matter. I do not find your facetiousness amusing. You have distressed my customers and caused havoc in my restaurant! I am reporting you to the police and..."

Yikes! Poppy half rose out of her chair, wondering what to do. She darted a glance at Henry, who was watching the whole scene with narrowed eyes. She didn't want Henry to realise that she knew the eccentric old man with the wandering ants—she didn't think Henry would realise that it was *she* who had unleashed the ants on him; on the other hand, she also didn't want him putting two and two together and making five.

Then she saw the waiters grab Bertie's arm and start to haul him away. Forgetting her reservations, Poppy sprang to her feet, but before she could say anything, a familiar deep voice rang out across the dining room:

"Wait!"

Nick Forrest strode over to the group of men. He stopped in front of the manager and gave him a conciliatory smile, saying, "Look... there's probably been some kind of misunderstanding here. There's no need to involve the police, really. Why don't we just go somewhere quiet and have a little chat—"

"Sir..." The manager gave Nick a hard look. "Do you know this man?"

Nick hesitated, then gave a weary sigh and said, "Yes."

"Son!" Bertie cried, beaming. "I didn't realise you were here! How wonderful. It's been so long since I saw you—" He peered at Nick. "Dear me, you're starting to go grey, you know—just at the temples—but you've still got a nice thick head of hair. Don't worry, though, if you do start losing it; I've invented a wonderfully effective formula for regenerating new hair follicles." He glanced at the restaurant manager. "Actually, *you* are going rather bald on top, aren't you? Would you like to try some of my formula?"

Nick took a deep breath and let it out slowly, then swung around to face his father. A strange mix of emotions played across his face. There was a pause, then he said, through gritted teeth:

"Hello, Dad."

***

Poppy breathed a sigh of relief as the red Porsche pulled up in front of Hollyhock Cottage. She could barely wait for Henry to come around and open her door. All she wanted to do was to get to her room and flop on her bed. She felt absolutely drained by the events of the evening.

Henry walked her to the garden gate and paused expectantly.

"Um... thank you... I had a lov—" Poppy broke off. She had been about to utter the usual polite phrase, but to say that she'd had a lovely time would have seemed like a bad joke. There was an awkward pause, then she stuck her hand out and said: "Er... well, thank you again—"

"Surely you don't expect me to shake hands!" burst out Henry with a laugh. "After a night like that, the least you can do is give me a kiss!"

Before she could react, he snaked a hand around her waist, yanked her towards him, and clamped his mouth over hers. Poppy went rigid with shock and outrage. She reared backwards, trying to push him away, but he was too strong. Squirming, she tried to jerk her head away from his, to break the kiss, but he held her so tightly that she could barely move and all she could do was make furious noises as he kissed her.

Poppy's heart hammered with fear. She had been kissed before, of course, but they were mostly chaste pecks from hesitant dates—no man had ever forced himself on her like this. She struggled again and was just wondering if she could pull one leg back far enough to kick him when something dropped out of nowhere and landed on Henry's head with a bloodcurdling scream.

"*N-O-O-O-O-O-OWWWWW!*"

Henry let out a cry of fright and released her. He reeled backwards, cursing and flailing his arms, then toppled over and landed with a thump on the ground. A big ginger tomcat sprang off his head and landed on the ground next to him.

"What the f—!" Henry gasped, staring at Oren. "Get away from me or I'll... I'll make you sorry!"

"*N-OW?*" said Oren, stalking forwards and eyeballing him.

Henry obviously had second thoughts about taking the cat on. He scooted backwards on his bum, putting as much distance as he could between himself and his furry assailant. Poppy almost wanted to laugh as she watched him crawl like a crab towards the car. His carefully cultivated languid manner was gone; his trousers were soiled with dirt, his hair was dishevelled, and there were claw marks on his forehead. He didn't stand up until he was safely on the other side of the Porsche, whilst Oren watched, his yellow eyes narrowed and his tail lashing from side to side.

"I'm going to report that... that *thing* to Animal Control!" spat Henry, jabbing a finger at the orange cat. "I'm going to make sure they come and put it down!"

He opened his mouth to say something else, but Oren let out a loud hiss and took a step forwards. Henry yelped, jumped in the car, and roared away, leaving Poppy and Oren alone in the lane.

"Oh *Oren!*" cried Poppy, scooping the cat up and burying her face in his soft fur.

He purred loudly, and she felt his whiskers tickling her as he sniffed her face, as if reassuring himself that she was all right.

"Thanks, Oren... you saved the day." She put him down again and smiled at him. "I think you deserve a big tin of tuna for that."

"*N-ow?*" asked Oren hopefully.

Poppy laughed in spite of herself and opened the garden gate for him. "Yes, now. Come on."

CHAPTER TWENTY-SEVEN

Poppy groaned as the curtains in her bedroom were whipped back, letting the bright sunshine in, and she heard Nell's voice saying:

"Time to get up, dear. It's past nine! Oh my lordy Lord, Poppy—look at this mess..."

Struggling to sit up in bed, Poppy yawned and rubbed her eyes. She looked blearily across the room to where Nell was picking up various items of clothing from the pile on the chair. Her dress from last night lay in a rumpled heap, next to various other outfits she had tried on and discarded, and her handbag and shoes were tossed on the floor next to the chair. The sight of them reminded her of the disastrous dinner date with Henry and she groaned again.

"I've made some pancakes for breakfast, dear,"

said Nell. "They're still warm; if you hurry—"

"I'm not hungry," Poppy mumbled, burying her face in her pillow again. After two very early mornings and her emotionally draining day yesterday, she was feeling a bit fragile and petulant. "I don't want to get up."

"Well, I'll just have to have tea with Inspector Whittaker myself then," said Nell placidly.

"*What?* Suzanne is here?" Poppy shot out of bed. "Why didn't you say so?"

Fifteen minutes later, after hastily washing and throwing on some clothes, Poppy hurried into the kitchen to find Nell facing Suzanne across the wooden table, grilling the elegant detective inspector about her love life. Suzanne looked slightly befuddled to be on the receiving end of a probing interview for once.

"...such a shame about you and Nick, although you do seem to have remained *very* good friends?" Nell was saying with an arch look.

"Er... yes... well, you see, we used to work together when we were both sergeants... and anyway, I don't see why a man and woman can't remain friends if a relationship doesn't work out," said Suzanne with a smile. "I'm sure we can all be mature about things."

"Ah, so is Nick understanding about your current boyfriend?" asked Nell slyly.

"Oh... I don't have a boyfriend at present."

"Really? Why not?"

"*Nell!*" gasped Poppy, stepping into the room and giving her old friend a scandalised look. "You can't ask people things like that!"

Suzanne laughed. "It's all right. I suppose it's a fair question. I guess... well, I work crazy hours and it's not really the kind of job that's very conducive to a social life, so it's pretty hard to meet people. Plus, I'm not sure many men would be happy to have a wife or girlfriend who rarely takes weekends off and spends all her time chasing murderers and crooks."

"But don't you think you'd like to settle down and have babies at some point?" asked Nell.

"*NELL!*" Poppy glared at her friend.

"All right, all right... it's just natural curiosity," Nell grumbled as she got up from the table. "Well, I'm heading off to work so I'll leave you two to chat. The pancakes are warming in the oven, dear." And she bustled out of the room.

Poppy gave Suzanne an apologetic smile. "Sorry. Nell is a bit old-fashioned."

Suzanne chuckled. "She would get on really well with my mother. Anyway, how are you? I'm sorry I couldn't return your call the other day. The conference was completely full-on—I've had to come back to work for a rest!" She laughed again, then sobered and added, "I've been catching up on things and I see that there's a new murder enquiry. Your name was mentioned in the reports—you found the murder weapon?"

Poppy nodded eagerly. "Oh, I'm so glad you're

back, Suzanne! Maybe now the investigation will be handled proper—er, I mean, make some progress." Quickly, she told Suzanne everything she knew, ending with the eventful dinner the night before.

"Bertie didn't have to spend the night at the station, did he?" asked Poppy as she finished. The last time she'd seen the old inventor was when he and Nick were being marched off to the restaurant manager's office.

"He was lucky he wasn't arrested for breach of peace," said Suzanne dryly. "I think Nick pulled some strings with his old contacts in the Force and managed to smooth things over."

"I was really surprised when Nick stepped in—I thought he didn't care about his father at all..." said Poppy.

Suzane gave her a wry look. "Well... things with parents are always complicated, aren't they?" Then her expression turned stern and she said, "Those ridiculous 'ants' aside, you know hacking equipment like the one you used on Henry Farnsworth's phone is probably illegal? If Bertie wasn't already in so much trouble, I'd feel obliged to take action against him—and you too! But as it is, I'm going to let it go this time."

"Thanks," said Poppy, ducking her head meekly. "I'm sorry—I just really needed to find out if Henry was the one who called Ursula that day."

"But doing what you did doesn't confirm anything anyway."

"What do you mean? It told me that it wasn't Henry who called her. Her number wasn't listed in his Call History."

"That tells you nothing. He could have easily deleted the record of her call."

"Oh." Poppy sat back, feeling foolish. She hadn't considered that possibility at all.

"I'm surprised Nick didn't think of that," said Suzanne impatiently. "He should have known better—"

"He did, actually," said Poppy, remembering. "He mentioned something but I... well, I wasn't really listening."

Suzanne sighed. "Anyway, all those shenanigans were totally unnecessary. The police can easily get hold of Ursula's phone records and check who called her just before she was killed. In fact, Sergeant Lee did that the day after the murder and I looked through the report this morning."

"And?" asked Poppy eagerly. "Was she talking to Henry?"

"No. She was talking to a recruitment agency in London."

Poppy sat back in surprise. "A recruitment agency? Was Ursula looking for a job?"

Suzanne frowned. "I'm not sure. It looks like Sergeant Lee didn't speak to the woman who called Ursula—just to a colleague. But she confirmed that the call was about a position on the committee of a large charitable organisation in London."

Suddenly, Poppy remembered the conversation she'd had with Ursula the first time she met the woman, as they were standing together in the marquee. She had complimented Ursula on the success of the fête and Ursula had said something about it being the first time she had organised an event of that scale. With charitable organisations relying on fundraising events, she'd said: *"...this kind of organisational experience is crucial for someone who wants a position on a committee."*

At the time, Poppy had simply thought that Ursula was referring to the experience benefiting her role at SOAR, but now, in light of what Suzanne had just told her, she wondered if Ursula's words had had a different meaning. Had she been referring to gaining good experience for her CV, so that she would be a more attractive candidate for a job in another charitable organisation? Perhaps one down in London?

Her thoughts jumped to Norman. Did he know that his "soulmate" was planning to leave Bunnington? He hadn't mentioned anything when she'd spoken to him—only warbled on about him and Ursula being "together forever". But in spite of his protests and pretences, Poppy was pretty certain that any romance between him and Ursula was only wishful thinking in his head.

So if Ursula *hadn't* welcomed Norman's attentions—maybe she had even found him annoying or repulsive—she might have been quietly making plans to leave Bunnington to escape him. A job in London would have been the first step...

"Poppy?"

Poppy came out of her thoughts to find Suzanne regarding her quizzically. "Sorry," she said with an apologetic smile. "I... um... I was just thinking about Ursula's murder."

"Anything in particular?"

Poppy hesitated, unsure whether she should share her theory with Suzanne. The mild-mannered antique dealer was always the last person she'd imagined as being the murderer and she had no actual proof that he was involved. If he really had nothing to do with Ursula's murder, then he had already suffered enough, and the last thing she wanted to do was add to his misery by encouraging the police to think that he had killed the woman he loved.

"Er... no, not really," Poppy said. "Um... so you'll be releasing Betsy now, won't you?"

"Yes, although I'm not striking her completely off my list of suspects. But for the time being, I'm willing to believe her story that she was framed. Which means that the real murderer was someone with access to the manor and who was familiar with the place, such that they could find their way to Betsy's room and hide the knife under her mattress."

Again, Poppy's thoughts returned uncomfortably to Norman, but she pushed them away and said out loud: "So will you be investigating other suspects now?"

"Definitely. I'll be going through all of Ursula's contacts—both at the manor and in the village—and examining her relationships with them." Suzanne smiled grimly. "I know it's a cliché but the statistics show that it's true most murders are committed by someone known to the victim. I'm going to speak to Henry Farnsworth myself, and to Paul Kirby too, and, of course, to Muriel Farnsworth. She may be able to shed some light on her niece's private life, which may give us a lead. I'll also be interviewing the other members of the SOAR committee—as well as any other village residents that Ursula had frequent dealings with. The postmistress in the village has been very helpful and she's given me a list of names."

Suzanne rose from the table with a sigh. "Speaking of which, I'd better get going—I've got a ton of things to do." Then she pulled a face and added: "At least I'm not having to deal with that gang of teenage vandals. My colleagues in Uniform are pulling their hair out on that one. It seems crazy to be outwitted by a bunch of teenage boys, and yet so far they haven't managed to catch them. And in the meantime, they keep being inundated with reports about the damage the boys have caused. This morning, there was a flood of calls to the station from angry villagers who had been vandalised in the night."

Poppy felt a stab of guilt. Perhaps if she had spoken up at Duxton House yesterday, the police would have caught the boys already. She remembered what Mrs Peabody had said, about petty crime progressing to something much worse, and asked anxiously:

"What did they do this time? They haven't hurt anyone, have they?"

"No, no one's been injured, but several houses in the village have had their rubbish sacks torn open and the contents tossed all over the garden and onto the street. Most people had a week's worth of rotting food and other rubbish in their bins and now they've got a huge clean-up job. I can imagine the smell is quite horrendous."

Poppy accompanied Suzanne out the front door and down the path, relieved that Nell wasn't around to launch another barrage of personal questions on Suzanne. As they approached the garden gate, she remembered something else and asked:

"Have the police found Ursula's phone? It *was* weird that it was the only thing that was stolen. I suppose that's why Sergeant Lee thought her attacker could have been the mobile phone thief."

"Yes, well, Sergeant Lee has been bit premature in some of his conclusions on this case," said Suzanne in a tone which suggested that the sergeant had received a sound reprimand.

Poppy felt a childish satisfaction at the thought of the smug sergeant getting his comeuppance.

"As for the phone—no, it hasn't turned up yet, although we are still searching. I understand that it's fairly distinctive as it was in a custom case?"

"Yes, Ursula had a matching case for her iPad," Poppy told her. "I saw it when I was at Duxton House—it's really beautiful: rose-gold embellished with Swarovski crystals in the shape of swirls."

"Well, that should be easy to spot. I'll put out a call for it. Of course, the murderer may have simply destroyed it, in which case we may never find it. But just in case... we'll keep looking."

A few minutes later, Poppy stood at the gate and watched as the dark grey Audi glided away. She felt a huge sense of relief that Suzanne was back in charge and would now be leading the investigation. She could forget all about the murder now and leave everything to the police while she got on with her own life. There were plug plants to transplant, flower arrangements to deliver, two naughty runaway dogs to find...

And what about Norman? Determinedly, Poppy pushed her uneasy thoughts to the back of her mind. Suzanne had said that she was going to check out everyone that Ursula had had regular contact with, and that would definitely include Norman. *Let the police deal with it.*

She turned away from the gate and was about to start walking back to the cottage when something moved in the bushes to her right. She glanced across and was surprised when a skinny boy with a thatch of brown hair stepped out from behind a large shrub. She blinked. It was the boy she had seen at Duxton House the other day—the youngest member of the teenage vandals gang.

CHAPTER TWENTY-EIGHT

Poppy looked quickly around for the older boys, wondering if she was about to become the victim of some gang prank, but she could see no one else. It was just her and the young boy in the cottage garden. He was regarding her warily, much like a wild animal deciding whether to flee, and she found herself instinctively giving him a friendly smile.

"Hi."

He hesitated, then muttered, "Hullo." He took another step forwards, then said, in a rush, "I... I came to say thanks."

Poppy looked at him in surprise. It was the last thing she'd expected to hear.

"For yesterday," he added, misinterpreting her

blank look. "When you saw me at the big house and... and didn't say anything."

"Oh... well... you're welcome," said Poppy, a bit inanely. She groped around for something else to say and came up with the tried and true British panacea for any situation. "Um... would you like a cup of tea?"

The boy shook his head. "Gotta go," he muttered. But he didn't move. Instead, he gave her an uncertain look from beneath that thatch of hair and asked suddenly, "Why?"

"Why what?" said Poppy, confused.

"Why didn't you say something? Like, why didn't you tell the police I was there?"

"Oh... well... I don't know, really..." Poppy gave him a crooked smile. "I guess... I didn't want you to get in trouble."

He looked slightly stunned by her answer. "But... you don't even know me. Why should you care?"

Poppy shrugged. "Sometimes you don't have to know someone to do the right thing... and... and sometimes you care, even if you don't know them."

He looked at her for a moment in silent wonder. Then he ducked his head and said in a voice so low that Poppy could barely hear him: "*We* weren't doing the right thing."

"No, it's not very nice what you guys have been doing around the village," Poppy said severely. "And you were at it again last night, weren't you? The rubbish at the houses?"

The boy nodded miserably. "I... I didn't want to do it. None of it!" he burst out suddenly. "I knew it was wrong, like spray painting stuff and chopping things up—"

"Then why did you do it?"

"Because it was sort of exciting, you know? Like... like when we were hiding and sneaking round and then running away and nearly getting caught... it was cool. At least in the beginning." He paused. "Then I started feeling bad about what we were doing. I told them we shouldn't do it, but the big boys just laughed and said that was how they have fun... They said if I want to be with them—if I want to be in the gang—then I have to join in too."

Poppy hesitated, then said gently, "Do you really want to be part of a gang like that, though?"

The boy shrugged and looked away. "It's better than staying at home... with Mum crying all the time and stuff..." he muttered.

"Oh... well, what about hanging out with your other friends instead?"

He didn't answer and Poppy realised belatedly that perhaps he didn't have other friends. She kicked herself mentally for her insensitivity. There was a long awkward pause and she was hugely grateful when a familiar demanding voice broke the silence:

"*N-o-o-o-ow? N-ow?*"

Oren came into view, sauntering down the garden path from the back of the property. He was looking very self-satisfied (no doubt from his recent second breakfast, courtesy of Nell!) and his ginger coat was freshly groomed and gleaming. He came up to them and eyed the boy curiously.

"*N-ow?*" he said, flicking his tail in greeting.

"Wow, that's a cool cat!" cried the boy, staring at Oren in admiration. "Is he yours?"

"No, he belongs to my next-door neighbour, although he seems to think he lives here half the time," said Poppy with a chuckle. "His name's Oren—would you like to pat him?"

The boy nodded eagerly and crouched down as the ginger tom approached him. He ran his hands over the glossy orange fur, then laughed as Oren headbutted him. Poppy was amazed by the transformation in him. Gone were the wary manner, the sullen voice and hunched posture—instead, his eyes were bright, his whole face open and smiling as he patted Oren and tickled him under the chin.

"I always wanted a cat or a dog," he said, his head down, still busily stroking Oren. "But Mum always said no—pets are too much trouble."

"I never had pets either when I was growing up," said Poppy, crouching down next to him and reaching out to pat Oren as well. "Then I moved here and... well, Oren sort of adopted *me*," she said with a laugh.

"Can I... can I come back to see him sometime?" asked the boy.

"Of course! Come whenever you like. He's usually

here in the garden somewhere, if he isn't next door." Poppy grinned at the boy. "Just knock on my door if you don't see him—he might be inside, sleeping in his favourite spot. And that invite for a cup of tea still stands, you know."

"Thanks," said the boy gruffly. "You're... you're really nice."

Poppy held her hand out. "My name's Poppy. What's yours?"

"Timothy." He put his hand in hers and solemnly shook it.

Poppy was struck by how small his hand was and was reminded once again that he was just a child. Up close, he didn't look any older than ten or eleven, although he had that slightly cynical air that was usually seen in adults and those who had suffered pain and disillusionment.

They patted Oren for a moment longer, then Timothy stood up and said regretfully, "I'd better get back. My Mum will be expecting me for lunch."

"How did you get here?" asked Poppy, standing up as well and glancing around.

"Oh, I've got a bike." He gestured to the lane outside the garden walls. "I parked it down at the bottom of the cul-de-sac. It's only about ten minutes' cycle from here to my house."

"Do you cycle to school as well?"

He nodded absently. His mind seemed to be on something else. As he was about to go through the gate, he paused and looked back at her.

"You know what you were talking about just now, with that lady? About the murder and stuff?"

"You mean Suzanne—er, Inspector Whittaker?"

He nodded. "You were talking about this iPhone with a bling cover."

"Yes, Ursula's phone. It's got a special cover in rose gold, decorated with crystals—why?"

He hesitated. "I think I saw it."

"*What?* Where?"

"At one of the houses we were... you know, when we were going around last night..." he trailed off uncomfortably.

"You mean, you saw it *in* a house?"

"No, with some rubbish. We were taking black sacks out of wheelie bins, see, and ripping them open and then throwing the rubbish around. We started doing it at this row of houses, then a car with big headlights came up the lane and the other boys got spooked, so we ran. We never went back to those houses. But I cut open a sack before I ran and I saw this phone, like you said, in there. I noticed 'cos it seemed like a weird thing to throw away. You know, like it looked expensive."

Poppy clutched his arm excitedly. "Do you remember which house it was? Can you show me?"

"Yeah. It's on the other side of the village but I remember it."

Fifteen minutes later, Poppy found herself following Timothy down a narrow lane on the outskirts of the village. It was an area that she hadn't been to yet. Unlike the houses near the village high street or those near Duxton House—many of which had been renovated and extended by wealthy city-types buying a house in the country—the dwellings here were small and shabby, probably original workers' cottages, with several in bad need of repair.

The lane they were walking down was not actually a main thoroughfare—it was a sort of back alley which ran behind the row of terraced houses and allowed easy access to their back gardens and the wheelie bins put out each week for the rubbish collection. Timothy didn't stop until he reached the end of the row and pointed at the last house.

"That's the one."

Poppy stood on tiptoe to peer over the wooden fence surrounding the back garden. On the other side was a threadbare patch of grass, surrounded by some overgrown shrubs and a couple of bedraggled petunias planted in too much shade but still valiantly trying to flower. The house itself looked much like the others in the row—grey, nondescript, and in good need of a lick of paint.

"Where did you see the phone?" she asked Timothy, who was standing on tiptoe next to her.

"In there—see?" He pointed at a faded green wheelie bin tucked into an alcove beside the back door. "It was in a black sack, in there. I was supposed to do this house and the other boys were doing one of the other houses each. But then, like I said, this car came down the alley and the big boys legged it. I only just started ripping my sack open—so I shoved it back into the wheelie bin and ran too."

"How did you get in the garden?"

"Oh, that's easy—this gate's unlocked." He reached down and showed her how part of the fence was in fact a concealed gate, which opened into the garden. There was a bolt but it was hanging loosely from rusty screws.

Poppy hesitated, looking up at the house. Was there anyone inside? It seemed to be completely silent. She glanced at her watch. It was mid-morning and most people would be at work. She knew she should go back and call Suzanne, notify the police, but now that she was here, the curiosity was overwhelming. She had to know if Ursula's phone was really in that bin.

She took a deep breath and slipped through the gate, then hurried across the garden to the wheelie bin with Timothy at her heels. She lifted the swing-top lid up, wrinkling her nose at the pungent odour of rotting rubbish, and reached for the black plastic sack inside. She heaved it up and immediately saw the long tear down the side. Bits of rubbish—empty cartons of milk, lemon rinds, crumpled plastic wrap, soiled tissues, an empty packet of "sour cream and onion" crisps—spilled out from the gap. Poppy frowned. She couldn't see anything that resembled a phone...

Then she saw it. Wedged between a withered apple core and a piece of cardboard was something that had a metallic gleam. Grimacing, she grasped it with the tips of two fingers and slowly pulled it out. It seemed to be stuck at first and she wondered with a sinking heart if she would have to reach her whole hand into the rubbish, but she managed to wiggle it out at last. She held it up to the light: it was a phone, all right—or at least part of one. Someone had taken a hammer to the phone and smashed it so hard that the case had cracked and detached from the body of the device. This was the main part of the case—and she assumed that the remaining section plus the rest of the phone was still in the depths of the rubbish sack.

Well, she wasn't going to go digging around to find them, Poppy decided grimly. Anyway, she had more than enough for a positive ID. Looking down at the broken rose-gold case embellished with sparkling crystals, she remembered seeing an exact match on the cover of Ursula's iPad at Duxton House. And the fact that it was smashed and broken, and hidden here in a rubbish sack to be thrown out, meant that whoever had had this phone in their possession had wanted to make sure that it was destroyed and never found.

"Is that the dead lady's phone?" asked Timothy in a hushed voice.

Poppy nodded. Her mind was racing. Ursula's phone had been taken from her on the day of the fête by the person who had killed her. Poppy drew a shaky breath and looked back up at the house as the implication dawned on her.

Whoever lived here was Ursula's murderer.

CHAPTER TWENTY-NINE

Poppy stared up at the large window that faced the back garden. The first level of the house was slightly raised up from the ground, perhaps because of the proximity of the river and the risk of flooding, so the window was placed above her head height and she couldn't look into the room. However, she could see several objects lining the windowsill of what was obviously a kitchen window: a bottle of dishwashing liquid, a ceramic jar holding a couple of brushes, the gleaming silver end of a long tap, a shrivelled plant in a pot, and—she caught her breath—a couple of vintage glass bottles, in clear brown and green.

Poppy felt her heart begin to pound. She had seen glass bottles almost identical to those recently: in Norman Smalle's shop. And... her eyes jerked back suddenly to the rubbish spilling from the tear in the black sack, especially to the empty packet of "sour cream and onion" crisps. She flashed back to her chat with Norman: he had been eating from a packet of crisps as he spoke to her; it was the same flavour...

All her uneasy thoughts from earlier came rushing back to her. What if she was wrong about Norman? He could have lied about his whereabouts at the time of the murder. He had told her that he had been up at the manor, trying to lie down and rest during the terrier racing, and had only come back to the fête *after* Ursula had been murdered and her body had been discovered. But what if he had actually left the manor much earlier? What if he had returned to the fête while everyone was busy watching the terriers, and had wandered into the marquee and overheard Ursula talking to a recruiter about a job in London...? In his quiet, obsessive way, Norman had fantasised about a life with Ursula—but when he'd overheard her speaking on the phone, he'd suddenly realised that not only did she not return his feelings, she was planning to move away from him!

Had he stabbed her in a possessive rage? Or even in a sudden fit of disillusionment and betrayal?

Poppy started to grope in her pockets for her own phone, then remembered that her phone was still on her bedside table. She had been so keen to get into the kitchen that morning to see Suzanne, she had completely forgotten to take it with her—and then when she'd met Timothy and heard about his discovery, she had rushed straight across the village with him, leaving her phone back at Hollyhock Cottage.

"Tim—I don't suppose you have a phone?" she asked.

He shook his head. "Mum says I can't have my own phone until I'm twelve."

Poppy stared down at the cracked phone case, wondering what to do. She needed to let the police know what she'd found immediately. But if she left and took the phone case with her, she would be removing incriminating evidence and she didn't know if that might affect things in court. She looked doubtfully at the wheelie bin again. She could put the phone case back where it had been... but what if it was no longer there when she came back with the police? What if by some terrible stroke of bad luck, Norman came home and got rid of his rubbish? She would lose all evidence tying him to Ursula's murder.

"Listen, Tim... I need to stay here to make sure no one throws the rubbish out, but do you think you could run back into the village and ask one of the adults to call the police? You should be able to find someone in the pub—or even just on the village green. There are always a few residents out and about there."

He shrank away from her. "I don't know anyone—"

"It doesn't matter. Just tell them that you've found important evidence about Ursula's murder—"

"They'll think I'm making it up. Maybe someone will recognise me and remember that they saw me with the big boys, and they'll think I'm playing another prank!"

"They won't. If you just explain to them—"

"They'll never believe me!" said Timothy, shaking his head vehemently. "Maybe they'll catch me and not let me go!"

He was getting so agitated that Poppy hastily changed tack. "Okay, okay—how about if you go back to my cottage, then? I've left my phone on my bedside table... and I've left the front door unlocked," she added guiltily. "Can you get it and bring it back to me?"

He nodded and slipped out of the garden. Left alone, Poppy wondered about the best thing to do with the phone case. She didn't really want to have to push it back into the rubbish sack, but on the other hand, she didn't want to be accused of tampering with evidence or even planting false evidence, which might happen if she placed it somewhere else. In any case, she would have to wrap it in something... She considered the soiled napkins protruding from the rubbish sack with distaste. Perhaps if she—

Then she froze. Were there voices coming from

inside the house? Poppy hunched instinctively and glanced up again at the window. She had been so sure that the house was empty; it had seemed so quiet...

Yes, there were definitely voices coming from the other end of the house... Perhaps Norman had just arrived home? Then Poppy realised that the sound wasn't muffled, as it would've been coming through the windowpane above her head, but much clearer, as if from an opening next to her. She jerked around and saw that the back door was slightly ajar. She remembered Mrs Peabody saying that most Bunnington residents still didn't lock their back doors. And through the gap, she could distinctly hear Norman's voice. She couldn't make out what he was saying but his tone was urgent. Then she heard him say "Ursula" and she stiffened. The next moment, a woman's voice rang out shrilly:

"It was you! You're the one who killed her—"

Sonia!

Poppy gasped. Had Sonia somehow figured out who had killed her only friend and had come to confront him? Then she heard Sonia scream and, without thinking, Poppy yanked the back door open and rushed in. She stumbled through the kitchen, down the hallway, and into the small sitting room at the front of the house, to find Norman and Sonia in the middle of the room. They were struggling against each other and hadn't even noticed her come in. Poppy shouted at Norman, then grabbed the first thing that came into her hand—a ceramic ladybird on a side table—and threw it at the antique dealer's head. She missed, of course. It glanced off his shoulders and fell to the floor. The impact surprised him enough, though, and he let go of Sonia.

"Poppy!" Norman stared at her. "What are you doing here?"

"Leave Sonia alone! It won't help even if you silence her—I know the truth as well," said Poppy.

Norman stared at her. "What are you talking about? Sonia's the one who jumped on—"

"I'm talking about Ursula. You murdered her, didn't you?"

"*What?* No! How could you think that? I told you, I *loved* her—"

"I'm not going to fall for your sob story again! My God, you really had me fooled that day—I really thought you were heartbroken about Ursula's death! I should have listened when everyone said you were probably faking it—"

"I wasn't faking anything!" cried Norman, his face going very red. He started towards her. "Listen—"

"Keep away from me!" said Poppy, edging back.

She spied a phone in the far corner of the room and wondered if she could reach it and dial 999 before Norman stopped her. She glanced at Sonia—if only she could help distract him for a moment!—but the orange-haired woman seemed to have gone into a trance, wringing her hands and staring blankly at Norman.

Poppy glanced around the room, searching for something that could be used as a weapon. There was a conventional fireplace-plus-mantelpiece-and-mirror arrangement on the other side—but the hearth looked decorative rather than functional, and she couldn't see a poker or any other fire tool. There was a narrow sideboard behind her, which held various books and ornaments, and a messy tray of opened mail. She looked eagerly at the last, hoping that there might be a traditional knife-shaped letter opener, but there was nothing. In desperation, she snatched up one of the books from the sideboard and held it in front of her, like a shield.

"Don't... don't come any closer," she said to Norman.

He shook his head. "You're mad!"

"You're the one who's mad," Poppy retorted. "Or obsessed, rather. You were driving Ursula crazy with your obsessive adoration, weren't you? And when she decided that she had to get away from your creepy attentions, you lost it and killed her."

"No, no! I never hurt Ursula—"

"Don't lie! I told you, I know the truth," Poppy cut him off. She groped for the phone case, which she had shoved unthinking into her pocket when she ran into the house, and held it up, brandishing it in his face. "I found this—it's the case from

Ursula's phone. What do you say now?"

Sonia gave a little gasp and gripped the mantelpiece for support. Norman stared at the phone case, his face pale.

"But... but... I don't understand," he stammered. "How did you—"

"It was in the rubbish outside. You tried to destroy it and get rid of it, didn't you? And I suppose if it had gone with the general rubbish collection, it would never have been found again, which is exactly what you wanted—"

"No, wait—there's been some kind of terrible misunderstanding," Norman cried. "I only came here because I got a note from—"

"What d'you mean you 'only came here'?" snapped Poppy. "You live here! This is your house!"

"No, it's not." Norman pointed at Sonia. "It's *her* house."

CHAPTER THIRTY

Poppy started to protest, then her gaze flicked around the room once more, and this time she *saw*—she saw the horseshoe hanging over the doorway, the collection of "evil eye" amulets on the sideboard, the cushion covers with a pattern of four-leaf clovers, and the waving "lucky cat" statue on the mantelpiece. Her eyes dropped to the book in her hands and she saw the title: *Curses & Omens— How to Remove and Counteract Them.*

A horrible realisation began to dawn on her. She jerked her gaze back up to the orange-haired woman standing by the fireplace. Sonia was still staring at Noman in that blank, unnerving way, but now he was staring back at her in horror as the truth dawned on him as well.

"Oh my God, it was *you*..." he said in a hoarse

voice. "*You're* the one who killed her!"

"No, no, no—it was *you*! If you hadn't brought the knife to the fête... it was bad luck—"

"For heaven's sake, it wasn't *bad luck* that killed Ursula—it was *you* grabbing that knife and stabbing her!" shouted Norman.

"I... I couldn't help it..." cried Sonia. Her face went blotchy as she began to cry. "I was so angry... I... I couldn't think... and then I saw the knife..." She gulped and sobbed. "Ursula was supposed to be my friend! She never laughed at me like the others... she was always kind... I thought she would help me... but it was all a lie!"

"What do you mean?" said Norman. "Ursula *was* your friend! She was always nice to you and—"

"I HEARD HER!" Sonia shrieked. "I heard her talking on the phone. That day at the fête, when Mrs Peabody sent me back to find her, I walked into the marquee and I heard Ursula talking to someone... about *me*! It was the recruitment agency from London—the one who was going to give me the job I needed—but Ursula was telling them awful things about me being hysterical and unreliable and believing in silly superstitions... how could she? *How could she?*" Sonia's voice rose shrilly.

"What did you expect her to do?" demanded Norman angrily. "She had to be honest if they were asking her for a reference. She'd worked with you and she knew what you were really like—any other member of the SOAR committee would have said the same thing."

"But Ursula was supposed to be my friend!" wailed Sonia. "She was supposed to help me—how could she betray me like that?" She clutched her head. "It was all a lie... all a lie! She was never my friend at all... I had no friends... I had nobody! Nobody was going to help me... nobody was going to give me a job... nobody cared..."

The woman looked so devastated, so despairing, that in spite of the situation, Poppy felt a flash of pity for her. She put out a hand towards her and said gently, "That's not true, Sonia. Ursula did care—"

"No, she didn't! She just pretended to, which is even worse!" snarled Sonia, her face suddenly changing. "She made me think she was kind, and then she let me down just when I needed her the most! I wanted to hit her... to hurt her, like she hurt me... and then I saw it... The knife. It was just lying there on the trestle table, next to Ursula... She had her back to me... I grabbed the knife... I was so angry..." Her hands clenched spasmodically, as if gripping the pruning knife once more. "And then... and then afterwards... I was scared—"

"So you hid the knife in Betsy's room," guessed Poppy. "You tried to frame her for the murder, didn't you?"

Sonia stammered, "I... I didn't know what to do... I thought if I just hide the knife, then nobody would know... and the phone... Ursula's phone... I had to get rid of the phone..."

And then she ran back to the crowd and screamed bloody murder, thought Poppy. And of course, no one suspected her because who would think that the poor, distraught woman who had discovered the body would be the one who actually committed the murder?

But now that she knew the truth, Poppy realised that the signs were there all along, like the way Sonia had been so jumpy and nervous in the village post office when the ladies had asked her about discovering the body, the way she had said: "*there was blood everywhere... I never realised there would be so much blood...*" Poppy remembered thinking at the time that it was an odd choice of words, but she had brushed it aside because, like everyone else, she had never thought of Sonia as a suspect.

"That was you that I heard!" Norman burst out suddenly. "I thought it was Kirby sneaking to the maid's room, but it was you going to plant the murder weapon... You killed Ursula, you heartless witch! You ruined my life—"

"No, it was *your* fault," insisted Sonia, shaking her head. "It was you who brought that knife to the fête. If it hadn't been there, I wouldn't have killed Ursula."

"What? What kind of crazy logic is that?" demanded Norman. "*You* were the one who killed Ursula!"

"No, *you* were!"

Poppy's head swivelled back and forth between them. This was beginning to feel like a farce. She couldn't believe that she had just exposed Sonia as a homicidal maniac and the two of them were arguing like squabbling siblings. Poppy opened her mouth to say something, but she was interrupted by Norman jabbing a finger at Sonia and shouting:

"Don't blame it on me, you crazy cow! I'm going to the police now to tell them exactly what you've done—"

He turned towards the door, but before he could take a step, Sonia flung herself at him with a screech. Norman staggered back and tried to push her off, but Sonia was like a wild animal, biting, scratching, clawing, and kicking. The antique dealer crumpled under her attack, hunching over, with his arms over his face, making squealing noises. Poppy groaned. She knew that Norman was a weedy chap, but this seemed beyond pathetic. She decided she'd better help him before Sonia beat him senseless. She started towards them, then hesitated: she didn't fancy getting too close to the shrieking woman herself. Maybe if she could throw something at Sonia's head and knock her out...

She cast around the room once more, but while the house seemed to be stuffed to the brim with all sorts of talismans and lucky charms, it didn't offer much in the way of weaponry. Somehow, she didn't think clobbering Sonia with a giant rabbit's foot or an inflatable lucky pig was going to help much.

Then her eyes lit up as she spied something on the side table: a box containing a pair of Chinese meditation balls! She pounced on them and picked up the small metal balls, feeling their reassuring weight in her palm. She raised one and paused, struggling to aim as Sonia and Norman lurched past her—then she threw the ball as hard as she could.

It sailed through the air... past Sonia's head... and hit Norman square on the forehead. The antique dealer slumped over.

GAH! Poppy stared in horror at the man out cold on the floor. How could she have hit Norman *again*? She raised her eyes to the panting woman standing opposite her. *Great.* Now that she had knocked out her one ally, she was completely alone with the homicidal maniac.

Poppy cleared her throat. "Um... Sonia... maybe we should just talk things over—"

Sonia made an inarticulate sound in her throat and came towards her, her hands outstretched like claws. Poppy gasped and jerked backwards, darting around the sofa and putting it between herself and the madwoman. She remembered that she still had one meditation ball left. She glanced at the metal sphere, decorated with a black-and-white *yin yang* lucky charm, took a deep breath and raised it, then hurled it straight at Sonia's head just as the woman lunged towards her.

It missed.

Aaarrgghh! Why can't I ever hit anything? Poppy wanted to kick herself. Then she flinched as there came a resounding *CRASH*, followed by the sound of shattering glass. The mirror above the mantelpiece cracked suddenly into several pieces and disintegrated, falling to the floor in a shower of broken glass. Poppy realised that the meditation ball, which had missed Sonia, must have smacked into the mirror behind her instead.

"Noooo!" cried Sonia, her eyes bulging as she turned to stare at the shards of glass on the floor. "No! Not the mirror! Ohhh... what am I going to do? It's seven years' bad luck! Seven years' bad luck!"

Poppy remembered what Mrs Peabody had said the other day and pounced on the opportunity. "You must break the curse immediately," she said quickly. "There's no time to lose! You need to pick up the pieces and... um... what are the options? We don't have any moonlight and there isn't any running water so... you've got to pound them up, right?"

"Yes, yes..." said Sonia breathlessly. "The broken pieces must all be pounded into tiny fragments so none of them can reflect anything ever again!"

Poppy retreated to the other side of the room and picked up the phone. She dialled 999 but she knew there was no urgency now. She glanced over her shoulder to where Sonia was still crouched in front of the fireplace, painstakingly gathering all the broken pieces of the mirror whilst she muttered to herself about curses and bad luck. Poppy shook her head and smiled. As far as she was concerned, breaking that mirror was the best luck she'd ever had.

CHAPTER THIRTY-ONE

"My poor Flopsy! Lost and hungry, with no orthopaedic bed or feather pillow to sleep on..." Muriel Farnsworth gasped. "And she won't have taken her daily Caninetamins or had a doga session for *three* days!" She whirled and paced back down the garden path at Hollyhock Cottage. "I don't understand. How could she have just disappeared like that?"

Poppy flushed guiltily and glanced across the flowerbeds to the area by the sundial, where the white poodle had last been seen. She wished that she had a better answer to give Flopsy's owner.

"I'm really sorry. I don't know—"

"What do you mean, you don't know?" Muriel demanded. "You were the one looking after her! You should have been keeping an eye on her!"

"Sorry?" Poppy looked at her in surprise. "I wasn't—"

"Oh, Kirby told me what happened. When he had to dash into the cottage to use the loo, he thought it would be safe to leave Flopsy with you for a moment... but you just tied her to the sundial and left her. How could you have done that?"

Poppy stared at the old woman incredulously. A surge of anger filled her. That man really *was* a snake! How dare he put the blame on her when *he* was the one who had been careless and irresponsible? She glanced towards the gate but couldn't see Kirby, only Muriel's chauffeur standing respectfully by her car. Well, of course the pet nanny would be too much of a coward to come with Muriel and expose himself. She wished suddenly that it was Kirby she had uncovered as the murderer yesterday, not Sonia. It would have been good to see the police put *him* behind bars!

"It wasn't me—it was Kirby who lost her," she told Muriel. "*He* was the one who tied Flopsy to the sundial and then went off to sunbathe on the bench. I wasn't even here; I was out delivering some flowers—"

"He said you'd deny it," said Muriel with a sniff. "He said you'd be scared to admit your part, whereas *he* has been honourable enough to take responsibility for the whole thing, even though it was not really his fault. He feels dreadful, just because he brought Flopsy to you. You would do well to learn from him, young lady—"

"That's ridiculous! I never... I can't believe he..." Poppy spluttered, so angry she could barely speak. "That's... that's just not true! I'm not trying to avoid responsibility! I feel awful too, but I swear to you, I wasn't here when Flopsy disappeared—"

"Are you saying that Kirby is lying to me?" asked Muriel in a quavering voice, clasping her trembling hands together.

"I—" Poppy broke off, staring at the distraught old woman in front of her.

Muriel had recently lost a niece and now her beloved dog; her life had been turned upside down, and all those close to her, who she had depended upon, had been torn away from her. Did Poppy really want to destroy the old woman's last vestige of security? Tell her that the man she had trusted and welcomed into her household in the past year was a two-faced liar? All for what? To win a petty game of "he said, she said"? Besides, to be honest, she *did* feel a bit responsible, because it *was* on *her* property that the dog had gone missing.

Poppy took a deep breath and let it out slowly, then said in a calmer voice, "I'm really sorry, Muriel. In a way, both Kirby and I are to blame, but the important thing now is to find Flopsy and get her home safely."

"But what if we never find her?" wailed Muriel. "What if she starves to death in the wilderness—"

"It's hardly 'wilderness'! This is the English

countryside, not the African desert, and there are farms all around, not to mention homes and pubs and shops. I'm sure there will be food scraps everywhere."

Muriel gave a little scream and put a hand to her chest. "*Food scraps?* Flopsy would never eat food scraps! She only eats organic. And she likes to be hand-fed. She doesn't eat out of a bowl."

Bloody hell. Poppy was beginning to think a stint in the "wilderness" would do the pampered poodle some good! Still, she kept her thoughts to herself and pinned a reassuring smile to her face, saying to Muriel:

"We've already put up posters everywhere, and Dr Noble—that's Einstein's owner—has been working around the clock to devise a way to find the dogs."

"As he well should!" Muriel gave her a dark look. "It was *his* dog who stole away my Flopsy. Mangy, thieving, sneaky little beast!"

"Er…" Poppy cleared her throat. "Well, as I said, the important thing now is to find them as soon as possible. And in fact, I saw Dr Noble earlier today and he was very excited because he is almost finished with a special device that he's sure will bring them back. So the best thing for you is to go back to Duxton House and wait there. That's the most likely place for Flopsy to come back to, anyway, and—"

Poppy broke off as Bertie suddenly appeared

around the corner of the cottage. He had obviously come via the gap in the stone wall between their properties, because he still had leaves and twigs clinging to his wild mop of grey hair, from the plants he had obviously crawled through. He was carrying a brown paper bag in one hand and something that looked like a megaphone in the other, except that it had a strange suction fan where the mouthpiece should have been. Bertie's eyes lit up when he saw her, and he hurried over to join them.

"Bertie, have you come up with a way to find the dogs?" asked Poppy eagerly.

He gave a solemn nod. "If you can show me where the poodle was last seen... I think that would be the best place to deploy it."

Poppy led him over to the sundial, then she and Muriel stood back and watched as he carefully pulled something out of the paper bag. It was a bacon sandwich.

"Your device is a... *bacon sandwich*?" said Poppy, confused.

"Ah yes, you see, my dear, Einstein can never resist a bacon sandwich! It is his absolute favourite! If he smells it, he is bound to come—and hopefully bring Flopsy with him too."

"But... he could be miles away! How is he going to smell it if he's on the other side of Oxfordshire?"

"Ah... that's where my Mega Diffuser comes in," said Bertie, brandishing the strange device in his other hand. "This is what I have been working on for the past two days. It has the ability to diffuse an odour in a wide radius—far beyond ordinary air currents."

As he was speaking, Bertie began winding something on the side of his "Mega Diffuser". A minute later, Poppy heard a noise like a tiny whirring engine, and then she saw the suction fan begin to turn. A wonderful aroma of hot, crispy bacon filled the air. Poppy almost began to feel her mouth water. Then, to her surprise and delight, she heard the faint sound of excited barking.

She turned incredulous eyes on Bertie. "I don't believe it—it really works!"

A second, higher-pitched bark joined the first, and Muriel gasped.

"That's Flopsy!" She began looking wildly around the garden. "Flopsy? Flopsy, where are you? Come to Mummy! *Come to Mummy!*"

The barking seemed to be coming from the back garden, behind the cottage, and Poppy hurried towards the sound, followed by Bertie and Muriel. She followed it all the way to the neglected shed in the very back corner of the property—the one covered by the prickly monster rambling rose—and was astonished to see two little dogs emerging from under the thicket of thorny branches. One was Einstein and the other was a dog that Poppy almost didn't recognise at first, with its matted curly coat of dirty brown... Then she saw the sparkle of a jewelled collar at the dog's neck and realised with a shock that it was Flopsy.

She couldn't believe it! Had the two dogs been at Hollyhock Cottage the whole time? The little buggers—they must have hidden in that hollow under the monster rambling rose when she and Kirby and Muriel's staff had all been searching the property. Since no one had wanted to brave the thick canes, bristling with sharp thorns, they had remained undiscovered.

Now Einstein came eagerly forwards, but he was hampered by Flopsy, who kept jumping on him and biting his ears, pulling his jowls, grabbing his neck, chewing his feet, all whilst whining and growling shrilly. Einstein looked very weary as he tried to fend her off and a look of relief crossed his face when Muriel swooped down and picked Flopsy up.

"Flopsy!" shrieked Muriel, squashing the poodle against her face. "Oh, Flopsy, you're alive!" She held the little dog up to get a better look at her. "Ohhh... my poor baby—look at the state of you!" She turned towards the front of the property and bellowed: "Harrison! HARRISON!"

A minute later, the chauffeur came hurrying into view from around the side of the cottage. "Yes, ma'am?"

"Call Diva Dogs Salon and book Flopsy a spa session immediately! Tell them it's an emergency. She needs the Deluxe Pawdicure, the Blueberry Facial, the Detox Bath with Conditioning Rinse, some Whitening Spritz—oh, and don't forget the Fresh Breath Treatment."

"Yes, ma'am!" said Harrison, disappearing back round the front of the cottage.

"Oh!" Muriel remembered something and hurried after him, carrying the toy poodle with her. "Flopsy also needs an urgent appointment with her canine therapist! She'll have to work through the trauma of her time in the wilderness—oh, I do hope this hasn't set back her progress on separation anxiety—and she also needs..."

Her voice faded away as she headed towards the front of the property with Flopsy in her arms. The poodle looked back at Einstein over her owner's shoulder and gave a couple of high-pitched yaps. Poppy glanced at the terrier, expecting him to rush after his beloved—but to her surprise, he looked uncertain. In fact, an expression more like relief than regret crossed his face.

"Come on, Einstein—let's go home and have this bacon sandwich," called Bertie over his shoulder as he set off for his house. He disappeared around the opposite side of the cottage and Poppy could hear his voice fading away too as he continued muttering to himself: "Hmm... yes... a successful trial, although one can't be sure that the parameters of radius were truly tested..."

Einstein hesitated again, then looked up at Poppy. She chuckled. Somehow she had a feeling that the terrier was discovering romance wasn't all it's cracked up to be—especially with a neurotic, high-maintenance female!

"You know, there's nothing wrong with a bachelor life," Poppy told him.

Einstein wagged his tail. Then he gave a stretch and shook himself. "*Ruff! Ruff-ruff!*"

Poppy smiled as she watched him scamper happily after Bertie's disappearing figure without a backwards glance towards Flopsy.

CHAPTER THIRTY-TWO

Poppy stood back and proudly surveyed the beautiful little area in front of her, filled with scented plants and herbs, and glowing with the late afternoon sunshine. Wide gravel paths meandered between several rocks and boulders, which provided interesting features amongst the clumps of aromatic foliage and fragrant flowers. It was hard to believe that only two weeks ago, this had been a neglected rock garden.

And I *made this*, thought Poppy, her chest swelling with pride. *I created this garden, I planted it all—and I haven't made any cock-ups this time. Not a single plant has died! Well, at least not yet...* she added silently, glancing at the two clary sages that she had planted, one of which looked slightly droopy. She hoped that it was just transplant shock and that with a bit of TLC, the plant would recover after a few days.

She'd read that clary sage should really be planted in spring, not autumn, but Muriel had been so impatient to have all the plants in as soon as possible that Poppy had sourced some advanced specimens growing in pots and had transplanted them into the garden. Since clary sage normally flowered in their second year anyway, she hoped that they would settle in and flower next spring and summer. And in the meantime, their large, aromatic leaves would still provide herbal benefits. According to her research, clary sage was supposed to be "good for highly-strung animals"—*which should make it perfect for Flopsy*, Poppy thought with a smile.

Speaking of which... She looked around for the guest of honour, the dog that all this effort was being made for, but she couldn't see the white toy poodle anywhere. There were plenty of other people around though—in fact, Poppy was surprised to see how many there were. She'd thought that this was meant to be a small celebration to mark the official completion of the canine scent garden, but it looked like half the village had come to Duxton House. And several people had dogs on leashes too! They were wandering around, encouraging the dogs to sniff the plants. Poppy eyed them with surprise.

"I didn't realise that Muriel was planning to open the scent garden to the public," she said to Mrs

Peabody as she joined the older woman at the trestle table set up on one side of the new garden, with tea and scones for the guests.

Mrs Peabody looked up from the cup of tea she was pouring and glanced at the other dogs. "Oh, not the public, dear—just the residents of SOAR who are still looking for adoption. Not all of them can be placed in foster homes, you see, and kennel life can be very hard on the shelter dogs, being cooped up in a cage or a run all the time. And many of them are quite anxious and nervous anyway, because of the experiences they've suffered—so anything that stimulates them in a positive way and gets them interacting with their environment is good." She smiled. "Muriel has been very generous and offered SOAR the use of the canine scent garden any time we like, so we can bring the rescue dogs down here to give them some natural therapy."

"Oh!" Poppy looked over to where the elderly lady was holding court on the other side of the scent garden and saw her with new eyes. Muriel Farnsworth might have been eccentric and overindulgent where her pet was concerned (and a terrible snob!), but her heart seemed to be in the right place.

"Poppy, you've done a fantastic job! This looks wonderful. If I ever spend enough time at home to actually be able to enjoy my garden, I might get you to come and give it a makeover too."

Poppy turned and smiled with pleasure to see an

attractive, dark-haired woman in an elegant trouser suit come up to her. "Suzanne! I didn't realise you were coming today."

"Well, I don't think I'm on the official invitation list," said Suzanne with a laugh, glancing at Mrs Peabody's retreating back as the older woman went off to join Muriel. "But I came with Nick, and when you're the guest of a bestselling author, people don't tend to ask questions."

Poppy followed her gaze over to where Nick had just politely joined Muriel and her group of cronies as well. All the older ladies were simpering up at him and she almost wanted to laugh at the expression on his face.

"I always thought writers were introverts," Poppy commented, still watching him. "I'm surprised to see Nick joining in with so many events in the village."

"Actually, Nick is pretty sociable when he's between books," said Suzanne, looking at her ex-boyfriend fondly. "It's when he's writing that he can get very tetchy. I've learned to just give him a wide berth when he's deep in a manuscript, until he resurfaces." She turned back to Poppy and her expression grew serious. "I'm really glad to see you, actually, as I've been meaning to pop around to Hollyhock Cottage but just hadn't had a chance yet. I wanted to let you know that thanks to your little friend Timothy, the police have finally identified all the boys in that gang and they have been remanded in custody."

Poppy raised her eyebrows. "Aren't they too young to be arrested?"

"No, the age of criminal responsibility in England is ten years old and some of those older boys are fifteen and sixteen, so they can certainly be arrested and charged with a crime, and possibly even do time in a juvenile detention centre. It depends partly on the nature of the crime—sometimes they are just let off with a caution—and on whether they are repeat offenders."

"So Tim could go to jail?" asked Poppy, concerned.

Suzanne smiled. "Well, he *is* only eleven so he's very young and—aside from the fact that he did help us track down the rest of the gang—he did not actually instigate any of the malicious pranks. One could argue that he was heavily influenced and controlled by the older boys. The judge has also taken his situation into consideration: his parents separated last year and he lives alone with his mother, who has been suffering badly from depression—so it's been a tough time for Timothy and he has had very little support. I think they are going to let him off with a verbal warning." She sighed. "Ironically, I actually think a community service sentence would have been good for him. There's still another month or so until the school term starts and it would have been good for Timothy to have some responsibility, some work to occupy him and give structure to his day. It's when kids spend all this time alone that they start getting into trouble."

"Hey... I know it's not a community garden, but maybe Tim could come and help me at Hollyhock Cottage?" suggested Poppy impulsively. "Then both Nell and I could keep an eye on him. In fact, I think just Oren alone could probably keep him busy for hours," she added with a laugh.

Suzanne gave her an approving look. "That's a lovely idea, Poppy. I'll speak to Timothy's mother and see what she says. I think she'd be very happy with the arrangement and it'll be great for Timothy. Thanks."

"By the way, there's something I've been wanting to ask you too," said Poppy. "It's about Henry." She glanced quickly around; she hadn't actually seen Muriel's great-nephew and she wondered if he wasn't at Duxton House today. Still, she lowered her voice before continuing: "It's been bugging me... Betsy the maid told me that she overheard Henry and Ursula arguing the night before the murder, and Henry practically threatened Ursula when she said she was going to tell Muriel something about him... Do you know what that was about? It was something to do with money, wasn't it?"

"Yes, I questioned Henry myself last week, just to tie up all loose ends. Ursula had discovered his secret: he's a compulsive gambler. He'd started gambling quite heavily during his travels around

Europe and it had become a full-blown addiction by the time he returned to England."

"Oh! Yes, of course, he mentioned that he'd ended up in Monte Carlo at the end of his travels," Poppy recalled. "That's one of the gambling capitals of the world, isn't it? And now that you mention it, when we were out at dinner, he insisted on making this ridiculous bet over my father's identity. I remember thinking at the time that it was a ludicrous thing to suggest, given that I might never find out who my father is and even if I did, Henry and I might not be in touch anymore to fulfil the bet... but he didn't seem to care. It was almost as if he had an obsessive need to bet on something, anything. It all makes sense now!"

"Yes, I think it's become a real problem and is dominating all of Henry's time and energy now. He wouldn't admit it but I suspect that he's been visiting all sorts of dodgy gambling dens down in London, when he's supposed to be at college—and constantly asking Muriel for extra money, of course, to cover his huge losses. Ursula found out about his gambling when she intercepted a phone call for Henry from a moneylender, by mistake."

"And what about when he was hiding in the woods on the day of the murder? Who was he talking to then? Was that tied to the gambling as well?"

"Yes, that was another moneylender. I think Henry is up to his neck, to tell you the truth. He's been borrowing money from all sorts of places in order to fund his habit and now he's being hounded to pay a lot of it back. Apparently, that day he had been on his way to Duxton House to see Muriel but got this call and had to pull over to spend some time placating this person. And then he felt too unnerved to return to Duxton House, so he went for a drive to give himself time to think and come up with a plan for asking Muriel for more money. Of course, he didn't expect to return home that evening to find the place a crime scene."

"So does Muriel know now?" asked Poppy.

Suzanne sighed. "Well, that's a difficult one. The police's duty is to uphold the law, not solve domestic conflicts, and arguably Henry's money troubles and gambling addiction are his personal business. If he chooses not to tell his great-aunt, it's not really in my place to interfere with that."

"But... but he's lying to her and taking her money!" said Poppy. "I heard him! I happened to be outside the room when he was asking her, and he pretended that the money was for some textbooks he needed for university."

Suzanne gave a cynical smile. "He probably isn't the first to pull that stunt on a parent or guardian—and he won't be the last. Lying to your family isn't an official crime and how Muriel chooses to distribute her money is her business." She sighed. "Unfortunately, this isn't a Disney movie, Poppy, where everyone gets their comeuppance, and everything is wrapped up nicely with a bow. This is real life and in real life... well, you can't always fix everything. People get away with bad behaviour. As long as they're not committing an actual crime, there isn't much the police can do about it."

Poppy remained where she was long after Suzanne had left her and chewed over what the detective inspector had said. It really narked her that Henry would be able to continue his lying ways, but she knew that Suzanne was right. There were countless "men-behaving-badly" scenarios and injustices in the world that she could do nothing about. And maybe Muriel spending her wealth on her spoilt great-nephew was no different to the old lady spending her wealth on her spoilt dog, paying for things with questionable benefits like canine spa facials and doga sessions...

Then she heard Muriel's loud voice carrying across the garden:

"...Flopsy? Oh, Kirby's just giving her a last little groom. There's a photographer here from *Pampered Pooches* magazine and I wanted her to look perfect for her photos. Kirby should be bringing her out any moment."

Poppy smiled grimly to herself. *Well, there might be things I can't do anything about, but there is one man who I can make sure gets what he deserves.* She slipped quietly away and headed back to the manor house. Inside, she made her way unerringly to the doggie playroom and grooming suite. As she drew near the half-open door, she heard a familiar impatient voice hissing:

"Hold still, you bloody little rat, or I'm going to slice your nose right off!"

Poppy slipped her hand into her pocket and pulled out the item she had borrowed from Bertie, hoping she'd find a chance to use it today. Carefully, she removed the wrapping around the object, then bent and placed it on the ground, just outside the door. She wrinkled her nose at the pungent odour that wafted up from the slimy-looking brown pile. It was hard to believe it was all made of plastic polymers—it looked (and smelled) so realistic!

She tiptoed away as fast as she could and rejoined the party outside. She had left her knapsack by one of the boulders, and now she hurried over and rummaged inside until she found the wireless speaker. She took it out, placed it on top of the boulder, where it had unhindered reception from all sides, and switched it on. There was a loud crackling sound which made everyone stop talking and look around in confusion, then flinch as the speaker squealed with interference, searching for the signal from the hidden transmitter back in the house.

The next moment, loud and clear, Kirby's irritable voice issued out of the speaker and filled the air.

"C'mon, c'mon... let's get out there before that old

bag Muriel starts bleating again... And if she gives me any more lip about your bloody mineral water, she can kiss my arse! Really, it's beyond ridiculous what I have to put up with—AAGGGHH! FUC—"

There was a stumbling sound, like someone tripping, followed by a door rattling, then came Flopsy's shrill yapping. Kirby cursed viciously and Poppy saw several of the older ladies in the garden wince and clap their hands over their ears.

"—you sodding dog! I can't believe you did it here on the floor! Forget the bloody dog spa... what you need is toilet-training!"

There was a thump, then squealing from Flopsy, followed by the sounds of a struggle.

"Shut up, you little piece of—I'm going to rub your nose in it until you learn!"

Muriel gave a horrified cry and seemed to come alive from where she had been standing frozen. She rushed into the house and, a moment later, they heard her furious tones coming out of the speaker too.

"KIRBY!"

"M-Mrs Farnsworth! I... I didn't see you ther... I mean... er..." A nervous laugh. *"Sorry we've been delayed, but as you can see, Flopsy's done a little accident on the floor, poor lamb. Maybe you'd like to take her out first while I clean up here—"*

"Don't try to pretend! I know the disgusting way you treat Flopsy behind my back!"

"What... what do you mean?" Another forced

laugh. *"You know I love Flopsy-pooh and I would never treat her badly—"*

"You're a liar! I heard everything you said just now, Kirby, starting from when you referred to me as an 'old bag'."

There was a strangled sound of horror. *"But... but... how could you have—?"*

"I don't know how and I don't care. I'm just glad I finally know what a filthy liar you are."

"What? No, I never—"

"You are hereby released from the tedious task of kissing my... bottom... or any other part of my anatomy."

"No, ma'am... Please let me explain—"

"Have I not made myself clear, Kirby? YOU'RE FIRED."

CHAPTER THIRTY-THREE

The tea party to celebrate the new canine scent garden at Duxton House was a great success, not least because of the exciting drama with Kirby that would probably occupy the village gossips for weeks. As the afternoon drew to a close and people started leaving, Poppy also began preparing to return to Hollyhock Cottage. As she returned her teacup to the trestle table, she was pleased to see Betsy collecting the tea service and leftover scones. It was good to know that the maid was back at work.

"Hi, Betsy," she said hesitantly.

The girl stiffened, then said with an effort at politeness, "Hello, miss."

"Betsy, I just wanted to say I'm really sorry again," said Poppy in a rush. "I've been feeling awful about it all. I know it doesn't make up for the horrible experience you had, but I honestly didn't think the police would arrest you. I thought Sergeant Lee would be reasonable and not jump to conclusions."

The girl's face softened slightly. "Well, I suppose you thought you were doin' the right thing."

"If you have any more trouble with the police or with Muriel, please let me know and I'll try to do everything I can to help. I'll vouch for you, I'll stand up in court and swear testament to your good character, I'll—"

"Ta, it's all right," said the girl, looking surprised but pleased. "Actually, Mrs Farnsworth has been really nice about everythin'. She said she never suspected me at all, and in fact, she's even given me a promotion!" Betsy beamed. "She's just told me that she'd like to give me the job of bein' Flopsy's next pet nanny."

"Oh... er, congratulations," said Poppy, wondering if commiserations would have been more suitable.

"Thanks," said the maid. Then her gaze went over Poppy's shoulder and she muttered, "Oh God, not him again..."

Poppy turned to look and was surprised to see Norman walking slowly towards them. He was stopping every so often to bend down and pick a flower as he passed various clumps of plants in the scent garden.

"I hope he's not pickin' those flowers for *me*..." said Betsy with a dark look.

"Norman's been giving you flowers?" said Poppy in surprise.

Betsy nodded, her face creasing with annoyance. "Yeah. All week. He's been hangin' around the manor too, comin' into the kitchen all the time... Keeps wantin' to read some soddin' poem to me—for God's sake, I haven't got time for that! I've got work to do, you know!" She grabbed the tray with the tea things. "I'm gettin' out of here before he sees me." And with another dour look in Norman's direction, she hurried towards the manor.

The antique dealer arrived at the trestle table a few minutes later and looked around in disappointment. "Where's Betsy?" he asked.

"Oh... um... I'm not sure," said Poppy with a bright smile. She glanced at the little posy of flowers he was holding and said jokingly, "Are you stealing from my scent garden, Norman?"

He flushed. "It's only a couple of flowers. I thought Betsy might like them—she's all alone, you see, and after her terrible experience with the police, she needs someone to protect her... like Sir Lancelot did with Guinevere..."

Poppy eyed him with disappointment, surprised to find that after his passionate words about his romance with Ursula, he seemed to have forgotten her and moved on to someone else already. Then she wondered why she was surprised—she should have realised from the way that Norman had talked that he'd never had any real depth of feeling for Ursula. She thought of the way he had accused Sonia of "ruining his life" when he'd realised she was the murderer. He had been more selfishly aggrieved than genuinely grieving. The whole thing had been like a shallow schoolboy crush, which existed mostly in his sentimental fantasies. And now those fantasies had found a new object of worship...

Leaving him still searching for Betsy, Poppy hitched the knapsack over her shoulder and began walking out of the scent garden. Then she paused in surprise as a tall man joined her.

"I thought you'd left ages ago," she said to Nick Forrest.

"Suzanne had to go first but I decided to stay on." He reached into a pocket and withdrew a small, flat envelope. "Here... I got this back from my friend this morning. I don't know if it'll help much but he's enhanced it the best he can."

"Oh, thanks!" Poppy took the envelope excitedly and extracted the two photos it contained. One was the original faded picture that had been in her mother's tin; the other was a copy—slightly enlarged and with the image brightened and sharpened. She peered closely at the latter, bringing it almost up to her nose, as she tried to make out more detail, particularly in the faces. But it was still too blurred to make out much and none of the men looked any more familiar than before.

She sighed and lowered the photo, giving Nick a self-deprecating smile. "I don't know what I was expecting—it's not as if he would have a label saying 'Poppy's dad' on his forehead."

"There might be other things, though, that could give you a lead," said Nick, taking the photo from her. He narrowed his eyes and pointed to one corner of the picture. "See that sign in the background? That looks like a logo of a bar or a club—and the décor suggests that they're in a nightclub of some kind. Perhaps some place that had bands playing." He brought the photo closer. "And on this side... if you look behind this chap's shoulder, you can see a bulletin board on the wall behind—see?"

"Yes..." said Poppy, leaning closer to look as well. "Yes, but I can't really read any of the posters pinned on the board."

He pointed at one of the rectangular shapes on the board. "No, but this looks to me like a Tube map. The London Underground," he elaborated at Poppy's blank look. "I'm willing to bet that this club was in London. So if you can track down the name of the place, you could contact them and see if they might have a record of the bands that played there around that time." He shrugged. "I know it's a very long shot but... it might be worth trying."

"No, that's a great idea. I'll start researching London nightclubs and bars, and see if any of their logos match... thanks!" said Poppy, genuinely grateful. She grinned at him. "You know, you make a pretty good detective... and actor too. I was really impressed by the way you improvised with Henry that night at the restaurant—by the time you finished, *I* almost believed that his name was Stewart!"

Nick chuckled. "I have my moments."

"I would never have managed to check Henry's phone without your help. It was really nice of you to come that night," added Poppy, feeling a sudden shyness come over her.

"Well... I wasn't that nice when you came to my house the day before," said Nick gruffly, running a hand through his unruly dark hair. "You caught me at a bad moment: I'd just got to the end of my first draft and realised that the motive for the murder doesn't work, which means I'm going to have to do some major rewrites—and my editor is already breathing down my neck, demanding the manuscript..." His mouth twisted. "Anyway, the least I could do was check up on you..."

Poppy realised that Nick was trying, in his own way, to apologise for his grouchy manner, and she was touched. She was also surprised by the fact that even though he had been under a tight deadline, Nick had somehow made time to follow her to the restaurant that night to make sure that she was all right. She stole a look up at the tall man next to her. Nick Forrest was such a strange mass of contradictions!

He caught her looking and raised an eyebrow. "What?"

"N-nothing," said Poppy, flushing and hastily dropping her eyes. "Um... that was really sweet of you to come after me. And it was really nice of you to speak up for your father too," she added.

Nick's expression hardened and he scowled. "Crazy old goat... I should have let him be locked up. Best place for him. He's a menace to everybody!"

Poppy didn't say anything, but she smiled to herself. Somehow, she didn't believe Nick's harsh words and hard attitude anymore. He might try to hide it, but she was sure that deep down, he still cared about Bertie. Whatever it was that had caused the rift, she was sure there was some way to get father and son back together again.

She started walking once more and Nick fell into step beside her, but they had barely gone a few yards when he stumbled over something at the side of the path, hidden under foliage spilling out of the adjoining flowerbed. He bent down to pick it up and straightened again with a wooden ball in his hand.

"Must have been one of yours," he said to Poppy with a grin. "You must have chucked this one so far, even the workers didn't find it when they were clearing up after the fête." He handed it to her, his dark eyes twinkling. "Shame they didn't have a coconut shy here again today... that would have *really* livened things up."

"Oh, shut up," said Poppy, trying not to laugh as she tossed the ball away over her shoulder.

There was a muffled cry behind them, then a loud thump. Poppy whirled around and stared, mortified. *GAH!* She rushed towards the man slumped on the ground.

"Oh my God—Norman! I'm *so* sorry..."

***

The gate creaked open at Hollyhock Cottage and Poppy sighed happily as she looked around, feeling the cottage garden work its familiar magic. *It's good to be home.* She wondered if Nell was back yet and started towards the house, then, on an impulse, left the gravel path and plunged into the flowerbeds, wading across to where she had crouched down to pat Oren on the day she had returned from the fête. She found the same spot and sank to her knees again, enjoying the sense of losing herself in a profusion of shapes, textures, and colours. Just like that day, the sun was low on the horizon and twilight was falling, like a dark gossamer curtain drawing slowly across the orange sky, melding the colours into salmon pink and deep purple.

She leaned back and realised that things looked very different from this vantage point, low on the ground. Several of the plants that had been waist-high now towered above her, their flower spires silhouetted against the evening sky. The shrubs loomed large, their dense leaves and branches coming into sharper focus, so that she noticed every vein, every bud, every crease on the leathery bark...

She noticed also the life teeming all around her: a trail of ants marching purposefully across the path nearby, an earwig rustling through some dead leaves, a spider dangling daintily between two flower stems, reeling out silk for a web to catch its dinner, and a garden snail making its slimy way up a blade of grass next to her... She gave a delighted laugh. She felt like someone discovering a world that they had never realised was right beneath their feet.

Rocking back on her heels, Poppy closed her eyes and listened to the soft *swish* and murmur of the tall grasses nearby as the evening breeze moved through them. Then she inhaled deeply, taking in the soothing fragrance of English lavender which still lingered in the garden (despite the butchered bushes!), mingled with the more pungent, woody aromas of rosemary and thyme.

She gave another happy sigh. Her plug plants had been transplanted and were thriving in their new pots, word about her flower arrangements was spreading, she was being inundated with orders, and this morning she had been delighted to see fresh green shoots growing from the bare, twiggy stems of the lavender she had overpruned. After the madness of the last week, it was nice to think that life might be finally getting back to normal—

The peace was broken by a blood-curdling yowl. Poppy's eyes flew open and she sprang up, just in time to see a big orange tomcat come racing around the corner of the cottage with a scruffy black terrier hard at his heels. Oren gave another gleeful yowl as he weaved between the plants, staying just close enough to wave his tail tantalisingly in front of the dog's nose but running fast enough to keep out of reach. Einstein let loose a volley of barking, promising all sorts of dire consequences when he finally caught up with the cat, and hurled himself even harder after Oren.

The two animals raced through the flowerbeds and towards the stone wall which separated Hollyhock Cottage from Nick's property. Oren sprang nimbly up onto the wall, leaving Einstein bouncing up and down at its base, almost howling with frustration. The ginger tom turned around and shot the terrier a smug look of triumph, then he turned and leapt gracefully for the open window in the house on the other side of the wall. He landed on the windowsill and tossed another disdainful look over his shoulder, then disappeared through the opening.

The next moment, there was a crash—the sound of a cup shattering and liquid sloshing everywhere—followed by a furious voice:

"YOU BLOODY CAT! I'm going to kill you!"

Poppy grinned. Oh yes, everything was definitely back to normal...

THE END

ABOUT THE AUTHOR

USA Today bestselling author H.Y. Hanna writes British cozy mysteries filled with humour, quirky characters, intriguing whodunits - and cats with big personalities! Set in Oxford and the beautiful English Cotswolds, her books include the Oxford Tearoom Mysteries, the 'Bewitched by Chocolate' Mysteries and the English Cottage Garden Mysteries. After graduating from Oxford University, Hsin-Yi tried her hand at a variety of jobs, before returning to her first love: writing. She worked as a freelance writer for several years and has won awards for her novels, poetry, short stories and journalism.

A globe-trotter all her life, Hsin-Yi has lived in a variety of cultures, from Dubai to Auckland, London to New Jersey, but is now happily settled in Perth, Western Australia, with her husband and a rescue kitty named Muesli. You can learn more about her (and the real-life Muesli who inspired the cat character in the story) and her other books at: **www.hyhanna.com**.

Sign up to her newsletter to be notified of new releases, exclusive giveaways and other book news! Go to: **www.hyhanna.com/newsletter**

ACKNOWLEDGMENTS

A big thank you as always to my beta readers: Basma Alwesh, Connie Leap, Charles Winthrop and Erin Preble, for always finding time to fit me into their busy schedules and for investing so much time and energy to help me create my stories—even reading manuscripts multiple times and coping with constant plot changes and character revisions! I am also grateful to my editor and proofreader for being such a great team to work with.

And last but not least—I can never thank my amazing husband enough for always being there for me. Without his unwavering support, encouragement and enthusiasm, I could never have achieved everything that I have. He is one man in a million.